# Captured!

A rough gloved hand snatched at Wren's bridle, jerking the horse's head down. The horse lurched sideways. She jumped free of the saddle and landed rolling.

Behind her she heard the sounds of desperate scuffling, and once the clang of metal on metal. Connor's sword! But next came the sound of metal ringing on stone.

"Get the girl," a voice shouted. Steely fingers grabbed her arms and yanked her to her feet.

*So Connor was right. They saw our tracks and came back. Remember that,* a voice insisted inside her head. She blinked hard, trying to banish the dizziness that had come with the fall from the horse. *Get up,* the voice went on. *Think. Think. What would Eren Beyond-Stars do?*

The hands on her arms forced her around. She saw one ruffian holding their horses' reins. Another man sat on Connor's back as he bound some kind of thong around Connor's wrists. A third held Tyron against the ground as he kicked fiercely, trying to squirm free. The man holding him down snuffled evilly, obviously entertained by Tyron's futile struggles. . . .

༄

# FIREBIRD
## WHERE FANTASY TAKES FLIGHT™

# Wren to the Rescue

## SHERWOOD SMITH

**FIREBIRD**

AN IMPRINT OF PENGUIN GROUP (USA) INC.

FIREBIRD
Published by Penguin Group
Penguin Group (USA) Inc., 345 Hudson Street, New York, New York 10014, U.S.A.
Penguin Books Ltd, 80 Strand, London WC2R ORL, England
Penguin Books Australia Ltd, 250 Camberwell Road,
Camberwell, Victoria 3124, Australia
Penguin Books Canada Ltd, 10 Alcorn Avenue, Toronto, Ontario, Canada M4V 3B2
Penguin Books (N.Z.) Ltd, 182-190 Wairau Road, Auckland 10, New Zealand

First published in the United States of America by Jane Yolen Books,
Harcourt Brace Jovanovich, Publishers, 1990
Published by Firebird, an imprint of Penguin Group (USA) Inc., 2004

1 3 5 7 9 10 8 6 4 2

ISBN 0-14-240160-9

Printed in the United States of America

To Janis Marie Robinson
because long ago, when she was eight and I was eleven,
I promised


and to T.K.K.
in affection and gratitude
for twenty-five years of
friendship, laughter, and Belief

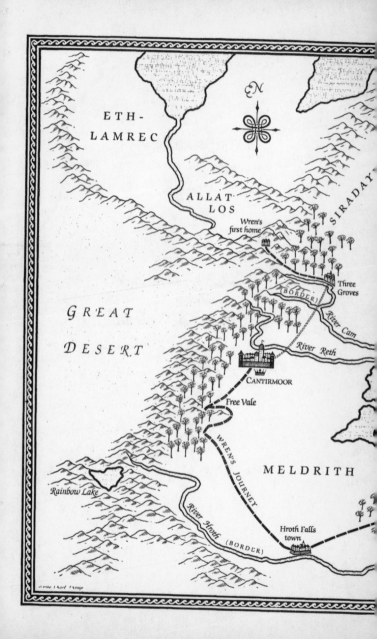

# ROYAL FAMILIES OF MELDRITH AND SIRADAYEL

## 👑 : MELDRITH

### Rhisadel

Varus (d)

Verne  Astren Shaltar*
— Teressa

### Rhistaris

Zhethrem (d)  Hyron  Sem (d)

Rora  Halle (d)
Farle
Tyron

### Rhiscarlan

Kaen (d)

Kaen (d) — Idres

Halle (d)

Kess (d) — Hawk

Les (d)

### Rhismordith

Sheris (d)  Garian (d)

Corenna  Fortian — Garian
Hileme

## Shaltar

Thidor (d) — Nerith

Merrian
Sheris
Astren*
Rollan
Lusra
Leila
Kerrith

Liam
Dareneth (d) — Connor

## 👑 : SIRADAYEL

👑 Current ruling family
* Listed twice
(d) Deceased

NOTE: This family tree only shows connections relating directly to the main characters in this book. The four families are old and have intermarried many times. Anyone who wishes to know all the connections and all the cousins would do best to consult the Heraldry Guild in Cantimoor.

## Chapter One

$W$ren stared at Tess in amazement. "You're a *what*?"

"A princess," Tess said again.

"Oh, I get it. A new game." Wren clapped her hands. "So how do we play? Am I a princess, too?"

Tess shook her head. "It's not a game."

"Tess," Wren said slowly, "if this is supposed to be a joke, it's not working."

The two girls stood under the spreading branches of their favorite tree and looked at each other in silence. Wren studied Tess's familiar face above the plain gray dress that all the girls at Three Groves Orphanage wore. She saw no hint of a smile on the curved lips, and Tess's blue eyes gleamed steadily and solemnly back at her. In front of Tess's white apron, her long hands clasped each other tightly. This wasn't any joke.

"Long lost?" Wren asked in a tentative voice. Images flitted through her mind, and she just had to add, "Lost . . . stolen away by the Iyon Daiyin, perhaps? And you've been rediscovered—here?"

Tess smiled at last, her own sweet smile that transformed her long face into something very beautiful indeed.

"*Not* long lost. Just—hidden."

Wren saw a glitter in her friend's straight blue gaze—a sheen of tears Tess was not going to let fall. *If she just found out she's a princess*, Wren thought, *the news doesn't seem to be part of a happy ending*. To make her best friend smile, Wren gave a loud and dramatic sigh of disappointment. "Well, then I'll still have hopes for *me*." She plumped down on a tuft of long green grass. "So you've had a secret, and now you're telling me. Can you tell me any more?"

Tess rubbed one of her hands up her sleeve and down again. "Yes. Mistress Leila is my aunt, and a princess in her own right. She's really Leila Shaltar—"

Wren knew as well as any child in Siradayel the names of Queen Nerith's offspring. "Princess Leila Shaltar, the Queen's youngest daughter? The one who was supposed to have gone off traveling and settled out of the country?" At Tess's nod, Wren's light blue eyes grew round as icebird eggs. "Are *you* a secret ninth child—"

Tess shook her head. "No. I'm the daughter of Princess Astren—"

"*Third* daughter of Queen Nerith!"

"—and King Verne Rhisadel, of Meldrith."

Perplexed, Wren frowned. "I thought . . . well, I guess I never thought much about Meldrith—it being so far away—but I remember, somehow, hearing that there wasn't any heir."

"There is an heir. Me. But I've had to live here in secret except for a short trip every year to see my parents. On my birthday, which comes day after tomorrow."

"I thought your birthday was in summer, just after Gerrin's—oh! That was a pretend one?"

Tess nodded slowly, solemn again.

Wren sighed, sagging like a cushion for a moment. She was a short girl, with a square face and small hands and feet. Her only remarkable feature was a great quantity of brown and blond streaked hair, as if—Zanna the orphanage pest said once—two scalps of hair had had a fight for possession of her head and both had become attached. Wren's braids were long and thick and heavy and seldom remained neat. In contrast, Tess's waving, shining auburn hair never seemed messy.

Wren looked up at her friend. "So you're leaving for good, is that it? That's why you're telling me?"

2

Tess said quietly, "I think my parents might try to keep me in Cantirmoor this time if nothing happens."

"Nothing *happens?*" Wren repeated, bouncing up from the ground. "A curse? Is that it? You've been under a *curse?*"

Tess nodded, her eyes now distinctly unhappy.

Wren said longingly, "Oh, how I *wish* it were *me*."

This made Tess laugh. She sank down onto a low rock and laughed almost soundlessly. Wren stopped bouncing about and regarded her with a mixture of mischief and concern. To Wren, Tess's laughter sounded uncomfortably close to tears. "I guess I shouldn't have said that—" Wren began.

Tess lifted her head. "Why should you stop saying what you wish?"

Wren spread her hands, giving her friend a funny, lopsided smile. "Well, things have changed."

"Do you think I've changed?"

Wren looked at Tess's intense face. "*You* haven't, but your *place* has. Unless you're about to tell me that I'm a princess, too." Wren made her voice and face sound comically hopeful.

Tess smiled again. "I wish I could. In fact, truth to tell, I wish we could trade places. You want a life of adventure—how many times we've talked about it. And I don't, really."

Wren was silent for a time, thinking over the past. She had been sent down to the larger Three Groves Orphanage from a small, overcrowded one in the high border mountains three years ago. There, orphans were trained to obey orders and to be good general helpers, and when they prenticed out on their twelfth or thirteenth birthdays, it was nearly always for unskilled labor. The mountain folk were very close: weavers, clockmakers, and other skilled artisans tended to take prentices from their own families first. No one in the mountains had much need for scholars or scribes. So it had not been thought necessary to teach Wren and her fellow orphans to read.

When she had been near nine—reckoning from the day she was first found—the Keepers had met with the Village Council, who had decreed that there were too many children and not enough jobs.

Wren was among those sent down to the larger village of Three Groves. She'd been happy about the change—hoping she might now be allowed to do what she wanted—but at Three Groves she'd found that, despite the larger numbers of children, the available positions were much the same. True, a small number of children, mostly girls, were trained to serve as scribes or governesses for noble families in the local great houses, but Wren was told that she was too old to learn the many skills needed. And traveling players? Three Groves children were prenticed out for *respectable* jobs! So Wren was once more employed in the garden, laundry, kitchen, and more and more often at the pottery.

At first she had not noticed Tess, not until she caught Zanna and her two toady friends picking on her. Wren had intervened, and later, in the course of conversation about bullies and how to handle them—there had been four or five of them in the mountains—Tess and Wren discovered some common likes and dislikes.

In a burst of confidence, Wren had admitted her secret desire to become a stage player. Tess had a revelation of her own: that she owned a book of historical plays. She volunteered to teach Wren to read them. That had sealed their friendship.

Now Wren looked up. "You always knew, didn't you? You were living in disguise."

Tess smiled. "Aunt Leila told me when I was five. Before then we made those yearly visits, but I didn't know who the strange man and woman in the pretty clothes were."

"When you go there, do you get to put on jewels and a crown and have people wait on your every wish?"

Tess got up and stared through the hanging willow leaves to the tumbling stream. "No. Nice dresses, but otherwise my visits have always been much like life here. No children, of course. I had to be kept in secrecy, and I was always on my very best behavior . . ." Tess hesitated, then stopped, shrugging suddenly. "It was not exciting. It was—strange. My parents are strangers, my true home strange as well."

Wren's quick ears heard the struggle against sadness under the soft voice. Mistress Leila, teacher of writing and deportment at the orphanage, had coached Tess to speak clearly and well, to never raise her voice. Tess had also learned to hide her feelings. Looking at her now, Wren realized that she didn't really *know* Tess. She'd thought her best friend a quiet, ordinary girl, content with things as they were; content with Wren being leader in everything they did.

"And here you've been spending all this time listening to me pretend to be people in history and watching me juggle and tumble," Wren exclaimed. Then she remembered the import of Tess's words and winced. "So I guess you'll be going away now. Is that why you're telling me? For good-bye?"

Tess said quickly, "I believe I am to go back for good, but Aunt Leila said I could tell you, in case you might like to come to Cantirmoor with me?"

Wren sighed happily. "*Would* I!" She wrinkled her nose. "Or would I have to be your maidservant? I *will*, if I must—but I don't know that I'd be a very good one. You know how they're always getting mad at me in the kitchen, and garden, for daydreaming."

Tess shook her head. "I wouldn't want you to come as that. I know you wouldn't be happy. Aunt Leila said we have to leave here as just Wren and Tess. No one here's to know. She said that there will be plenty of opportunities for you to try other things in Cantirmoor."

Wren clasped her hands. "The *stage players*." She danced across the grassy space, then did a cartwheel. "Not those old, mean traveling players, but *real* players, with beautiful clothes, speaking poetry, and performing before the toffs." She struck a proud pose, then grimaced. "Though I thought you had to be beautiful. And no matter how much I try, I will never be able to sing."

"You'd do well, I should think, because your memory for long poems is so good," Tess said loyally. "And you know by heart all the plays in my—"

In the distance, a bell clanged.

"Dinner." Wren groaned.

Tess got up and straightened her skirts with smooth, automatic movements. "Aunt Leila said we could come here to talk privately just until dinner."

Wren looked around the small space where they'd shared so many games. "Nobody *knew!* But why . . . how . . . your parents—" Wren stopped and drew a deep breath. "I think my head is going to pop from all the questions growing in it. Let's begin with *one*. The curse."

"Not a curse, precisely—a threat," Tess murmured, pushing aside a curtain of leaves. "Does the idea frighten you? Would you rather not come?"

Wren said fervently, "Not likely!"

"Then let's talk more tomorrow, as soon as we can find time alone." Tess waited until Wren passed, then let the leaves fall. "We'd better go to dinner now, or we'll be missed."

Wren's answer was a muffled groan of impatience as she bounced up the rocky slope behind their Secret Tree. Tess smiled and followed more slowly.

♛

# Chapter Two

*L*ooking at her narrow bunk that night, Wren whispered almost soundlessly: "Last time for you."

She started to undress, stopping when she heard a shriek of rage next to her. She turned in time to see Zanna's golden head duck and her fingers tweak viciously at Mira's braid while Mira's nightgown was still over her head. Mira gave a muffled squawk and tried to fend off the bully, but Zanna skillfully and surreptitiously tripped her so that she crashed into two other girls. Skipping quickly out of the way, Wren caught Zanna's arm just before she could duck around the side of a bunk.

"I saw that," Wren said. "Leave Mira alone."

Zanna glowered at Wren for a moment, then sniffed and flounced back to her side of the room. Around Wren, the girls quickly finished undressing.

Climbing into bed, Wren thought: *Strange—this is the last time I'll defend anyone against Zanna and her pals. Now they'll have to learn how to handle bullies on their own because tomorrow I'll be gone.*

A moment later the door opened, and Mistress Lith swept in, demanding to know why there was so much noise. Voices rose, but as usual only her favorite, Zanna, was allowed to speak. After she told her version, everyone was threatened with extra kitchen duty if it happened again. Then Mistress Lith blew out the lamp and left.

Wren lay quietly, smiling in the dark, and listened to the familiar hasty rustlings as the slow girls finished getting into their nightgowns, the creak of the wooden beds, and last the soft hiss of breathing.

*I'll be gone*, she thought again, savoring the strangeness of the idea. She fell asleep trying to imagine life in a real royal palace and only worrying a little about Tess and the curse.

The next morning, instead of racing out while braiding her hair, Wren jostled for a place in front of the little mirror to make certain her braids were neat and her apron and bodice laces straight.

At breakfast Tess gave her only a brief, shy smile as Wren passed by to sit with her own dormitory.

Afterward Wren dawdled in the hall until she felt a light touch on her shoulder. She turned to look up into Mistress Leila's face. Mistress Leila was the youngest Keeper, with bright red hair worn in the customary severe Keeper's bun. Her smile was rare and usually wry, and though she never raised her voice, she had a way with sharp words that had earned her a formidable reputation among the children. Even the rowdiest boys seldom gave her trouble.

*She's really a princess*, Wren thought wonderingly as Mistress Leila said in a very low voice, "Tess is waiting for you in the Keepers' parlor. I'll be there presently." Then she glided smoothly by as red-faced Master Milvar bustled in, shouting orders at a string of youths running after.

Wren put a hand up to hide her grin. *No more digging out carrots with him bawling and squalling at me to be faster*, she thought as she walked with sedate steps to the Keepers' parlor.

Opening the door, she looked around with brief interest. Ordinarily the orphans were not allowed in there. The room was much like the staid downstairs parlor, where the orphans were interviewed by potential masters when it was their turn to prentice out. Tess was sitting by the window, staring down into the road. When Wren came in, she looked up, smiling a welcome.

Wren plopped down onto one of the straight-backed chairs and said, "Now! Tell me about the curse."

Tess gave a quiet laugh. "It *wasn't* a curse—I'm glad, I must say—it was a threat. From King Andreus of Senna Lirwan."

Wren felt her jaw drop. "Truth?"

Tess nodded.

Even in the orphanage, Wren had heard of the wicked King Andreus of Senna Lirwan, though orphanage children were given only the scantiest lessons in history or current affairs. She had listened eagerly, however, whenever rumors or fireside tales were told in the village. She had also enjoyed sneaking glances at the single, ancient, much-repaired map in the scribe students' room, imagining adventures as her eyes roamed over the orange-painted Great Desert lying far to the west. Now she shut her eyes and pictured the map in her mind: Senna Lirwan, land of the wicked King Andreus, lay across the high mountains to the southeast of Siradayel. Like Siradayel and Meldrith, it was landlocked. She recalled bits of gossip about how the wicked king was trying to expand his country at the expense of his neighbors.

"Why did King Andreus threaten your father?" Wren asked.

"It has to do with something my father did. Aunt Leila told me only that he once rescued someone from Andreus's castle. She said my parents will tell me more—when they think I'm old enough." Tess wrinkled her upper lip a little, and Wren snorted in agreement. "All I know about the curse is that Andreus threatened to take any child that my father had as a return for this rescue that happened before I was born. That's all I know—*now*. I've planned for a long time to look in the records as soon as I can and find out what happened."

"So they think the threat is over now?"

"Well, that's what they hope. Aunt Leila told me he did try to steal me away with some kind of magic spell just after I

9

was born. Luckily Halfrid, the King's Magician, was ready for that. But they decided to send me away soon after."

"But why here? I thought those magicians have places where nobody can get in."

Tess shook her head. "Like the Free Vale? But other *magicians* can get in. Aunt Leila told me, when I asked her that same question, that most rulers don't trust any magicians besides their own. If I were sent to one of those faraway magic strongholds, my father would worry that any ambitious magician could grab me. But *nobody* knew about Three Groves except my parents and Aunt Leila. Anyway, nothing has happened on any of my visits to my parents in Cantirmoor, so they're going to try to keep me. But, at first, no one is to know who I am. Aunt Leila told me last night." Tess smiled lopsidedly. "People are going to think that you and I are new heraldry prentices, sent to the palace from the north country. It happens sometimes. That's *if* anyone sees us. We're going to be kept away from people for a while."

"Ah!" Wren exclaimed. "Is *that* why I'm to go, too? As a kind of disguise? What fun!"

"We'll be able to read all the history records and plays that we want—" Tess broke off as the door opened.

Mistress Leila came in. Closing the door behind her, she studied Wren for a moment with steady dark gray eyes. "Well, Wren, would you like to come to Cantirmoor as a companion for Teressa?"

"Yes, Mistress," Wren answered promptly.

Mistress Leila's eyebrows were long and slanted, and when she smiled as she did now, they slanted even more steeply. There was no mistaking the humor there, though her mouth stayed serious. "You understand that you will have to be circumspect. That means you must talk to no one until you are given leave. You will also have to behave like a young scribal prentice: no acrobatics when you think the adults aren't looking, and no juggling pieces of fruit, or glass weights, or whatever you might find handy. Do you understand?"

10

"Yes."

Mistress Leila nodded once. "Very well. Let us go."

"Now? But won't everyone know we're going?" Wren exclaimed.

Leila smiled. "Did you ever notice us going in the past?" After Wren shook her head, she went on, "And can you tell me where everyone in Three Groves is right now?"

Wren shook her head slowly. "Maybe some—but mornings are always so henlike around here." She flapped her hands crazily.

Mistress Leila laughed. "Exactly. But *I* know where they all are. And they all think the three of us are somewhere else. So now, if I may request a pause in the questions, we will go."

She gestured for the girls to stand up. Tess's hand reached for Wren's and held it; her other hand slipped into Mistress Leila's. Tess gazed out the window, her shoulders braced stiffly. Wren watched in amazement as Mistress Leila made a quick gesture with her free hand, then spoke two words very softly.

A sudden sense of light and wind and sound all at once nearly overwhelmed Wren, but almost as soon as it began it stopped. She blinked and discovered that they now stood in a room with high, round-topped windows down one long wall. All around the walls of the room were low shelves with books in them, more books than she had ever seen. At each end of the room round glow globes, set on spindly silver rods, gave off soft light, adding to the light that streamed in the windows. Under her feet lay a carpet, but Wren noticed that it was distinctly threadbare. The walls were plain whitewash unadorned by any pictures.

Mistress Leila murmured, "Wait here, please, girls," and walked swiftly toward one of the doors.

Nudging Tess, Wren whispered, "Is *this* the royal palace?"

"No, it's the Magic School," Tess whispered back through tight lips. Wren looked at her pale face in surprise. Tess drew a slow, careful breath and then added, "I think she's finding out if anything has happened before we go on to the palace."

11

"Are you ill?" Wren asked anxiously.

Tess smiled, just a bit. "It's that magic transfer. Doesn't it make you dizzy?"

"I like it." Wren stopped talking when she saw a tall man in brown tunic and hose meet Mistress Leila at the door. The man had a bushy beard that seemed to fluff out as he cast a quick smile at the girls. He and Mistress Leila held a low-voiced conversation.

*So this is the Magic School?* Wren thought. *And that was real magic.* She stretched her hand out, trying to mimic Mistress Leila's gesture. She remembered the two words clearly.

Mistress Leila returned, moving with such a straight-backed briskness that Wren decided to try practicing that walk when she was alone. *It would be the way to show a princess in disguise walking, if I ever do get to be a player.*

Once again Mistress Leila took Tess's hand. Tess's other gave Wren's a squeeze. Then Mistress Leila's free hand made a gesture in the air. This time, she was looking away as she spoke, and the words were indistinct.

The strange sensation of light, sound, and almost-wind was faster. Wren barely registered it before they stood in yet another room. This one was everything she had hoped for. High, vaulted ceilings curved over them with painted green and gilt leaves twining upward in vines along the groins. Mosaic-outlined high archways graced each wall, and a parquet floor with different shades of wood in a wonderful star pattern glowed clean and polished underfoot. Through some of the archways Wren glimpsed other hallways, and on two distant walls she noticed huge tapestries.

Mistress Leila turned to face the girls. "I will not be staying with you this time, Teressa. Your parents have made their own arrangements. Obey them as you have obeyed me. I must return to Three Groves for a few days, until they can find a replacement for me, then I will be back to see how you are doing. The others at Three Groves will be told that you two prenticed out early. Remember what I said!"

This last was addressed to Wren. Then Mistress Leila walked through one of the archways and disappeared.

Tess, meanwhile, sank down gratefully onto an embroidered sofa nearby. "We're to wait here," she said.

Wren dropped happily onto the comfortable cushions beside Tess, admiring the fancy stitchwork on the pillows—spring leaves and golden buds—that even the Sewing Mistress at Three Groves would not have been able to do. Then she heard a rustling of skirts, and a smiling woman in a quiet-hued gown entered the room.

"Princess?" She smiled at the girls as she bowed to Tess. "Young Mistress? The King and Queen await you."

Tess's face lit with her sudden, transfiguring smile. She got up swiftly and started after the maid. Wren followed, looking around at the fine furnishings and decorations. At the end of a hall there was a wonderful door carved with more gilt leaves and a splendid room with a long row of painted flowers, birds, and growing things high on the walls, the colors of which were worked into the embroidery on the curve-edged furniture.

Wren's eyes went to the two people in the room—a man and a woman, both beautifully dressed. At first they seemed impossibly handsome. But as Tess ran forward and the woman's arms closed around her, Wren noticed that the Queen had a much longer face than Tess and big knuckles on her hands.

Wren hung back. She couldn't hear the soft words the Queen murmured to her daughter, or the replies that Tess made into her mother's velvet-clad shoulder. Then Tess transferred herself to the King's arms, and she was caught up and swung round in a wide circle.

"My brave girl!" the King exclaimed. Tall and thin, he had a short gray-streaked brown beard. Narrow, dark eyes crinkled with good humor when he looked over Tess's head at Wren. "Come forward, child," he said genially. His voice was clear and loud, but somehow reassuring. "So, you're the one who wants to be a pirate, eh?"

Wren's face went hot. "Well, only when we play adventure

13

games." Startled at how different her voice sounded in the large room, she added belatedly, "Your Graces." And she bobbed into an awkward curtsy.

The King laughed. "So once did I, child. We'll have to compare tales. Now I fear I must return to duty—it wouldn't do for the curious to know that I was here to welcome two heraldry students. Tomorrow, though, I have arranged a surprise. We will have time to talk then." He bent down to kiss Tess and left.

"Let us get you settled, my dears," the Queen said. Her voice sounded low and musical to Wren's sensitive ears. She spoke to both girls, but her eyes remained on Tess as she led the way through one of the high arches. Tess slipped her hand tentatively into her mother's, and the Queen clasped it tightly as they walked.

Wren looked down the hall at the tall pillars along one side. In the wall beyond them stretched a row of long diamond-paned windows. Through these she saw an ordered garden and more of the palace bordering it. She wondered how soon she could go exploring.

Two maidservants in gray and green gowns appeared. One opened a tall door to a suite of rooms. These rooms were smaller and simpler than the one in which the King and Queen had welcomed the girls, but they were still far more splendid than anything Wren had seen before.

"Fleris and Lur will stay with you here in the guest wing." The Queen indicated the two maids, who both curtsied. "They know who you are, but they will address you as Young Mistresses from the city of Chancebridge. Until Halfrid feels it is safe, I must ask you not to talk to anyone else unless one of us is with you. Now I will leave you alone, for I also have other duties, and I imagine you would like a chance to refresh yourselves. We will dine together tonight, just the three of us. Welcome back, my sweet dove." The Queen bent to kiss Tess's brow.

Wren felt something in her throat tighten. Not since she

was very small had she even thought about parents or families. Inside her now was a strange mixture of pleasure at how nice the Queen seemed and of loss that no one would ever kiss her that way. Then she noticed Tess surreptitiously dashing tears from her eyes.

*She's been a kind of orphan as well,* Wren thought. *And in some ways, it's been worse for her. She knew she had parents—wonderful ones—and never got to see them.*

But Tess sniffed only once, then lifted her chin. "Well, shall we go in? Just *wait* till you see what the bathtubs are like here."

"What? No more nasty wooden tubs with splinters and cold water?" Wren matched her friend's tone.

The maid Fleris, who was only a few years older than the girls, was plump with a big smile and blue-black hair. Lur was older, tall and gray-haired. They showed Wren and Tess into a tiled room with a wide pool into which water poured from a spout cleverly worked into a statue of tumbling fish.

When Wren stepped cautiously into the clean, swirling water a few minutes later, she found it warm and scented.

"I think I approve." She laughed before ducking her head under.

"I think it won't be too hard not to be a princess yet," Tess answered, and joined her in the tub.

## Chapter Three

*T*he dinner with Queen Astren was the most wonderful event of Wren's life so far. The Queen had her harp brought in, and after they ate a delicious meal—with several plates to choose from, a rare occurrence for orphans who had been raised to eat what was on the plate before them, like it or not—she sang and played for them. Wren had been right in her guess about the Queen's voice.

When darkness fell, a quiet servant came in and lit three lamps. That was when the Queen turned the talk to the orphanage.

"Tell me everything," she said. "For instance, what nasty things did Zanna get away with this year, and is Noker still playing his awful practical jokes on everyone?"

At first Tess and Wren took turns talking, but Tess seemed more content to lean against her mother and listen. Soon she waved off her own turn. "Tell Mama the time the rain made the roof crash in just when Mistress Lith gave us extra laundry duty!"

Encouraged by the Queen's laughter, Wren stood up and acted out the best incidents. When the girls finished, the Queen said, "Teressa told me you wish to become a player, Wren. Besides becoming a pirate captain, an adventurer, and a hermit in a haunted castle with several treasures."

Wren grinned. "I suppose my mind changes now and then.

I decided about being a player when I realized that I wasn't going to learn to manage a charger—never even seen one—nor find a magic sword. Mistress Varu, when she measured me for my last dress, said I probably wouldn't grow much taller. I know that Eren Beyond-Stars in my favorite play wasn't much older than I am when she had her adventures, but she was really a princess and had lots of magic knowledge. I didn't think that orphans who are supposed to prentice to the pottery when they reach twelve ever find much in the way of adventure."

The Queen said, "Being a player is a fine vocation. There would be long years of difficult training, but I don't think you're afraid of that."

"No. It certainly can't be harder than years of mixing clay."

"The Keepers did *not* consider it to be fine." Tess pressed her cheek against her mother's shoulder. "They always told Wren that her dreams were foolish and that they would get her into trouble if they kept her from the work at hand."

Queen Astren smiled. "Many would praise that practical attitude. But there's only one 'practical' idea I wonder if you've considered, Wren, and that is: only one person in your favorite play can be Eren Beyond-Stars. All the other players take the roles of villains or silly courtiers or cooks."

Wren shrugged, grimacing a little. She was pleased to be taken seriously by the Queen of Meldrith, but at the same time she admitted to herself that she had *not* considered this. Her preparation had always been for the heroic roles. Nevertheless she said firmly, "I'll do my part, whatever it is, if it just keeps me from having to darn any more baskets of black orphan hose."

They all laughed, and then a special treat was brought in: warm milk with dark, rich chocolate from the faraway Summer Islands. Wren slurped hers right up after the first astonished and delighted taste and was given a second cup. The Queen had them leave soon after, telling them that they needed a good night of rest.

"Tomorrow is Teressa's twelfth birthday, and we have special things planned."

Wren thought privately after hearing *that* she'd never be able to sleep. And, as she lay down in the soft, big bed—in a room all by herself, but with Tess within shouting distance— she realized that in a long evening of talk and song, one thing had not been mentioned: the wicked King Andreus. But then her eyes closed, and she fell asleep.

The next day dawned clear and, though the season was early spring, warm. Wren wondered whether the weather in Meldrith was different from what she'd grown up with in Siradayel, or if this was just a lucky day. Meldrith! She was in a different *country*.

*And all at once, too*, she thought. She flexed her fingers and tried to copy the gesture she'd seen Mistress Leila making the day before. She was moving her fingers in the air, wondering if she had it right, when Tess came in, smiling happily and wearing a fresh green dress.

"Is something amiss with your hand?" Tess pointed.

"I was trying to do that magic thing that Mistress Leila did. Did you notice it? Or hear the words?"

"I guess I've never paid much attention to her hands. Magic makes me feel so nasty, like I've eaten a bad pie and had a nightmare at the same time. When she does it, I try to keep my mind on seeing my parents again. Anyway she never seems to *talk*. Hums, more like . . ." Tess's brow creased faintly as she thought it over.

"She spoke, all right. I heard *that* much," Wren said.

"Well, I suppose you could ask her. She'll be here at the end of the week, Mama said. Meantime, get dressed. Shall we go down and have a look at the garden?"

"Yes," Wren exclaimed, swinging her feet out of the bed. Then she frowned. "My dress from yesterday is gone."

Tess laughed. "Certainly! You're in the palace now." And, putting her nose in the air, she added, "The high-born *never* wear a thing twice. Twice in a row, at least, for the likes of

18

heraldry prenties. Look in that chest there. You should find some gowns."

"I was afraid to touch any of the furnishings," Wren admitted, moving to a big carved chest at the other end of the room. Lifting the lid, she smelled sweet wood. Several folded dresses lay in the chest, all made of soft, heavy polished linen. The top one was a nice shade of pale blue. "Like the eastern sky just before the sun comes up," Wren said in delight, lifting it out.

The skirt dragged across the tops of her feet, and even laced up tightly, the bodice was loose, but Wren still thought she looked grand. She turned round and round, admiring the square-cut neck and the long, slightly belled sleeves. Then she looked at Tess, whose gown was equally bare of decoration but equally well made.

"We look like toffs, don't we?" Wren said.

Tess smiled, shaking her head a little. "Well, to Three Groves orphans we would. To some of these courtiers, we'd look like servants. They can be quite horrid, some of them. But we don't have to think about that yet. Come, let's explore that garden and maybe act out one play before we get called for breakfast."

Wren pushed her feet into her slippers, tied them quickly up her ankles, then paused and looked up. "Are we going to be told *exactly* what happened to your father and why the wicked king did his threat, or shall we try to nose into the records?"

"Mama promised we'll hear the full story tonight, at the special dinner they have planned."

Wren smacked her hands and rubbed them, thinking: *I hope if this is a dream I never wake up*, as she followed Tess out.


The garden was full of early blooms, which the girls admired, but what interested them was the grove of light-leafed aspen trees at the far end. Here they explored, playing Morayen and Tre Resdir discovering the Rainbow River, until they had gone over the entire grove.

Finally Wren exclaimed breathlessly, "I'm getting hungry," and flopped onto the soft, well-clipped grass. Tess dropped down beside her.

"Princess Teressa," a low voice said respectfully.

The girls looked up. Sun dazzled their eyes, making it hard to see any more than a short, plump person in a gray and green gown.

"Is it time for breakfast, Fleris?" Tess asked. "We're ready."

"Your father desires your presence," Fleris replied. "You must come quickly. Halfrid is there also."

Tess exchanged looks with Wren.

"I wonder if something has happened. I guess I had better go."

"They won't want me or they would have asked." Wren shrugged. "I'll go in and see if the breakfast is coming."

"Good idea. If there are sweetberry rolls, save me two," Tess called as she got up and followed Fleris.

They disappeared immediately among the trees. Wren watched, thinking: *That's strange. Why would Halfrid want to have Tess there? And for that matter, why did Fleris forget to call us 'Young Mistresses from the city of Chancebridge'?*

She was tempted to follow them and ask, but hesitated, fearing that if an emergency of some sort really was at hand, her interruption might not be welcome. *I know, I'll ask Lur,* she thought.

Back inside the cool marble hallway, she saw the older maid carrying fresh towels into the tiled bathroom. "Good morning, Lur. We're ready for breakfast any time you can point us to it." Wren grinned. "That is, soon as Tess gets back."

"Gets back, Young Mistress?" Lur said blankly.

"Fleris just came out to us in the garden and whisked Tess away. Said the King and Halfrid needed her right now."

20

Lur set her towels down carefully on a gilt chair in the hallway. She said slowly, "Tell me again, of your courtesy, Young Mistress. Fleris *came* to you? She was not out in the garden *with* you?"

"No! Should she have been? We were playing a game—went out soon as we woke . . ." Wren stopped speaking as Lur's eyes changed from worry to horror.

"Wait here, child," Lur said abruptly, whirling about. She stopped. "No, you had better come with me."

Surprised, Wren followed her outside into the garden again. The woman nearly ran as she led the way from path to path, and then to three empty archways in adjacent wings of the palace. At last she stopped, slightly winded, and said only one word: "Gone!"

A strange knot tightened in Wren's stomach as she followed the grim-faced, silent woman inside. Lur rarely checked her pace as they descended two flights of stairs and hurried down the length of another set of halls. Through one handsome door Wren could see that the halls were suddenly full of paintings and carpets again; they entered a long dining hall with servants busy clearing away plates. Lur walked past them all without speaking until she reached a short, fat man wearing a silver chain of office about his neck, who was giving orders to two waiting servers. As soon as he saw them, he stopped.

"Lur? Was something amiss with the food preparations this morning?"

"The food never arrived, and someone seems to have sent Fleris to fetch . . . *her* . . . to the King," Lur said in a hissing voice.

The fat man's cheeks purpled. "Not to *my* knowledge," he said. Ordinarily Wren would have been secretly delighted with the way he hitched up his belt above his round belly and blew out his jowls importantly, but now she sensed that something was very wrong.

The fat man turned on her suddenly. "This is the other one, yes?"

"Yes—" Lur began.

"Tell me what happened," the man said to Wren.

Even the Keepers had not such an air of command. Wren said hastily, "We got up, dressed, and went into the garden to play. It was getting kind of late when Fleris came and said . . ." Wren repeated the conversation with Fleris, ending with, "So Tess went off with her, and I came in to see about some food."

The man's cheeks turned pale, and then the whole world seemed to explode. In a thundering voice the fat man issued orders to the waiting servant. "You! Take a message to the King. You! Deliver these trays. Lur! Take this child to the Guilds anteroom."

This meant another fast walk until Lur led the way into an empty room with rich pennants hung at intervals on the high walls. The room contained a number of chairs. Lur pointed distractedly at them and asked Wren to sit down, which she did, while the woman walked back and forth before the entry door.

After a long silence, Wren said, "What's happened? Nothing to Tess . . . I hope."

Lur stopped and looked at her. "Fleris was supposed to be with you soon as you rose up. Breakfast ready for you. One of us was to be with you all the time—did the Queen not tell you?"

Wren's eyes stung: it was an accusation. But before she could answer, Lur took a deep breath and added, "Not your fault. You were new-arrived. While I was down in the laundry rooms, she was to be with you. When she took the trays back, I was to be with you. Those were the Queen's orders."

Wren said in a small voice, "She called her Princess Teressa, not Young Mistress."

Lur spun about, clasping her hands tightly. "*That* will have to be answered for as well."

"Well, maybe she forgot about that if there was such an emergency," Wren said, hoping that someone would come in and say that all was well.

Instead, a tall, frowning guard in polished helm and clinking mail under a green surcoat opened the door and said in a deep voice, "Follow me."

Lur sent one frightened look at Wren. Before long they entered a small room with books lining the walls, below shuttered windows. The King stood in the center of the room, looking more like a king than the ordinary father he'd seemed before. The friendliness was gone from his eyes.

Wren stopped near a knot of people, in the midst of whom sat Fleris with a bandage round her head. Fleris's eyes were red-rimmed. She was trying not to weep as another woman whom Wren had not seen before but who wore the same kind of gown as Lur and Fleris, bent over her, talking in an earnest whisper.

Lur was telling her part to the King. As she finished, she curtsied deeply and backed away.

The fat man gestured Wren forward to tell her story. When she got to the part about Fleris in the garden, Fleris's voice burst out, wailing. "It *wasn't* me, it *wasn't*. I woke up just now, with cold water in my face and Marrit standing over me. The last thing I knew was going down to get the trays from—"

"We've heard your tale," the fat man interjected. "Be silent."

Wren turned back to face the King. His eyes were still cold and stony, but his voice was even and patient. "Now, child, would you tell us again? This time, describe everything exactly as it happened when Fleris came."

At the sound of her name the servant burst into tears again, quickly muffled.

Wren's shoulders hunched; her stomach now felt like a pit of writhing snakes. She said, "Now I've heard it, the voice isn't right. *She*"—Wren pointed at Fleris on her chair—"has that high voice. Out in the garden, the voice was kind of flat and much lower. Anyway, the woman we thought was Fleris said, 'Princess Teressa?' And we looked up. The sun was just behind her. All we—I—could really see was her shape and her dress. Then she said what I told you before, 'Your father requires your presence—'"

"Your pardon, Young Mistress," a new voice cut in. Wren turned, recognizing the bearded man she'd seen Mistress Leila talking to at the Magic School upon their first arrival. "Did you at any time see her features clearly?"

Wren shook her head. "I didn't. I don't like looking into the sun. Hurts my eyes. I looked at Tess, right until they were gone."

"Shape-change illusion. A simple one," the man murmured.

"That's possible here?" The King frowned. "Never mind. Halfrid will answer that when he arrives." To Wren he said, "Thank you."

Wren sensed the dismissal in his voice, but her sick feeling made her daring. "She isn't . . . gone?" She flushed when her voice came out squeaky, just like a baby's.

The King actually smiled, just a little. "So it seems. I trust we will restore her to you shortly."

Now she knew she had been dismissed. He had turned to address some low-voiced comments to the bearded man, but Wren performed her very best curtsy and backed away to find Lur waiting.

Lur took her back to the rooms that she and Tess had enjoyed for such a short time. There Wren was left largely alone. She wandered about aimlessly. All the enjoyment had gone out of the place, the new things, and the sunshiny day.

Somehow the hours passed. The shadows changed and the light turned gold, then faded. Lur brought food in once, but Wren found that she could not eat.

At sunset Fleris appeared, her eyes still red-rimmed. Both Lur and Wren greeted her with "Any news?"

Fleris shook her head quickly. "Except that new runner from the kitchens is also missing. And poor Mavin, who was supposed to have met me with the tray, was found in her room half dreaming and moaning from some terrible sickness that took her during the night. They think she was poisoned. And they believed this!" She pulled her bandage down and pointed to a big, purple-red bruise at her hairline. "We're to wait, to act as if nothing's happened, until the steward tells us further." She spoke to Lur when she said that.

Wren felt peculiar, as if she had momentarily disappeared.

By the next day, that feeling had increased. *They don't know what to do with me*, she thought as she prowled around her room once more. She'd tried to go to the garden, but Lur told her to stay inside. Later, when Fleris brought a tray of food in, Wren said, "Is anyone looking around for that wicked Andreus?"

Fleris said quickly, "That's up to the King and Master Halfrid. And the Scarlet Guard."

Wren said nothing more, but she thought about that. Another thing bothered her as well. What would they do with her if the days stretched on and they still could not find Tess? *I won't go back to Three Groves. Not until I know what's happened.* But in her mind the urge grew stronger not just to ask, but to do *something*.

Night fell with her again unable to sleep. After several long and twitchy hours she sat up in bed. *I know I remember that spell, and trying anything has got to be better than this.*

She rose, rummaged in the trunk for a fresh dress, put it on, then stretched out her hand in the darkness. In her mind she saw very clearly the way Mistress Leila's capable fingers had sketched that gesture in the air. Wren mimed it carefully. At the same time she murmured the two words.

She disappeared.

## Chapter Four

While Wren was still sitting in the dark trying to decide what to do, Queen Astren sat alone in her own splendid room, staring out the darkened windows.

She jumped up when a soft knock sounded on the door and opened it herself. Standing outside was her youngest sister Leila.

"I came as soon as I got your message," Leila said. "Halfrid and Falstan and the rest of the Magic Council are all gone. What's happening now?"

The Queen lifted her hands as her sister sat down. "They are reasonably certain that the person who took Teressa was a new kitchen runner known as Jasran. She was quiet, polite, neat, and it turns out no one really knew her. We questioned Tam, the footman who originally spoke for her, and found out that he did not remember having done so at all. Shown the records—clearly stating that he stood for her—he just repeated that he did not know any Jasran, and the only two people he'd spoken for were his cousin's twins, out in the stable."

"This fresh?" Leila gestured toward the tea on a side table.

The Queen nodded. "In hopes you'd arrive soon, little sister."

Leila smiled briefly while pouring out and stirring her tea. "So they suspect a dream spell was put on your footman? I take it lower servants aren't checked for traces of magic on being hired?"

"That's what I heard over the supper I could not eat."

"Eat, Astren. You'll only get sick, and if Andreus *is* behind this, he'd probably just love hearing how everyone in Cantirmoor either wilted or panicked. Besides, one of Andreus's chief charms is his long memory for those who've crossed him." She leaned forward and pushed one of the fresh rolls into the Queen's hand. "Come now. Eat, or Mama will be *most* displeased."

The Queen smiled a little. "Mama. How frightened I used to be of her. Has she been told?"

Leila smiled wryly as she sipped her tea. "Who knows? She can't help—unless Teressa was taken as part of a nasty plot by certain of our cousins. But *they* would hardly show this kind of finesse."

The Queen took a small bite of her roll, then put it down. "Halfrid feels that magic was done. The shape-change spell was mere illusion, which escaped the old wards against real transformations laid over the palace. Just the illusion of Fleris's shape was enough to convince the girls, it seems."

Leila frowned. "Your note said so little. Tell me everything."

The Queen repeated Wren's and Lur's stories as they'd been told her by the King. She ended with, "Verne is questioning some of the courtiers while Halfrid has Falstan putting new spells on the palace. Halfrid himself is out somewhere, trying to trace Teressa by magic."

Leila nodded and set down her cup. "Then my place is back at the school until he calls me."

"Was there a stir at the orphanage?"

Leila smiled. "There was not. Halfrid would have my hair for sloppiness. I told them I was leaving to get married, and they were all so stunned no one thought to ask a direct question. They'll make up their own husband and future life for me, knowing *them*." She looked up suddenly. "What bothers me is I can understand Teressa following instantly if she thought her father might want her, but I would not have expected Wren with her quick eyes to fall for something like that so easily."

The Queen said, "Maybe not at Three Groves. This is new territory—"

"—And she was on her best behavior thanks to my threats." Leila winced. "But I suppose we are lucky she did not interfere, or she too might have been found lying unconscious—or worse—somewhere." She poured a second cup and studied it. "Halfrid must look for his proof, but I'll wager he and the council believe that Andreus is behind this, and timing and method constitute a message."

"A threat."

"Precisely. How much further he'll carry this out, we can only guess. It's not his style to send an army over the mountains, knowing the reputation of Verne's Scarlet Guard. He'd do it readily enough if he thought it would be an easy win, but I understand he prefers to show his conquered enemies how much *smarter* he is."

The sisters looked at one another for a long time. Finally the Queen said in a soft voice, "Idres might know."

"Dear 'Dishonorable Idres'?" Leila said, brows raised. "Apparently the last message she deigned to answer, ten years ago, was to tell Halfrid to dig his own hole and jump into it. She hasn't answered anything since. Just sits there in the Free Vale, doing nothing."

"Which at least proves that she is not out to conquer kingdoms, as some still maintain."

"Who knows?" Leila lifted her hands. "Halfrid fears she might just be waiting for her chance. At any rate, he has forbidden any kind of communication with her until we *do* know." She rubbed her eyes. "Well, if two cups of tea have no effect, then I should go back and try to rest until I am summoned." She stood up and raised her hand, then paused. "Tut! Must I *walk* across town at midnight? Did you not say that Falstan bound the palace against transportation spells?"

The Queen smiled unwillingly. "Do not try to draw me, Leila! Use your horrid magic transport with my good will, but leave me to walk even if the weather is blizzard-bad." As her sister laughed, the Queen went on, "I believe the new wards only concern people coming in. The transport spell to the Magic School is permitted, it being unlikely that any possible villain loose in the palace would want to go *there*."

"Good." Leila stooped slightly to kiss her tall sister, who was still sitting down. "I'll see you tomorrow. Do try to sleep." She transferred herself to the Magic School.


A few minutes later, Wren also appeared in the Magic School.

She blinked and looked about her, recognizing instantly the worn carpet, the rows of books, and the glow globes in their silver rods. *I did it*, she realized. Out loud, she cried: "I did it! I did magic!" and spun around.

A moment later a bearded man rushed in from an adjacent room, followed by Mistress Leila. They stopped when they saw Wren, the man looking stunned. Mistress Leila's eyes widened in surprise.

"It's my other charge from Three Groves, Falstan," Mistress Leila said. Despite her tired face and crumpled dress, she was her usual straight-backed, brisk self. "Who sent you, Wren?"

"No one. I saw and heard what you did when we first came."

The adults exchanged a look, this one expressive of surprise—and warning.

"Then you were right about her," the man said in a low voice.

Mistress Leila made a slight silencing gesture and turned to Wren. "Does anyone know you are here or that you tried magic?"

"No. I've been alone what seems years. No one has told *me* anything, and I want to help find Tess."

Falstan laughed. It was not a mean laugh. It was more helpless than anything, but Wren scowled. Somehow—for the first time—she felt the threat of tears, and she fought it down by getting angry.

"And do you have information that will aid you where the King's guard, the King's magician, and a good part of the court nobles as well have all failed?" Falstan asked.

Wren answered truculently, "I want to know what happened, and how I can help find her."

"We don't know much more than you do, child," Mistress Leila said, adding firmly, "listen, Wren, you must *never* use that spell again. It can be dangerous, for a number of reasons I'll explain to you later. It is late, and we'd better send you back—"

"Entry spells are now routed through the steward," Master Falstan said quickly.

Mistress Leila nodded. "Ah, yes. Thank you for the reminder. No use in rousing the palace. We'll keep you here tonight and send you back in the morning."

Rubbing his eyes Falstan added sympathetically, "It was a kind act, young one, but you must see that there is nothing that you can do. I wish there wasn't so little that *we* can do."

Mistress Leila gestured, and instead of embarking immediately on a rescue quest, Wren was led off much the same way she'd been led off all her life. Soon she was lying in a narrow bed in a tiny room, staring at a low, plain ceiling by the light of a single candle. She was too disappointed to take an interest in the new sounds and smells of this magic-laden place. Finally falling asleep, she dreamed about Tess being lost in a forest of aspen.

When she woke, early sunlight glimmered through the small round-topped window. She put on the dress she'd pulled so hastily from the chest in her palace room. It was a plain linen dress of a soft yellow color that ordinarily she would have liked, but now she just made certain it was tidy. Her spirits were lower than ever. There'd be no chance to explore even. Before she'd left last night, Mistress Leila had said in her firmest mistress-of-deportment voice, "Wait in this room until you are summoned."

At least Wren did not have to wait long.

She was sitting on the edge of the bed, rebraiding her hair, when someone knocked rapidly on the door.

Hastily tying her second braid tie, she opened the door. She was surprised when the person on the other side, a boy of about her own age, glanced furtively behind him in both directions before pushing his way past her and entering her room.

"Hey—" she began.

"Shh!" he responded. He had brown eyes and shaggy brown hair even more unruly than hers. "I heard you came by magic. How much d'you know?"

Wren shook her head slowly. "Just that bit I learned when Mistress Leila brought Tess and me here—"

The boy slumped down on the bed and regarded her in a sort of amazed disappointment.

"You learned a spell on *one* hearing?" he repeated.

Wren shrugged. "So? Seems easy enough if you pay attention."

The boy gave her a slow grin. "Some people can 'pay attention' for years, and they don't 'hear' the commands. Or if they do, or they think they do, they can't get it spoken right."

"Well, I only heard the one," Wren said. "And it just brought me here. Anyway, what are you looking for?"

"Another magician. One who could help me."

"What's wrong?" Wren asked.

The boy made a sour face. "What's wrong is Masters who think they know everything and who *never* forget mistakes," he said bitterly.

Since Tess had disappeared and everyone seemed to know it, Wren did not think it was breaking the secret to say: "Does this have to do with Tess—with the Princess's disappearance?"

"Everything!" He lifted his hands dramatically. Then he bounced up, his chin jutting with determination. "Well. Then I'll just have to act on my own."

He had spoken under his breath to himself, but Wren backed away and blocked the door.

"Wait," she said. As he looked at her, startled, she went on, "If you think that you can do something as mean as come in, say mysterious things about the person I came to rescue, then just stomp out again like a cabbage-nosed cactus . . ." She stopped, unable to think of a threat that was large enough to express her disgust.

The boy studied her warily. "You want to help, is that it?" Seeing her firm nod, he added, "But what can you do?"

"I'll try anything if it will help," Wren answered promptly. "Is she your friend, too? I don't see how she can be when she was with us at the orphanage—"

"You're that girl, that Wren," he said slowly, now staring at her with interest. "You *know* her. So *that's* why Mistress Leila had you put here in the special guests' wing."

"Of course—we were friends. Why else d'you think I want to rescue her?"

"For the reward—for a position—who knows? A lot of those court clods from the palace searching so hard for her didn't know her," he fired back impatiently. "But . . . if you did know her, then maybe we can do a—well! If you want to help," he announced quickly, "we have to go *right now*." He opened the door. "Just follow, and don't say anything."

Resolving to keep quiet for the moment, Wren stared around in appreciative curiosity as they began walking down long, cool halls. Through arched windows she caught glimpses of trees, and down other halls and in open rooms she saw more people, young and old, boys and girls dressed like this boy in brown tunics and hose even plainer than the orphanage uniform from Three Groves.

They passed a large room from which delicious breakfast smells wafted out. Wren's stomach growled in instant protest. A few steps from the dining room doorway, someone suddenly gave a shout: "Tyron!"

The boy beside Wren jerked to a stop as footsteps pounded

up. Another boy caught up. His face was red, and he was nearly breathless with laughter. "Tyron, I *had* to tell you. Ol' Crazy was out on final test for Basics—"

"I know, I know," Tyron interrupted, glancing down the hall again. Wren thought about telling him that that looked more suspicious than anything, but she remained silent.

"But you can't have heard what happened last n-night." The boy leaned against the wall, wheezing. "T-turned the Master into a turtle!"

Tyron snorted a laugh, then said with a faint frown, "So they're back? Is that it?"

The boy nodded, nearly doubled over. "There's more—"

"Tell me later? I've got to . . . run a message," Tyron said.

The boy nodded and lurched toward the dining room, still laughing.

As they started off at an even faster pace, Wren whispered, "You sure don't know much about sneaking."

"Huh?" Tyron threw her a distracted look without slowing his steps at all. He was busy looking to both sides and even behind, rather than right in front of him. Wren was afraid he might run into a wall if she spoke again, so she stayed quiet.

At last they reached a heavy wooden door. He pushed it open and motioned her out first. Sunlight greeted her. She got a glimpse of a secluded grassy area surrounded by tall firs; then Tyron grabbed her arm and pushed her behind a high, thick-leafed shrub. "Can you ride?"

"Ow," she protested as the sharp leaves scratched her. "Ride what?"

"A *horse*," he whispered with fierce urgency.

"No—"

He sighed, short and sharp. Before he could say anything more, Wren spoke. "Are you going back inside?"

"Of course—I have to get my bag."

"Then listen," she said grimly, thinking back to the false Fleris hurrying Tess away. She could see this boy's face clearly, and he didn't seem like any villain—but still. "Two things. *One.*

33

You know who I am, and I'm glad you invited me along, but who are *you*, and why are you going after Tess?"

Tyron was silent for a moment, the worry creasing his wide forehead changing to thoughtfulness. In surprise Wren also glimpsed a flicker of sorrow in his eyes, just for a moment. Then he gave a sharp shrug and just looked determined. "I am Tyron, and I'm training to be a magician. I want to help find that princess and prove something to some stiff-chinned, unlistening senior magicians when I do it."

Wren hesitated, still thinking of the false Fleris and remembering what Tess had said about those pretty, smiling courtiers sometimes being enemies at heart.

She studied Tyron closely, not caring that he saw her doing it. He was a skinny fellow half a head taller than she, with a sharp-boned face that reminded her of a fox. As she stared at him, he turned once to glance anxiously behind him, then just stood, apparently willing to give her this time to think.

So what did she think? Should she just go off with him, without a word to Mistress Leila?

It was that last statement of his, about "stiff-chinned, unlistening seniors," and the brief glimpse of loss in his eyes before he said it, that decided her. *But, I'll keep my eyes and ears open*, she thought, remembering that no adventure in the history plays began with anyone saying: "Here's your path. Follow the signs and everything will be easy."

"Second thing," she said. "I don't know much about riding—though I'm ready to learn—but I know *lots* about sneaking, and . . . and acting. If any people see you, they will know *immediately* that something is wrong. You keep looking around and stalking like ten fanged tigers are after you."

Tyron said, "But we've got to hurry if we're to—"

"You don't need everyone to see it, do you? Walk like you're busy, but not like you're desperate."

He gave a brief grin. "All right. Got it. Stay here while I get my stuff. Don't let anyone see you. I'll be back just as fast as I can. Be ready to climb up behind me. We are going to ride."

## Chapter Five

*W*ren stood listening to some unseen birds scolding and wondered when Mistress Leila would discover her absence. She felt a twinge of worry at the thought of being found and sent back to the orphanage in disgrace, but shook off the fears. *No use borrowing trouble. Could be I'll see plenty soon enough.*

Then she heard the thudding of a horse's hooves on grass, and Wren had to keep a new, sharper fear from making her hide. Orphanage prentices had little to do with horses, unless they were training for stable work. Horses were expensive, and only the rich rode them.

But here was Tyron on a brown horse that looked as tall as a house. He reined it in and held down a hand to Wren. She swallowed in a dry throat, looking at the horse's large eyes and tossing head, then thought: *Eren Beyond-Stars never showed fear.* Keeping her face unconcerned, she stepped forward firmly.

She didn't know how to climb on something that moved and had no corners or branches. It took Tyron pulling hard to get her up. Once aboard, she clasped her arms around his waist.

"Here we go," he said.

The horse began to move, and the bouncing terrified her for a short time. But when she realized that she had not been dashed to the ground yet, she slowly opened her eyes.

Her grip must have loosened at the same time, for up front there was a sudden and explosive sigh.

35

"Whew!" Tyron yelled. "I thought you were going to cut me in half."

"You could have said something," she shouted back.

"Too much of a hurry. As long as you held on, I didn't want to squawk about how tightly you did it."

Conversing was hard, so she said nothing in return. Instead, she began to notice things like the rhythm of the horse's gallop and the countryside around them.

Tyron's horse raced across fields. They crossed two roads but did not turn to follow them. On one side Wren saw a gleam of river between groves of trees, and further on a small village, but Tyron kept the horse well away from any buildings.

About the time Wren felt she was getting accustomed to the headlong pace, the horse slowed. For a while this meant some nasty bouncing, much worse than the galloping actually, then the horse slowed to a walk.

Now they were on a narrow road. Along one side of this road grew tall trees with long, dark green leaves that rustled in the breeze, and Wren thought the trees smelled sharply of summer weeds. "Where are we?" she asked.

"On the way to the Free Vale," Tyron said.

"Where's that?"

"You don't know about the Free Vale?" He turned in the saddle to stare at her.

"Do you," she replied promptly, "know about Three Groves Orphanage?"

"It's not just a place." He waved a hand. "It's a Free Haven."

"Oh yes, those magician hideouts. We read about those in the plays."

"The Havens," Tyron said, "are safe areas where really important people can go, not just magicians. People who've been exiled or who want to get away, usually from some villainous despot or other. Lots of magic protects the Havens. You'll feel the magic when we pass the border," he added with a grin that made her suspicious at once.

She did not ask about that immediately, however. The horseback ride was still on her mind. "If you're going to be a magician, you must be prenticed at the Magic School, right?"

"Yes." He looked surprised.

"Then why didn't we leave by magic? Don't you know any yet?"

"I know lots!" He kicked at the saddlebag that hung between her right knee and his. She saw corners and lines that suggested books in the heavy cloth bag. "But they'd trace us at once and then bring us back. No one can trace us if we travel without using any magic at all. They could track us—which is why I am trying to keep away from roads—but they couldn't use magic. And I said a ward spell against Halfrid scrying me," he added, his changeable face suddenly reflecting regret.

"Halfrid?" Wren repeated. "The King's Magician?"

"Right." He turned to the other side and reached into the bag that hung on the left side of the saddle. "Hungry?"

Wren groaned with artistic fervor.

Tyron laughed, the moment of forehead-puckered worry gone. "Here." He handed her a small round loaf of bread.

She took it and inspected it with interest. The loaf was slit in half, and cheese, greens, and tomato slices had been packed into it. She took an enthusiastic bite. In front of her, Tyron gave his attention to another loaf. He looked at least as hungry as she felt.

They ate silently. The horse kept walking, Tyron sitting sideways with one leg thrown carelessly over the front of the saddle in a way that Wren thought looked dangerous. She noticed that they were gradually approaching some low, rounded hills. She was used to the high, rocky mountains of Siradayel. These hills were covered with grass and low shrubs and looked as if they'd be fun to run on.

"Tell me more about this Free Vale," she asked at last, "and what this has to do with Tess—or with me."

"Someone is there who would be the best person to find the Princess and free her. What I need you for is to help me try

37

to scry the Princess tonight, so we can tell Id . . . the person exactly where she is."

"Scry? What's that? And who's Id?" Wren asked.

Tyron was silent for a moment or two. He was still chewing, but Wren wasn't fooled. *He didn't want to tell her. Why?*

"If I'm going to help—" she began.

"At least with the scrying," he said.

"Then *at least* tell me what *that* is."

"Scrying is . . . I don't know how to explain it," he replied, scratching his head distractedly. "You use a scrying stone usually, though you don't have to, I understand. But *I* sure can't without one."

"And?" Wren prompted, trying to control her impatience at his backward explanation.

"You use magic, and look in and focus on the person—or thing, if you're *really* good—and sometimes you can see it. Or them. Her, in this case." He shrugged. "Though I'm good at the magic part, I'm not too great at the *seeing* part. Sometimes two can do it better, especially if one person knows the person you're trying to see."

"So who's Id?"

"No one—" He paused, then seemed to reach a sudden decision. "Idres Rhiscarlan." His tone indicated he expected a certain reaction.

Wren just shook her head. "So who's that?"

His brown eyes went wide with surprise. "You mean you don't know—"

Wren sighed noisily. "Spare me a list of all the people in the world, *and* all the places, that I don't know."

"I'm sorry," he said, obviously trying not to laugh. "It's just that your being the Princess's friend, I thought you'd know about *that* piece of history since it kind of concerns her. The wrong version, to be sure," he added under his breath.

Wren said, "I don't know *any* version, and I don't think Tess does either. We were in Siradayel, you see, not Meldrith, and we weren't even told much of Siradayel's history. It being thought," she added with ominous sarcasm, "that preparing us for a life of weeds, pots, and darning was all that was needed. Though Tess did say, the other day—" Wren cut herself short as her voice went unexpectedly high. *A week ago we were playing quests and rescues.* Wren gave a fierce sniff and went on firmly, "Her aunt said that history talk would come from her parents."

Tyron now regarded her with clear sympathy. He said nothing embarrassing, though, and quite suddenly Wren decided that she liked this funny-looking, moody magic student. Tyron, meanwhile, said, "Some people consider Idres to be a figure of great controversy."

"You mean no one knows if she's a villain or not?"

"That's close enough." He looked around. "We can wash our hands and get a drink there in that stream. Then we'd better ride again. I was hoping we'd be well into the hills before dark. No one will find us there."

"We *will* talk more when we camp?"

"I promise."

He kept his promise, too. Dark was still early these days of early spring, and neither Wren nor Tyron wanted to sleep immediately. He found a grove of close-growing trees to camp under. Wren silently followed his directions as they cared for the horse. The sunlight was fading rapidly, and they wanted to be done before they could no longer see.

At last they lay on either side of a tiny fire that Tyron built, each wrapped in a blanket.

"I was able to grab an extra blanket, but not any extra food," he apologized as he tore the last loaf in half.

Wren swallowed, thinking: *This is good practice for real adventuring.* "That will be fine. I'm sorry my half today will make you go hungry tomorrow."

He shrugged. The firelight flickering on the lower part of his face made him look very much like a fox. "Once we're well into the hills, we might find some early berries or something. And we'll reach the Haven by tomorrow afternoon as long as we don't have rain slowing us down."

"Rain?" She squinted up at the sky, where stars like fire-lit gemstones glittered peacefully.

"Dew." He touched a nearby blade of long grass. "When it's like this, it usually means rain in a day."

"In the mountains, rain comes very suddenly," she said. "Now, how about telling me more about the Free Vale. How does one get in?"

"I don't really know how they decide to allow someone in permanently. Vote, I guess. As for people like us, no one with ill intent against an inhabitant can enter. The magic over it is very powerful. No one has broken it yet, and lots have tried."

"So, who exactly is this Idres person, and why is she the best to help find Tess if she's thought to be a villain?"

"She was once on the side of King Andreus of Senna Lirwan," Tyron said.

"Ugh!"

"But she changed." He waved his last bit of bread in the air. Grinning, he added, "She made a hash of his rotten plans before she left. She's one of us now. But some people—" He frowned into the fire. "Some people don't seem to be able to remember that." Then he looked up. "She knows more about Andreus than anyone else. I thought she'd be the best to get the Princess back and also, at the same time, overcome the grumbling that still attaches to her name."

"Grudge holders," Wren said firmly, "are stinkweed."

Tyron snickered. Popping his last bite of bread into his mouth, he reached over and pulled his bag to his lap. First he dug out two thick books and set them carefully on his blanket. Then he pulled out an apple-sized object, wrapped in dark cloth. When he opened it, Wren gasped in pleasure. It was a round stone, milky white and softly glistening in the firelight.

She pointed. "What's that? It's beautiful."

"My scrying stone," he said. "Maybe this won't work, and

40

you're not to feel badly if it doesn't. Some magicians can't scry at all."

Wren nodded. "Let's try," she said firmly, thinking: *An adventurer is ready for anything.*

Tyron kicked dirt over the fire and for a few minutes they just sat, letting their eyes adjust to the dark. Wren waited in silence, feeling the soft spring air moving around her and listening to the leaves murmuring overhead. On the other side of the grove she heard a thud as the horse shifted his weight and clopped one of his hooves down on the ground.

"Now," Tyron said quietly.

Wren looked up. She saw Tyron's body outlined in the soft, multicolored starlight. Still with her blanket wrapped around her, she inched closer until she was sitting next to him. She gazed curiously at the stone he held, seeing stars reflected and refracted to its depths. As he moved the stone about gently on his palms, the stars winkled and stretched into lines of blue and red and green fire, as if they were melting.

"Think about the Princess," Tyron whispered.

It was hard for Wren to think about anything but the beauty of starlight, reflected deep inside the stone. The moving, flickering lights . . . melting together, bright as the sun in the morning . . .

*Tess.*

Wren was distantly aware of a gasp from Tyron. She ignored him: *Tess!*

The facets of the stone were gone, and inside it Wren saw the Princess looking around in perplexity, her eyes worried and her mouth solemn. Tess's hair hung down uncombed, and she wore the same green linen dress she'd put on the morning she'd disappeared. It looked rumpled and slept-in.

"Now concentrate on location," Tyron whispered, but Wren scarcely heard him. Her attention was wholly on her friend.

"Tess?" Wren murmured, and as the girl did not react, Wren called in her mind: *Tess?*

Tess jerked as though she'd heard a voice. She smiled hopefully—

The next moment Wren felt a sudden feeling of hot, terrible rage—

Tyron yelled "Break!" and jerked the stone away.

Wren fell back, dizzy and bewildered. "Tess?" she muttered. "She heard me. I know she did."

"Yes," Tyron said grimly, but with a new tone in his voice. Caution—respect. "That was your first scrying?"

Wren was too upset by what she had seen to respond to his change in attitude. "Yes. She wasn't happy. And never, ever, did she get dirty at Three Groves."

"Do you remember her surroundings?"

Wren squinted, trying to recall the vivid scene. She was aware of a thin, persistent pang in her temple, but it was fading rapidly. "Stone, I think. Yes. Smooth stone. Not much else—" She broke off and rubbed her eyes. "How could I see even that much? Does this thing make a window?" She pointed to the stone as Tyron wrapped it carefully and stowed it away.

"No, what you're seeing is not a completely *physical* vision, like looking through a window. It's more like . . . well, how the other person sees herself. That's the simplest way to explain it right now."

"What was that nasty business at the end? Someone was mad."

"That was Andreus," Tyron said, even more grimly than before. "We won't be able to try it again."

Wren sighed. "Tess was *not* happy."

"Let's go to sleep. Soon as we have light, we'll ride, as fast as we can. Maybe she can be free in a couple of days."

Wren lay back, wrapping the blanket more tightly around her. Almost at once she dropped into a heavy sleep.


In a cold, dark room, Teressa sat up shivering. Pulling the single thin, mildewed blanket about her shoulders, she fought

42

against the sting in her eyes and the tight fist deep in her chest. *No blubbing*, she thought sternly. *If that wasn't really Wren thinking at me somehow, then it was a nice dream. But I know she thinks about me—*

She heard sounds outside the door. Boots, clanking keys. As the heavy door began to open, Teressa made a sudden decision and lay flat again, feigning sleep. Strange yellow light flared unevenly on her eyelids, and a familiar voice, tenor, slightly metallic—as though a knife had been melted into it—spoke.

"Teressa!"

She hated that voice. "Uhn," she mumbled, turning to the wall.

She heard a step, and hard fingers shook her shoulder. She sat up, rubbing her eyes so she wouldn't have to look at him.

"Who was that?" the voice demanded. "The scry contact."

*So that really was Wren.* A sunburst of gladness and triumph warmed her inside, banishing the awful fist that had lived there since she had been put out of consciousness in her parents' sunny palace garden and had awakened in this room. Still rubbing her eyes, she kept her face blank. "Huh? Who?"

"The person making the scry contact, you witless fool! Who was that?"

Teressa had a sudden memory of Aunt Leila at her crispest, teaching a class of unruly boys: *Don't sit with your mouth open, Noker! Did your wits fall out?*

Teressa let her jaw drop, so she'd look like Noker. "I guess I had a bad dream," she mumbled, squinting against the glare of the lamp. "Why are you here? Did I yell?"

A long, nasty pause stretched out as she stared upward at angry brown eyes. Twin lamps glittered in those eyes, tiny fires. It was an awful moment, but then, suddenly, the lamps swung away. No further words were spoken. Teressa sat silently, listening to the thud and clank of the door being closed and locked.

Once again she was alone.

# Chapter Six

$\mathcal{A}$s daylight faded the next day, Wren and Tyron, shivering and soggy on their head-drooping horse, crossed the border into the Free Vale. Wren had awakened that morning with a mild headache, and now, after the cold rain had slashed at them for most of the endless afternoon, she felt as if boulders had appeared out of nowhere and lodged in her skull.

They'd had nothing to eat, either. Still, Wren did not complain, nor did she wish she was elsewhere. The memory of Tess's unhappy face had made turning back impossible.

As they passed through the border, she felt a vertigo akin to the transportation spell that had brought her from Three Groves to the Magic School: briefer, but more intense. Accompanying the vertigo was a creepy sensation, as though some kind of net had passed through her mind. She flinched, the headache worsening. Then Tyron shouted against the hissing of the rain, "We're through. We're here."

She looked about her, saw nothing but darkness, and huddled into her wet blanket again. It seemed much later when she finally heard voices. A man said, "I'll fetch her over. You come inside. You're not to go any farther. She lives a good half hour's walk when the weather's fine." And Tyron muttered something in reply.

Two strong hands lifted Wren from the horse's back. A short time later she found herself in a warm room with a soft quilt wrapped around her, while a comforting old lady's voice murmured gently. Wren's wet clothes were taken somewhere, and someone combed the rain out of her hair, and then strong, wrinkled hands pressed a mug of something hot and good-smelling into her own tightly clenched fingers.

"My special soup," the voice said. "Drink."

Wren drank obediently and felt warmth course through her. She drank again, her tongue scalding just enough to feel pleasant. More warmth spread into fingers and toes, and the headache began to dissipate like summer thunder fading away.

She looked up. She was in a small room, across from a wonderful wall painting of people in a garden. On a stool in front of her a tiny old woman sat, light blue eyes expectant.

"Well," the woman declared, her accent slow and pleasing, like a song. "Your friend is in the front room, with my brother Gastarth. They await Mistress Idres. You like my soup?"

"Very much, thank you," Wren managed.

"You would like some more? Or to sleep?"

"Thank you, no." Wren looked to the doorway, where she heard a sudden noise. Tyron's familiar voice, now excited, was followed by a man's gruff tones, and a cool, low, woman's voice. "I'd like to hear—oh." She looked down at herself.

The woman chuckled. "No one will mind the rose quilt. It is prettier than most gowns, I do think."

Wrapping the quilt around her more securely, Wren grinned. The hem dragged on the ground as far as any court gown's train as she crossed the room.

"But you have to!" was the first thing Wren heard plainly. This was from Tyron, in a voice of dismay. He was sitting in front of a mighty fire, wearing a green and scarlet embroidered tunic much too large for him, his bare feet propped on the hearthstone. Clasped forgotten in his hands was a mug like hers, half filled with the thick soup.

Facing him stood a tall, thin woman with a straight back and a pair of steady dark eyes. Shining black hair fell in a thick braid halfway down the skirt of her black dress and lost itself among the folds. The woman ignored the short, white-bearded man leaning against the opposite wall and kept her gaze on Tyron's face.

She said, "Were you forbidden by Halfrid to approach me?"

Tyron's jaw tightened. Wren realized suddenly that that was exactly what had happened.

The woman gave him a faint smile. "More fool you, then. I meant that vow. I will never lift a hand against Verne Rhisadel, King of Meldrith, nor yet in his aid. If you know that much about me, then you must know that I keep my word."

Tyron looked up in dismay. "But this is his daughter."

"She will have enough champions."

"But none of them have been able to do much good."

"That is a tragedy, eh? Perhaps she will survive and turn the situation to her advantage. I did."

"Advantage," Tyron said bitterly, in a voice strained and almost unrecognizable. "Sitting here and s-sulking, when you have the p-power to do anything. It makes me sick."

"Then have the goodness to keep your sickness to yourself, Tyron ner-Halfrid," she said coldly. "I did not ask you to seek me out. You had best return to your teacher and beg forgiveness. Blame the unrealistic altruism of youth." She smiled again, very faintly, but with no warmth whatever. "If he cannot remember such an emotion, you may assure him that I do."

"Mistress—" the old man began tentatively.

"Are you interfering, Master Gastarth?" Idres Rhiscarlan addressed him in a frosty voice.

The older man bowed, with slow dignity. "Your pardon."

The woman turned abruptly and from a hook by the door plucked a black cloak with raindrops glistening on it. She threw the wrap about her shoulders and disappeared into the wet night.

Tyron slumped down, head bent over his soup cup.

"I knew Halfrid a little, years ago," the old man murmured. "In truth, he will forgive you."

"It's not just that," Tyron muttered. Looking up again, he grimaced with a faint return of his usual humor. "Though he will be fierce with me. It's . . . oh, I guess I hate unfairness. And I despise the waste of wars. I was *sure* that she would know the best way to sneak past that rotter Andreus's magic defenses, and she'd know the most about his citadel, so we could get in and out fast. The King must not be pushed into marching in war against Andreus."

"Why not?" Wren asked.

Tyron looked across the room and seemed to see her for the first time. "You look like the queen of the mudlarks with that wet hair all over and those silly roses on that blanket."

"Never mind what I look like," Wren said tartly. She was not really angry. She recognized instantly that he was trying to recover his sense of balance, just as she did when she was upset and trying to hide it. "Why shouldn't our King go to war against the creep king? It's not like King Verne's trying to conquer anybody—unlike Andreus of Senna Lirwan."

"Andreus made the vow about the Princess after King Verne sneaked into Senna Lirwan and convinced Idres to change sides," Tyron said. "So Andreus maintains that he is getting his own back again. He'd *say* he's only defending himself. Meanwhile, people on both sides get killed—and nothing gets resolved, because Andreus will just come back again." Tyron scratched his head fiercely. "There are so many reasons. In short, the King wants to get his daughter back, well and good, but he should be helped to do it without causing a war."

"A war with Andreus would be difficult to win," Master Gastarth put in, nodding his head slightly. "He's organized the country entirely around the preparation for military conquest."

"Which can be discussed as well in the morning, after you have refreshed yourselves with sleep," the old lady announced, coming forward. "You children took a terrible soaking, and anything you wish to do will be the harder if you are sick."

Tyron protested only faintly. He finished his soup and was led up a ladder into a loft. Wren, lying in the narrow, warm bed allotted to her, heard creaking footsteps overhead, which reminded her of the old orphanage in the mountains. Her mind wandered back there as she drifted off to sleep.

For a while Wren slept in her usual manner, which was like a lump. However, as the night progressed, her dreams turned threatening. It always seemed to be raining, and though she burrowed down under the warm quilts, her hands and feet still felt vaguely chilled. Then she started dreaming about Tess, and about that glittering scrying stone, glistening like ice. Tess was trying to speak to her, and Wren knew she had to get to the stone in order to hear. But there seemed to be something else trying to hear Wren, something she had to avoid.

When it seemed she couldn't fight against the dreams any longer, she became aware of a gentle, old voice singing a high, compelling melody. The voice was too soft to make out words. As Wren strained to hear, she woke up completely and felt the dream terror slide away like shadows after a bad storm. The voice had stopped, leaving Wren wondering if she'd dreamed that as well. She sat up in bed. The window showed the faint blue light of impending dawn.

Finding her yellow linen dress fresh, dry, and laid neatly over a low chest, she dressed hastily. The room and the floor were cold. She picked up her shoes and stockings, tiptoed to the door, eased it open, and saw warm orange light.

Tyron lay on his stomach before the fire, his books open before him. He was writing in one. Wren sat down on the hearth to one side, so as not to block the firelight from his steadily scratching pen. As she put on her stockings and shoes, she glanced down at the pages. The book he was writing in had tiny, badly formed letters, with some crossing out. The other book also displayed tiny printing, but in a neatly rounded hand.

"Who made that book?" she whispered.

"I did." He did not look up from his writing.

"You made both books?"

"Yes." Now he looked up. "Ready-made books are expensive. And besides, we are supposed to learn better if we make our own. This one is my practice book, and *that*"—his fingers brushed the one with the neat lettering—"shows what I've learned."

"Magic," she breathed. "How I'd like to see some more."

"Maybe later. Before we leave."

"I thought we'd be traced. Or does that no longer matter?"

"We're in the Free Vale. No outside magic penetrates in here. I can do as much as I like while I'm here. And anyway, it *matters*." He grimaced. "Did you think I was giving up?"

She drew her legs up under her skirt and hugged her knees tightly. "Well, if you're not—why not? When you first laid eyes on me, you asked *why* I wanted to rescue Tess. And I told you. But now, since that Idres isn't going to blast into Senna Lirwan like thunder and lightning with her magic to rescue Tess, I've been wondering the same thing about you."

Tyron scratched above his ear with his pen end as he stared into the fire. "Some of my reasons I can't say. Promised not to. And there are some I guess I'd rather not say." He looked up at Wren. "This I can tell you, though. I won't get anything out of it if any plan I make does work—if you were thinking that."

"So why—" Wren began.

"Because I made a promise not to when I—" His face changed again. His mouth smiled a little, but the humor reflected the kind of bitter irony that made Wren all of a sudden think of Idres. "When a thing happened last year. Anyway, I won't give up either. It's just that it's not going to be easy—not that it ever would have been *easy*. That's the wrong word. But now, it will be harder."

Wren nodded. "Hard or easy, after what I saw in your magic glass, I won't stop trying until she is free!"

Tyron slammed his book shut and wiped his pen carefully before stopping his tiny crystal bottle of ink. "Who is your family, may I ask?"

She shrugged. "Nobody knows. Me and one other, a boy

49

who was older, were found on a battlefield. They thought it might have been a caravan attacked by thieves. But no one was able to find out who they were. Foreign merchants, maybe."

"What about that boy, was he your brother?"

"Nobody thought so. He was tall and skinny and had pale hair. He was also dull as old oatmeal. Prenticed to the village weaver before I was sent to Three Groves. Why?"

"Because nobody, ever, has read so clearly in a scrying stone, much less made a contact, that I know of—particularly on a first try. It was a first try?"

"Yes." She sighed. "I always dreamed I might be a long-lost princess, or even a duke's daughter who'd been captured by the Iyon Daiyin . . ."

Tyron grinned with some sympathy. "Well, you probably aren't. For one thing, those nobles and royals always take pretty good care to find out where their relatives are. They don't get 'long lost' so much as 'long hidden.' "

"Like Tess," Wren said softly.

"True. As for the Iyon Daiyin, if you believe those stupid stories about stealing babies for ransom or whatever, then you don't know much about *them*. And furthermore, a trait for magic—such as scrying—doesn't necessarily run in those ruling families. In fact, in some countries, the rulers regard magicians with suspicion."

Wren sighed, this time in mock sadness. "Too good to be true. Besides, what princess has striped hair?"

Tyron shrugged carelessly. "Probably as many as not."

"Princesses are always lovely—and Tess certainly is."

"That's because her mother is. Some of 'em, in true-written records, are plain-looking people, like you or me."

"But the stories and plays—"

"Are written to make everyone look better, or worse, than they are. And you get stories about the people in governments not because they are prettier or better but because people are interested in power."

"That," Wren said, forgetting to whisper, "is a boring way to look at things."

"But it's true."

"And I suppose all adventures did not really happen and were just accidents? And evil magicians are just people with bad stomachs that make them crabby?"

"No, but what has that to do with how nobles look—"

"Would you children like something to eat?" The calm voice of the old lady broke into what was fast turning into an argument.

Tyron flushed, scrambling to his feet.

"I'm sorry if we woke you," Wren said.

"No, no, I always rise at dawn. A beautiful time of day, don't you think? So peaceful . . ." The old lady murmured on as she handed Wren a kettle to fill from the pump outside and pointed out the firewood for Tyron to bring in.

After a time Mistress Selshaf's brother came downstairs from the loft, and the four of them ate a hearty breakfast. Wren liked the old people and found them so comfortingly ordinary and kind that she wondered why they were living in a Haven that was meant for prestigious exiles and other mysterious figures.

Tyron and Wren helped to clear the dishes, and their borrowed bedding, and then Tyron found a chance to whisper to Wren, "I'm going to see Idres alone. Then we'll leave."

Wren's first instinct was to insist on coming, too, but she realized she did not really want to see cold and imperious Idres Rhiscarlan again. So she nodded, and a few minutes later Tyron hefted his bag of books over his shoulder and set off briskly down the road.

Mistress Selshaf picked up a trowel and a basket and said, smiling, "I must go out to the vegetables now, or they will feel neglected. Will you come and tell me about life in the mountains?"

Wren assented politely and just as politely helped the old lady with pulling weeds. She certainly knew plenty about vegetable gardens from the orphanage, but hereto she'd hated the work. It was boring, and if she daydreamed and pulled a carrot instead of a weed, she inevitably earned a sharp rebuke. This gardening was different. Mistress Selshaf asked her questions as they worked, and smiled with enjoyment at everything Wren said. Before long Wren was coaxed—easily—into performing some of her juggling and stunts.

The ground was uneven, and Wren did not always have good luck, particularly with the juggling, but she kept trying. Thus, she was determinedly trying to get six beetroots flying through the air, as the old lady watched and clapped, when a voice interrupted.

"Ho, Wren."

"Yipe!" The beetroots went scattering. "What—"

Tyron ran toward them, his face red and sweaty.

The old lady's face crinkled with interest and silent amusement. "Had you success, then, with our neighbor Mistress Idres?"

Tyron grimaced. "Of a sort. She's not going to budge—but surprisingly she did tell me some things about Andreus's border protections."

Mistress Selshaf's smile suddenly changed from mirth to concern. Reaching for her basket, she said, "Come inside, young ones. It is time and past for the noon meal."

## Chapter Seven

*T*he old man met them inside the little cottage. Wren's sensitive ears caught a drift of softly murmured words from Mistress Selshaf to her brother, but Tyron didn't seem to hear. His hands rubbed absently on the sides of his bag of magic books as he sat down next to the hearth.

"I will fetch the food." The lady disappeared into the kitchen.

Master Gastarth said slowly, "A rule binding those who live in the Haven is that we do not interfere in one another's lives without an invitation. That rule exists for guests as well. Therefore, though you have accepted our roof and board, you must not think that we expect you to heed any questions that you would rather not answer."

Tyron shook his head. "Some, I wouldn't," he said firmly. "But you're welcome to ask."

The old man smiled, his snowy beard moving on his chest. "You are a good choice, I think."

Tyron's face turned crimson, and Wren thought, *For what?*

"You have decided to free Princess Teressa from King Andreus of Senna Lirwan, though Mistress Idres had denied you her aid?"

Tyron gave a jerky, awkward shrug, but Wren answered. "We have."

"His borders," the old man said seriously, "are nearly as

protected as are the Free Vale's against magical penetration. And they are watched carefully, even in the mountains."

"I know." Tyron was still fidgeting with his bookbag. "And I know the mountains are dangerous. But if a person is careful and prepares and plans, then I think it's possible to get past. The Lirwani border guards will be watching for armed intruders, and his spies on our side of the border will be taking note of parties of adults. I think a couple of prenties could slip in unnoticed."

"You cannot use magic. You do not know enough to ward off his tracer spells."

Tyron did not deny it. "So I won't use magic. My advantage is that he doesn't know who I am. He can't have warding spells set for me, like there are for Halfrid and Falstan."

Appearing silently, Mistress Selshaf passed out bowls of good-smelling stew.

The old man went on. "What of the citadel?"

"Idres gave me a detailed description of it," Tyron said. "She told me the best ways in and out."

"That will be of use only if he has not changed his stronghold," the old lady murmured quietly. "Idres has not seen it for ten years."

Tyron's jaw tightened. "We'll manage," he said. Then he cast a questioning look at Wren, who nodded firmly. "He won't be watching for prenties."

Master Gastarth set his bowl down and placed his hands on his knees. "Andreus of Senna Lirwan may not be watching for prenties, but you will not know for sure until you enter his stronghold. He is a clever man, and a dangerous one as well. His plans extend far beyond the trouble he is making with Verne of Meldrith. And anyone who is daring enough and lucky enough to oppose him and win free again will have his enmity not for days, or months, but for years. The disappearance of the Princess is proof of that."

"I've read as much about Senna Lirwan as I could find." Tyron's voice was stiff.

"What if Halfrid comes here looking for you?"

"I plan to send a message to him anyway. To tell him my plans changed a little, but I am acting on them just the same."

"A good choice," the old man repeated, almost too softly to hear.

This time Tyron did not blush. Wren watched in silent question as he rubbed hasty knuckles across his eyes. Then he looked up. "Maybe once. He won't think so now." His voice was thin, as it had been the night before when he faced Idres, but steady. "I can't go back, so I'll go on and help Wren find the Princess. I still think this is the only way, and the King should not be pushed by those court toffs to go to war."

Mistress Selshaf gave them her wide smile. "Eat your stew, young ones, while I pack you some provisions. You have before you a good day for travel."

Not very long after, Wren and Tyron walked briskly down the road toward the border. Wren's first question was, "Why aren't we riding?"

"Because the horse belongs to the Magic School," Tyron said shortly. "Halfrid will take it back when he comes."

"Is that why you left your magic books there, and that stone?"

"No. Those belong to me. They promised to keep them safe for me. On this journey, I must not use any magic. When . . . when it's over, then I can return to the Free Vale and fetch them." He frowned slightly, and Wren could tell he did not want to discuss his magic anymore. "Show me what the Mistress gave you—and *why* did you ask for a packet of yellow pepper? We won't be cooking, and I don't believe you sprinkle it on your oatcakes for taste."

Wren laughed. "When I lived in the mountains, I found out that pepper was a good thing to have about for anyone short, young, and not real strong. Orphans aren't allowed to learn to use weapons, so every village bully picked on us."

"*Pepper* as a weapon?" Tyron said doubtfully. "*That* I should like to see." Then, with more interest, "What else did she give you?"

"Well, first thing she gave me was this apron." Wren patted the plain white apron she now wore over her yellow dress. "When I told her this gown isn't really mine, but belongs to the palace, and I thought I should try to protect it, she gave it to me. Said she has two spares." Wren then pulled a long, silky fringed scarf from one of the apron's two roomy pockets. "She gave me this as well. Isn't it pretty? I've never had *anything* like this before."

Wren held up the scarf and admired it as it waved in the breeze. It was a soft bluish gray, with thin gold embroidery around the edges in the shape of vines. Tiny flowers of crimson and blue made a pattern among the vines, and the fringe was made of soft strands of dark blue silk. "So that's three gifts," Wren finished happily, indicating with pride the knapsacks she and Tyron now wore. "*Four.*" She corrected herself. "Mistress Selshaf packed a cloak in each knapsack along with a packet of oatcakes. Anyway, how *lucky* for us we met them first, when we rode in that night."

Tyron's eyes seemed somber again as he watched Wren carefully fold the scarf and put it in her pocket. "Yes. Lucky. I think," he murmured.

"Imagine if we'd managed to find our way straight to that awful Idres, and she put us right back out into the rain."

"She isn't awful," Tyron said promptly.

"Anybody who could help Tess and refuses is awful," Wren retorted.

Tyron said nothing.

They walked for a while in silence. Wren looked around appreciatively, though Tyron's gaze remained on the ground before his feet. The Free Vale was located in a shallow river valley, with forest growing dark green and mysterious along the tops of the farther hills. In the other direction the low hills were grassy, and here and there sheep grazed peacefully. In the distance, on a bend of the river, she saw a house that had to have been erected by magical means, for it looked to be made of spun glass.

After they had walked for some time, she said, pointing to the forest, "Will we be entering it?"

"No." Tyron looked up for a moment. "Too dangerous, once we're past the Haven border. If I could use magic . . . but I can't."

"Danger? What—beasts?"

"And robbers, on the southern part of the frontier. We are near the southern border of Meldrith—" He frowned at her, not angrily, but in question. "Do you know where that is?"

"Far from home," she said, smiling. "I've been enjoying it ever since yesterday. *That* way lie the mountains where I first lived"—she pointed north—"and further than that, but a bit east, is Three Groves. And now," she finished up triumphantly, "we are near the southern corner of Meldrith, because all around on the horizon I see mountains, but the highest ones are in the east. That's the border of Senna Lirwan."

"You do know your maps." His face relaxed a little.

"Map. We had just one." She waved her arms wide. "But I did love to look at it and imagine myself on tremendous adventures, seeing wondrous new things." She made a face. "Except, I just thought of something. When we get beyond the mountains, nobody is going to speak Sirad."

"I thought of that as well," he said. "We'll be going southeast along the Hroth River road for a time, until we reach a trading town called Hroth Falls. I thought we might pay a visit to the magician there, who can give you the language spell. You won't have any problem with that spell, not the way you read that stone."

"A language spell?"

"Yes. Some people can't accept them. It will make your head feel strange for a little time, but afterward you will know Lirwani."

"What about those magic tracers you were afraid of the other day?"

"Tracers only work against one type of spell—whatever it

is you want to trace—or in a magically enclosed space, like Senna Lirwan."

"So, the other day, if we'd gone by magic transportation, someone at the Magic School could have put a transportation tracer on us and found out where we'd gone?" Wren asked, and at Tyron's nod, she said, "That makes sense—I think. So do you know Lirwani?"

Tyron nodded. "I know seven languages, three of which I learned by study. At the School we have—had—to learn three before we could try the language spell."

"Had," Wren repeated. "You're not going back. Is *that* why you're so grumpy whenever I mention your magic?"

He shook his head violently. And as that same stiff look came into his face that he'd had when Master Gastarth talked about Halfrid, Wren added hastily, "How about if we make up some stories to pass the time?"

"Why?" he asked, scanning the distant line of dark forest.

"Why?" she repeated. "Because it's fun, of course."

"Making up stories?" He looked at her in disbelief.

"Sure. Pirates, and mysterious ghosts, and—"

"But what's there to learn in something that never happened?"

"Learn?" she repeated, as if it were a foreign word.

"Learning," he said impatiently, "makes it possible to *do* things." Then eying her apologetically, he amended, "It's a good idea, to do something to pass the time while we walk. Would you like me to teach you some of the old sign language?"

"Sign language?"

"From the bad old empire days, when magicians were always in danger. That's how they recognized each other and how they conveyed messages and so forth. It's fun. We used it to talk secretly in class, when lessons were dull at the School."

Wren had lived with other children all her life, and she knew a peace offering when she heard it. Besides, her curiosity was sparked. "Let's!" she exclaimed happily.

"Then here's your first." He held one hand out flat and

moved it forward in a quick gesture. "That means, 'Let's get going!' "

Obligingly, Wren walked faster.

Tyron showed her several more signs, some of them letters of the alphabet and others general phrases. In this way the distance as well as the remainder of the day passed quickly. When the sun was about to set, they decided to stop. They were just inside the Haven border and, as Tyron pointed out, were perfectly safe from bandits or other threats. "Why not stay the night here and leave the Haven at daybreak?"

This remark made Wren reflect on his not using magic as she wrapped herself up in the fine gray-brown cloak that Mistress Selshaf had given her. *What that must mean is that he might not know how to defend himself by ordinary means. That's one thing we learned young in the mountains,* she thought.

They each ate one traveler's cake, then lay down on the grass to sleep.


When Wren woke in the morning, the field around them was white with delicate dew, and the rising sun orange and bright on the horizon. It was going to be a warm day, and already the dew sparkled as it began to fade. Sitting up, Wren was delighted when she realized she was perfectly warm and dry inside her cloak. "Hey—these keep water out!" she exclaimed.

Tyron snorted and sat up abruptly.

"I'm sorry," Wren said. "Did I wake you?"

"Had trouble falling asleep." He shrugged. His hand ran down the outside of the gray-brown cloak that he was wrapped in, a twin to Wren's. He said, "There must be magic woven in. A fine gift indeed for two strangers." He frowned slightly as he folded his cloak and stowed it in his knapsack.

"What's wrong? Danger? Tracers against the magic in *these?*" She patted her cloak before folding it carefully.

"Oh, no." He rubbed his head, which made his thick brown hair look even more like a birds' nest. "I doubt anyone would set up tracers for any magic cloaks . . . but . . ." He turned and stared at his knapsack. "There *are* certain kinds of powerful spells that will sense any magic either done or acting, and I imagine Andreus has them on his border. The strange thing is, these cloaks won't set them off: the magic in them is *different*—" He fought for words for a moment, then shrugged sharply. "It's very hard to learn." He looked perplexed.

As Wren waited for him to continue, she hastily unbraided her hair, fingered it smooth, and braided it again. When she bent to take a cake from her knapsack, Tyron copied her absently.

For a time he munched in silence. When he spoke, it was suddenly. "All these things we were given—and some of the things they said—I get the feeling it wasn't any accident we met them first. But why?"

Wren said practically, "Do you think their mysterious reasons are bad or good?"

Tyron blinked at her for a moment. "Well, good—of course—"

"Then why worry?"

Tyron sighed. "All right. I won't. You done eating?"

They found a stream in which to wash their hands and get a drink, and then set out at a brisk pace. At first they walked in silence, but after a time Tyron looked over at Wren, and his face changed to a funny grin. "You look like you're smelling something really terrible," he commented. "Something amiss?"

"I'm waiting for that border magic," she said. "Feels like worms in the brains."

He laughed. "There are no spells of intent for people leaving. We won't feel anything."

"Great," Wren said, and they picked up their pace.

Not much was said for an hour or two. Tyron's face was downward again. He was obviously thinking hard. Wren looked around with interest—until she thought she saw something.

"Tyron!"

"Riders." Tyron's head jerked up. "Here's my plan: when anyone appears on the road—we hide."

For answer Wren led the way to a clump of close-growing shrubs halfway up a small rise. They crouched down and waited until the four riders had passed and the sound of the horses' hooves had died away. Then they resumed their walking, and Tyron immediately began teaching Wren more of the hand signals.


"They've been found." Mistress Leila greeted King Verne and Queen Astren with the news late the next day. The three of them were alone in the King's private audience chamber.

Queen Astren closed her eyes in relief.

"Together?" the King asked.

Leila smiled briefly. "As we'd guessed. Also as we'd guessed, they went straight to the Haven. Halfrid received a sending from Tyron yesterday morning and went immediately to investigate."

"So now they're where? Returned to the School?" The King walked back and forth in front of the heavily curtained window. "I trust Halfrid has locked up this wayward prentice of his on bread and water for a month—" He stopped speaking when he saw Mistress Leila's slowly shaking head.

"What has happened?" the Queen asked.

"What has happened is simply that Tyron and Wren have decided to carry on their rescue quest alone."

"And Halfrid allowed this?" The King whirled about to glare at her.

Though Leila had renounced her royal title in order to become a magician, she was sometimes more imperious than mere rulers. One of her eyebrows went up. "Must you use that field command voice in this tiny room, Verne?" she asked pleasantly. "I fear for those exquisite glass windows."

Reluctantly, the King said, "Your pardon, Leila."

61

"Thank you. Halfrid has returned empty-handed—much to his own bemusement—because it seems that Wren and Tyron were sheltered and sent off on their quest again by none other than Selsheris and Jestarth Sendimeris of Starborn Island."

The names seemed to linger, echoing, in the silence that greeted this news. Then the King said quietly, "Starborn Island . . . where the Iyon Daiyin come from."

"Well, not come from," Leila said, trying to interpret his tone. "But they originally settled there. And it's true that the Sendimeris twins are descended from—"

"I thought they were dead." The King turned around, obviously deep in thought.

"No. Old, yes. Old-looking, anyway. And disappeared from public life, yes. It seems they've been living quietly in the Haven these six or seven years, in a cottage, as Mistress Selshaf and Master Gastarth."

"Did Halfrid ask why?" Now the King looked up at her.

"Indirectly. He was not expecting to find *them*, you understand. Nor did he get a direct answer, really. What seems to be important is that they know what Tyron and Wren wish to do, and they sent them on their way with gifts and good wishes. And hinted that we'd do well not to interfere."

"Why?" the Queen murmured. "Wren and that boy are so *young*."

"You could always ride to the Haven and ask them." Leila smiled. "For myself, I can't help but remember that Tyron is merely two years younger than I was when I went, alone, to live with your daughter at Three Groves. As for Wren, no one knows how old she really is."

The Queen shook her head in amazement. "Yet it seems very strange. The Sendimeris twins . . . I'm not familiar with half the legends that have grown around their names, but one I've always remembered is how she defeated a terrible sorcerer called Syngus of the Steel Claw—"

"While she was three seasons along and about to give birth." Leila smiled again. "I recall you talking about that before

62

Teressa was born. What was I? Ten years old? I was *very* impressed."

"I told that story to give *me* courage. I was scarcely able to move at three seasons along."

While the sisters talked, the King stopped before a window and drew apart the brocaded curtains to look out on the shadow-dappled garden. When the Queen stopped, he said, "So we're to wait on these two young prentices. Alone and unaided prentices. Is that their advice?" The King's voice remained quiet, but anger hardened his next words. "Do these legendary figures know that I just received an insulting communication from Andreus of Senna Lirwan, forbidding me to make any move *at all* against him?"

"I can only tell you what Halfrid said their advice seems to be," Leila said calmly.

"Ah, fine. I now know that the enemy who holds my daughter, and some mysterious figures from the other side of the world about whom more stories are known than truth, all desire me to do nothing." The King snapped the curtain shut again.

He finished on a note of detached humor, but Leila sensed that he was still furious. She hesitated. Before she could frame an answer, the Queen, who had been watching her closely, spoke up.

"There's something more, isn't there, Leila?"

Leila laughed ruefully. "I wasn't sure you wanted any more news of disappearances—but you always did read me well, Astren. The last bit of news is this: it seems that Tyron and Wren are not to be alone after all. I just found out from Halfrid that this morning our wayward youngest brother rode out to join them."


Wren and Tyron walked steadily southeastward for six days, hiding only when travelers approached from either direction. As they lay on their stomachs watching, Tyron pointed out the origins of some of the passersby. The capital messengers, for instance, always rode in twos, and they wore bright green surcoats.

On the last day they started down a winding road toward a large town that spread along one side of the gleaming silver river South Hroth. Wren had never seen such a large river, or a town of that size for that matter, and gazed about her with interest.

Traffic increased as they approached, and they no longer bothered to hide. They saw plenty of youths their age, or near their age, as they walked: mostly prentices, wearing the colors and garments of their chosen trades. Twice carriages containing wealthy people raced past, drawn by matched horses galloping their fastest. Tyron and Wren had to walk off the road and wait for these carriages to pass, for the horses did not stop.

When they reached the outskirts of the town, Wren noticed how Tyron carefully scrutinized certain buildings. Nearing a particular house, he paused, gazing up at the windows. A murmur of voices drifted down to them.

Wren couldn't stand it anymore. "What are you looking for?" she asked.

She was surprised when his face went red. Instead of answering, he grabbed her arm and yanked her away as his other hand flashed up in the hand signal for *Keep silent!*

# Chapter Eight

*O*w!" Wren said sharply. "That *hurts*."

Tyron responded by clapping his hand over her mouth. "Listen. I heard—*oof*."

Wren's palm smacked his chin upward, and one of her knees poked him hard in the stomach. He folded and sat down jarringly in the dust of the alleyway. "Oh," he gasped, looking up at her in hazy reproach.

"Don't shove people around," Wren said. "Or warn 'em first."

They gazed at one another in silence for a time, Wren's mouth a grim line, and Tyron trying to recover his breath. "Your pardon. Where'd you learn *that?*" he managed finally. "Ouch," he added, getting up slowly.

"Mountain orphanage," she said briefly. "Don't you magic prentices learn anything about defending yourselves? Or is magic supposed to do that for you?"

"Come away—please." He was still whispering, and he looked anxiously over his shoulder at the house with the window boxes. As Wren followed, he said, "Well, we do exercises, of course, and I was considered a good hand with a staff, but that was yard practice, you know. We really are supposed to stay out of danger, using magic and our wits."

They walked down the narrow alley between buildings and stood in a little brick-covered courtyard. Overhead, lines of

65

washing crisscrossed, the brightly colored lengths of material flapping in the breeze.

"What was that house, and why did you yank me away?"

Tyron looked around carefully. The only other people in the court were a group of very small children, playing with some barrel hoops. Their voices echoed up the sides of the enclosing buildings. They paid no attention to Wren and Tyron, but Wren was diverted very briefly by the accent common to this region, and by slang words whose meaning she could only guess at.

"There was a sign—a certain combination of letters, worked into one of those gateway carvings—on the way into the town. It means that a magic worker lives on this street," he said softly. "And the same sign was worked into the iron railing on the stairway of the house we just passed, meaning the magician lives there. In the old days especially, magicians practiced one trade publicly and magic secretly. Anyway, we have this courtesy, among magicians, to offer hospitality to one another. But I heard someone's voice—someone I know—inside."

Wren silently studied Tyron's unhappy face. Her delight in this evidence of more secret signs dissolved. When he said nothing more, she prompted, "Some toad-wart of a Lirwani spy, maybe?"

Tyron sighed and rubbed his eyes tiredly. "No, nothing like that. I don't know *how* he managed to find me. He's got the most amazing knack for nosing things out."

"And his name is—" Wren tried again.

"Connor," Tyron said dully. "Until now, he's been my best friend. And he's a great fellow. But he's also a prince of Siradayel."

"*That* Connor?" Wren's eyes widened. "Youngest son of Queen Nireth?"

"Right, which means he *must not* go into danger because there'd be political consequences, and also he is the worst, bar none, magic prentice in the history of the school. The students call him Crazy Connor," he finished somewhat weakly.

Wren frowned. "That boy. The day we were at the school,

the boy outside the eating room. He said something about someone named 'Crazy' having turned a master into a . . . a turtle?"

"That was definitely Crazy Connor. The masters had decided to go ahead and try him on the test for Basics since he's already fourteen, and most of us pass that test when we're twelve or so. A disaster, apparently. Not that anybody would be surprised."

"Why's he still a prentice and not sent away? Because he's a prince?"

Tyron nodded, rubbing his hand through his hair. "I guess they've been hoping that he'd be able to learn eventually. He says—quite cheerfully—there's no princely land or position left at home for him to inherit, so he has to think up some other calling. I expect magic is not going to be it. None of that matters now." He looked up at the sky. "The main thing is, he was against my plan to see Idres." He hesitated, ending shortly, "So he's either here to help or, worse, to try to stop me."

"And you're afraid he'll try to help with his terrible magic?"

Tyron shrugged.

By now Wren could tell when Tyron did not want to talk about a subject anymore. "So what'll we do? Continue on?"

"I don't know," Tyron said, looking skyward again. "I can feel rain coming again, lots of rain. Whenever high clouds get hazy like that, you can wager on getting wet. I thought we'd be able to wait out the storm with the local magician, get your language spell, and . . . and news, at the same time."

"Rain," Wren said. "I know our cloaks keep out dew, but I don't want to have to try them with rain. I haven't any money, have you?"

Tyron shook his head. "So an inn's not going to have us."

"Well, we can't pay," Wren said, then added firmly, "but we can try to earn our night's stay."

"How?"

"Entertainment . . ." Wren began doubtfully.

"If you mean your juggling, watching you try to keep beetroots in the air wasn't very entertaining." Tyron shook his head. "Until you dropped them, that is."

"I guess what we'll have to do is offer to work for our keep and offer the entertainment if the innkeeper wavers," Wren said.

There was no more talk about Idres, magic, or Crazy Connor as Wren and Tyron walked from inn to inn, trying to find one that would allow them to work for a night's stay.

It had been Tyron's idea that they try the humbler sorts of places, the ones close to the fishy-smelling docks. Wren's private judgment was that people who had little money were usually tight-fisted, but she'd agreed reluctantly.

It soon became apparent, though, that they were not likely to meet with success. Meanwhile, Tyron seemed to be learning for the first time what it means to be just another anonymous and moneyless urchin, instead of a prentice from a respected profession.

Wren felt bad about Tyron's increasingly frequent over-the-shoulder unhappy looks as they walked along. She said nothing more about trying to remain inconspicuous, not when they had to tramp from place to place and endure rude shouts of "We don't want beggars here!" or worse, snorts of loud laughter from red-faced innkeepers. She made a game of trying to mimic the local version of Sirad; if Tyron noticed, he said nothing.

The shadows were long and blue and the breeze had strengthened steadily into a cold and clammy wind as the unpleasant voice of the last innkeeper echoed in their ears. "You? What can *you* do but get underfoot? Hie, Timar, chase them out of here." The spit boy had been all too happy to run them out of the refuse-strewn court of the inn, taking whacks at their shoulders and backs with a stick as he chased them away.

Tyron's features were pinched with misery. Wren could tell he was not used to cold, hunger, or the abusive treatment. She was cold and hungry as well, but she'd been cold before, and occasionally hungry. And all orphans who'd had anything to do with the local villagers knew something about abuse.

At last Wren said, "We could try just one of the toff hostels. They can't be any ruder than these cactus-noses have been, and, who knows, maybe some lord will have overpaid and they'll feel generous."

Tyron did not even argue with this unlikelihood. He shrugged silently, and as the first cold drops of rain spattered down on them, they turned and found their way to the wide, handsome main boulevard. Raindrops were plopping steadily in the street when Wren spotted the golden-lit stable doors of a large inn. Tyron would have hurried right on past, but Wren was drawn by the atmosphere of the place. It seemed somehow warm and welcoming. She pointed, and now Tyron was the one willing, however reluctantly, to follow.

They walked past the carved doors and made their way to the huge kitchen. Wonderful smells assailed them. As they watched, cakes were pulled from a gigantic oven. After seeing that the last tray of pastries was safely out, the red-aproned innkeeper looked up and spied them, her smile of satisfaction changing to a smile of curiosity.

Wren was scarcely conscious of her shoulders relaxing as the innkeeper said, "What have we here. . . ?"

An hour later the storm outside broke in earnest, but Wren sat with Tyron in the long, cozy attic room shared by the cook and stable prentices, their stomachs full with the first hot food they had eaten in a week. Two cook prentices slept peacefully on the far side of the room.

Tyron bent toward Wren and whispered, "That was quick thought, what you told that innkeeper."

Wren grinned wickedly. "All I did was tell her the truth, minus the Free Vale and magic and Tess—"

"—and plus our being cousins, and a sweet and lonely grandmother waiting for our help in her spring planting. And you somehow sounded like you'd been born hereabouts. I didn't even think we'd have to give anyone reasons for being here."

"If people give charity, they like to feel generous. We

69

learned that at Three Groves. She had to feel sorry for us *and* for the grandmother, and she won't ask any more," Wren said.

Tyron sighed softly. "I didn't think of any of that."

"Another thing," she began hesitantly.

The light of the one candle danced over his foxlike features as he winced. "Something else I've forgotten?"

"Overlooked, more like," she said. "I hate sounding like a know-it-all, but it's our clothes. Well, yours. Nobody seems to be able to recognize mine for palace togs—especially covered by Mistress Selshaf's spare apron—but if you don't want any Lirwani biddiepeepers to see you, then shouldn't you get something besides that magic prentice tunic?"

"I don't know," he said, head drooping. "It's usual for us to wear our formal white if we go out on magic business. Certainly no one in the town recognized me as anything but a beggar. But there's no telling what Lirwani spies know. Truth to tell, I overlooked that, too."

"Well, as you say, it's the plainest of togs. Could be any spies'd never notice, especially since you don't have that bag of books." Wren looked at the top of his tousled head. He was sitting hunched in a knot on his pallet, staring down at the worn quilt he'd been given by the kindhearted innkeeper. Wren said cautiously, "You're not giving up?"

His head came up abruptly. "No!" Then, softer, "No. It's just that I seem to have planned badly."

*And you're feeling bad, too, but that can't be helped*, she thought. "Well," she whispered in a practical spirit, "you included me, for which I'm grateful, and I'd just as soon not be extra luggage."

He smiled a little. "But what's a biddiepeeper?"

"Oops. Didn't mean to say it out loud. Peepers are noses, or spies, where I come from. You know, rotters who like to sneak on you to the Keepers when you break the rules. And biddies . . . well, what's the silliest animal you can think of?"

"I don't know," he murmured, looking mystified.

"For me, the silliest animal is a broody hen. A biddie. Ever

70

since I was small, if there was someone who scared me, I'd think of what was as nearly opposite as possible, and I'd call them it in my mind."

"Biddiepeepers." Tyron grinned. "But Andreus's soldiers aren't *hens*, which are girl chickens."

Wren shrugged. "So we'll call them *baddie*peepers."

"Baddiepeepers!" Tyron's shoulders shook with silent laughter. "I haven't called people names since I was little—but it works."

"Sure it works, even if you only do it in your own mind," Wren agreed. "Who can be scared of a baddiepeeper?" She curled up in her quilt and heard scrunchings as Tyron wrapped himself up and lay down on his own pallet.

"Baddiepeepers . . ." she heard him murmur, followed by a chuckle. Then they both fell asleep.


In Cantirmoor at dawn the next morning, Leila found a place next to a square stone battlement atop the high wall before the royal palace. Glancing up against the weak, watery sunlight—rain was on the way, from the south, she noted—she caught her sister's eye. Astren, of course, gestured an invitation to join her on the royal balcony. Shaking her head, Leila patted the battlement beside her to indicate that she was pleased where she was.

Down below, along both sides of the wide cobbled main street, citizens gathered in excited clumps. Brightly dressed adults talked and gestured, and behind them small children raced back and forth or engaged in noisy mock battles. The citizens had all donned their formal guild colors or best clothing in honor of Queen Nerith's promised army, which was shortly to arrive.

A moment later the press of palace servants on either side of Leila eased abruptly. She looked back—and up into the gray eyes of her favorite brother.

"Here you are," he exclaimed, squashing her in a giant hug.

"Shouldn't you be up with them?" As he let her go, he gestured up at the King and Queen and their honored guests in the banner-hung royal viewing balcony.

"I'm a magician, not a princess," Leila said softly. "But *you* should be up there, Rollan."

Prince Rollan shrugged. "Verne's the one those people want to see today. As for my band, they'll see *them* shortly."

"I heard you'd arrived last night," Leila said. "I hoped to see you before your muster duties completely overtook you."

"That'll be soon enough." Rollan grimaced. "And us scarcely ready! Oh, the Mountain Browns look tough as always, but much of the rest of 'em seem to have spent most of their time at their tailors'. That, and practicing sitting a horse aright. And Verne said last night that he wants to ride for the border as soon as Beshar and Eth-Lamrec get in with their cavalcade."

"I don't think the city can feed three armies for too long," Leila began.

She was interrupted by the distant, sweet sound of silver horns. A fanfare trembled brightly on the air. Below, the citizens fell quiet for a moment, then roared their approval in one great voice.

"Here they come." Rollan wedged in next to his sister, leaning his elbows on the stone parapet. Leila glanced up at his face. Wind and sun had etched laugh lines around his eyes and jaw, making him look older. There were some who said that his famed good nature had a lot to do with his having walked straight into an heirless duchy at age eighteen, but she had known and loved this brother best of any of her siblings until the birth of the youngest. She knew Rollan would be good-tempered even if he were in a field somewhere planting wheat instead of commanding the forces that his mother had sent to her son-in-law's aid.

Now they heard a distant thunder. Once again quiet fell over the crowd, and heads turned toward the south, where the main gate was wide open to receive the riders from Siradayel.

"Mine are first," Rollan murmured to his sister. "Setting the standard." He winked.

"Sounds like a full gallop," Leila returned. "At that pace, you'd be too tired to engage anyone."

"Oh, they've been camping in the hills since yesterday afternoon, waiting for my signal. Full and frisky . . . though, in truth, six days for our own muster is not so shameful for a country that hasn't faced war in thirty years."

Leila's reply was lost as a clatter of horses' hooves rang on the cobblestone street, a sound nearly matched in volume by the voices of the crowds lining the walkways.

Long purple and silver banners were the first things to be seen, gleaming and streaming in the wind as the outriders thundered down the street. Behind them, four abreast, rode the fit young soldiers of Rollan's own guard. Their duchy colors had been superseded by hastily made surcoats of purple and silver, the Siradi colors, but their straight backs and fine horses made them look splendid. After them came other groups, some riding in twos, some in no real order at all: these were the soldiers of different nobles of Siradayel. Rollan named each group for his sister as it passed.

Last came the Browns, the highly trained mountain patrollers who guarded the main pass between Siradayel and Meldrith, and the higher pass between Siradayel and Allat Los. Leila looked at the erect, tough-looking young men and women and thought suddenly of Wren. An unexpected pang shook her as she remembered how the orphan girl had been found, ten years ago, by some of these Browns. Maybe even by one of those riding below, their faces upturned stiffly toward Verne, who dipped his hand in salute.

*Did I do the right thing to bring her into this? I know my instincts are right about her potential, but will she want to do anything with her talents? If I see her again . . .*

"Disapprove?" Rollan was looking directly into her face. The last of the riders had disappeared into the garrison courtyard. Out in front the citizens were moving about, preparing to start their day as a fine mist began to fall.

Leila stirred, banishing her thoughts. "Not at all," she said quickly, "though you know how I feel about the subject of war."

73

"We did have some arguments, didn't we?" Rollan said appreciatively. "So you have not changed your mind? Think you magicians can solve *all* our problems?"

"No. But our tries won't lose lives," she responded automatically, seeing how he was studying the viewing balcony. "What is it?"

"Looking at old Halfrid," he murmured. "Grim-faced as you just now."

Leila's eyes went involuntarily to the short, stout old man with the thin fringe of curling silver hair. Halfrid was leaning toward the King, listening to him talk.

"Reminds me," Rollan went on. "Wanted to ask you something. You've been gone these last few years, but I'll swear it was you who landed little stepbrother Connor in with those wizards. What a disaster! Word of his exploits has reached even me. Is it true that our stepfather desired Connor to be magician-trained? I take leave to tell you I don't believe it."

Leila thought of the old duke, Liam Dereneth, with whom the Queen had made an unexpected second marriage, followed a year later by an unexpected eighth child. Some of Leila's siblings had been outraged or disgusted, despite the fact that their mother and her duke had been very happy during the short years left to them; the duke had died when Prince Connor was scarcely five.

"No," she said slowly. "He made no such request. But yes, it was my influence that placed Connor with us."

"Why? To make the House of Shaltar a laughingstock?" Rollan lowered his voice further. "We've often agreed that our Uncle Fortian is a prime stinker and his son worse, but he has never yet lied outright. He was telling me last night that Connor's been seen on the roof of your Magic School, squawking and cawing at passing birds."

"The Shaltar family's royal reputation will survive, and so will the school's," Leila said calmly. "A good deal of what you hear about are practical jokes, dreamed up by fertile minds precisely to enhance Connor's growing reputation for eccen-

74

tricity. Connor, I might add, usually serves as the butt of these jokes, though he does dream some of them up as well. For instance, if he thought his cousin were sneaking around spying on him. As for why he is at the Magic School . . . well, he has proved that he has no *magical* ability, but until such time as he decides what to do, he's been safe enough with us."

Rollan had not missed the slight emphasis on the word *magical*. He studied Leila silently for a moment, then said, "Let's go in, shall we? This mizzle is going to dampen my one good tunic, and we've still the oath audience to get through. Where is Connor, Leila? I didn't see him up there with Astren, and we know he's not any magician yet. For that matter, where's that scrawny fox-faced Tyron, Halfrid's prentice, that Connor was shadow pals with last time I was here?"

Leila's face did not change, but inside she felt the warmth of pride. *So the school students have indeed kept Tyron's and Wren's disappearance a secret. If Rollan did not hear of it in one long night of drinking and gossip among the courtiers and garrison officers, then no one will.*

Out loud she said, "Everyone's got duties, of course. I trust you'll see them before long." She led the way inside.

On the same day, Wren woke up just before dawn as two figures tiptoed by and started downstairs to a day's work. Rain still drummed steadily on the roof. Wren could just make out Tyron's sleeping face over on the next mat. She had heard him tossing and turning restlessly much of the night, so she did not waken him, but picked up her shoes and followed silently after the inn's prentices.

Soon she was sitting on a high stool, eating a thick slice of honey-smeared fresh bread and relating an improbable story about her background for the busily working cook staff. The cook was obviously the innkeeper's son, and as friendly and kindhearted as his mother. A good deal fatter, as well. He offered Wren a taste of this and that, enthusiastically accepted, while the prentice asked her questions. Wren figured out very quickly that they were interested in the truth far less than they were a good story, and so she was happily telling them about her pirate grandfather and minstrel mother when the innkeeper entered the kitchen and gave Wren a rather odd look.

"Would you step into the morning parlor, Young Mistress?"

Wren heard with surprise the formal, polite request, so different from the friendly and familiar treatment of the night before. Other than Fleris and Lur at the palace, nobody had ever called her Young Mistress before.

Wishing Tyron were awake and here to consult with, she cautiously followed the innkeeper into the front of the building. Had she not been apprehensive about her sudden and mysterious change in status, she would have enjoyed the sight of fine new carpets and a wide, glorious tapestry along the main hall.

The innkeeper paused beside a door, opened it, and bowed slightly.

"Wren?" Somebody inside spoke.

The innkeeper was waiting for her to enter. Wren passed by slowly into a pretty room, and the door closed behind her. Wren's eyes were immediately drawn to a large bay window filled with soft grayish morning light. Rain ran down the frosty diamond-shaped panes of glass. Outlined against the glass was a tall boy.

He stood before the windows with his hands clasped behind him, impressive in a fine gray tunic over a fresh white shirt and new dark hose, a sword at his side, and lots of curling dark red hair.

He turned to smile at her. "Good morning, Wren. I'm Connor. Where's Tyron?"

She swallowed and offered him a blank face. "Who?"

# Chapter Nine

*P*rince Connor Shaltar, eighth and youngest child of the Queen of Siradayel, had wide-set, dark-lashed gray eyes. Despite the seriousness of his mission, the expression in those eyes was merry, and his mouth mock-solemn as he bowed. "You doubt my credentials. You think, in fact, I'm Andreus of Senna Lirwan."

Wren tried not to laugh in response. He seemed taller than any fourteen-year-old, but maybe it was just those nice clothes and that sword. "What? Do you have the wrong person?" It was the best she could think of.

"My sister Leila," Connor said patiently, "told us that the head Keeper in your mountain orphanage was fond of naming new orphans after birds, bird names being unusual in either Siradayel or Meldrith. What does Tyron think—I'm here to curse him with my magical ministrations?" On saying this, Connor grinned and with a smooth motion pulled and flourished his sword. "Not so. I've come—"

"Watch the curtains," Wren said in a squelching voice.

"—instead to offer the able assistance of my well-trained arm." He sheathed the sword with a practiced gesture.

Wren sighed. That mention of Mistress Leila effectively doused inspiration. For once not even a single story suggested itself. She was considering just turning and running for it when the parlor door opened and there stood Tyron.

Connor smiled brilliantly. "Greetings and a thousand fortunes, friend of friends."

Tyron's face was almost comical in its mixture of worried forehead and unwilling smile. "The innkeeper just told me you'd hired proper bedrooms for us and ordered a lavish breakfast to be served in here. She doesn't know what to make of us at all now."

"I assure you I was exceedingly discreet. Said merely that your *grandmother* lives on my family's land, and I'd been charged with your welfare. You'll note I am dressed anonymously—nothing about me marked with the family device."

Tyron sighed and sank into a chair, shaking his head. "Connor . . ."

Connor raised his hand and made the truth sign. "I am not here to assist sorceretically."

Tyron groaned, scratching his head so that his hair looked more like a bird's nest than ever. "I—oh, I don't even know what to say. Except, how *did* you manage to find us?"

Connor smiled. "Town was easy to guess. Only big one on the southern border, and I was certain there'd be a magician here, South Hroth being close to Senna Lirwan as well. Figured six days' walk would bring you from the Haven. And, once I was here, I asked in one or two places and found you."

"So the entire town is probably talking about us."

Connor's mirth showed again in his crinkled eyes, though he did not laugh. "I give you my word, no one will have gossiped in this town as a result of my search."

"But they're all talking about us at the school."

"You must have expected it," Connor said gently.

Tyron just shook his head and jerked his shoulders up and down. Wren, watching silently, saw Tyron folding into his familiar knot of stiff arms and legs, head down, which indicated that he was upset. Looking up at Connor, she said crisply, "Very kind of Your Highness to unpocket money for rooms and such, but we were comfortable as we were. And we'll soon be gone on our business."

Connor smiled at her, bowing again. "A hundred pardons, Mistress. I intrude. May I try to convince you of the value of my aid?" His eyes went from her to Tyron, his long, dark brows lifting in question.

"Look, Connor, I—" Tyron broke off as a quiet knock sounded at the door.

The innkeeper and two of the staff came in, bearing three covered trays. These they set down on a buffet at the side of the room. The kitchen helpers then whisked themselves out silently. The innkeeper said, "Shall I pour?"

"We'll do for ourselves, thank you." Connor turned his smile on her and got a prim one in return as she bowed and left.

Wren watched in amazement. The differences between the jokes and questions of those two helpers just an hour ago and their stiff demeanor now made her feel strange. And as Connor and Tyron helped themselves to the food, she thought: *This Crazy Connor's a toff, all right, though a nice one, it seems. Still, with that sword and all, he'll soon be offering to take the place of an orphan girl who can't do much besides throw lumpish pots, weed gardens, and juggle five clay balls.*

*So why shouldn't he?*

She walked over and stood before the windows, looking at the tapping, streaming rain. *I'm here*, she thought. *I just can't go back without trying something. If it were anyone besides Tess, I'd feel I don't belong, but . . .*

It wasn't Princess Teressa of Meldrith that Wren thought about, it was her old friend Tess: talking about their favorite stories while sitting under the Secret Tree; reading plays; sometimes just smiling at each other across the noisy dining room for no particular reason.

Tess . . .

The uneven gray-silver window glass glimmered . . . shimmered . . . and there, suddenly, with rain running in streams over her image, was Tess. Face thin and pale, and behind her the dull uncompromising gray of a granite wall.

Wren called in her mind: *Tess!*

Tess jerked, looked around wildly.

*It's me, Wren. I'm seeing you in glass, and calling in my mind—*

As she thought the words, she wondered how this weird form of communication worked—and the image dissolved. She frowned hard at the window, trying to will the vision back, but all she saw was the frosty glass with rain running down it and, beyond the window, the waving green of tree branches. Turning away, she felt as if the floor were turning with her, and she sat down rather quickly in a chair. Deep inside her head a faint throbbing pinged. She brought a hand up and rubbed slowly at her eyes.

Behind her Tyron was talking in a low, rather flattened voice. ". . . and then I forgot completely about bringing different clothes. For someone who wanted to stay undetected, I've been a washout, I guess . . ." He paused for a sip of his drink, then suddenly said sharply, "Wren? What's wrong?"

She opened her eyes to find both boys staring at her. "One of those scryings. I did it in the window."

"The *window?*" Connor and Tyron said together. "What happened? Did you see the Princess again?" Tyron added.

Wren nodded and told them about the brief contact. Then she saw the creamy hot chocolate in their cups and poured some for herself.

"The window . . ." Tyron said excitedly, straightening up from his slump. "I've heard of people who could scry in water, or ordinary glass, but I'd never met one. And *contact*. Do you think—no."

Connor said, agreeing with the unspoken thought, "Without training, there's danger."

Tyron looked grim. "When we tried the first time, that cursed Andreus nearly scorched us. He's quick. I think it would be better if you did not try it again, Wren."

"It makes my head ache," Wren said.

Tyron and Connor exchanged obvious looks of relief.

Wren, glancing from one boy to the other, knew immediately what they wanted, which was a chance to speak to one another alone.

"I think I'll go gather my things," she said, and left.

The moment that they were alone, Tyron crossed his arms and faced his friend in a way that meant he was bracing for an argument. "It's great to see you, Connor, and thanks for the food and all," he began. "But if you've come to try to talk me out of my plan, then I'll wish you'd stayed in Cantirmoor."

"I meant what I said." Connor smiled. "I am here to help you. As for our former disagreements about your rescue plan, shall we agree to leave them back in Cantirmoor?"

Tyron moved to the window, his sudden sharp shrug indicating that he still was upset. "Idres wouldn't come. She didn't care—about *anything*."

Connor was one of the few people who knew just how much that *anything* meant. "So now you intend to try to rescue the Princess yourself?"

Tyron turned around, his expression fierce. "How can I not? They keep saying they don't want a war, but isn't the King calling in the Scarlet Guard? I heard bits of gossip as we walked about yesterday."

Connor nodded gravely. "It seems that the King of Senna Lirwan sent him a frightful scorcher of a message, thanking him for sending his daughter as a prentice and promising to return her well trained in a few years, and he'll appreciate the changes, and so forth. Implying he'll turn her into something nasty. Then he cautioned against any 'unfriendly gestures' like sending armies over the border. Such a sight, he said, might very well frighten the King's gently nurtured daughter to death."

Tyron whistled. "A scorcher indeed. What's the purpose? You'd think he's *daring* the King to send an army."

"That no one seems to know. Nor does anyone know what the King really has in mind. Some say defense preparations—

some say attack. Meanwhile, he also received promises of aid from three rulers, my mother among them. They all seem to feel that Andreus must be attacked and defeated before he does something worse."

"So what will happen to the Princess when Andreus sees those people come over the border? He made it fairly clear he isn't going to let her sit by and wave a flag."

Connor said, "I don't know."

Tyron scratched his head vigorously. "So it's back to us. We've got to try. It's more certain every word you say. But, well, there's Wren. *She's* going to go, no matter what. She keeps talking to me about the Princess. I've never met her, but now I feel as though I know her . . ." Tyron shrugged sharply again. "Another thing. All those arguments you and I'd had the night the Princess disappeared, I argued like that—worse—with Halfrid the night before Wren and I left. I still believe that magic and brains can make a difference, without anyone getting hurt. He agrees with that much. But Idres—well, Halfrid said that we couldn't even *ask* her. I couldn't agree, and now I can't let it go!"

Connor watched his friend's stiff fingers sliding along the windowsill. He asked gently, "About Wren. Does she know the danger she faces?"

"No, how could she? That's another thing. She alone of anyone can say that the Princess is her *friend*. How am I supposed to face down such loyalty? Do I croak out dire warnings like some old crow, or do I keep mum? Wren's funny, and she's as stouthearted as any three magic prenties, but she's also a short girl from a place that trains orphans to be farm servants and oh, I do wish she'd go back to Cantirmoor so I wouldn't have to feel blame if something happens to her." He took a couple of steps forward, rubbing his head again. "Then there's that scrying. Have you ever seen the like? She really should be seen by Halfrid—" He paused, looking hopeful.

Connor said, "Perhaps that's the way to talk her into returning."

82

Tyron straightened abruptly. "Right. Anyone might be proud to be told to take their talents straight along to the school. Here, let's get it over now, before my insides twist into something so knotted I turn into a crow."


Wren was just coming out of the room that had been set aside for her when she almost collided with Tyron and Connor. She saw both boys look surprised at the cloak about her shoulders and the knapsack on her back.

"Leaving?" Tyron said. "Ah, going back to Cantirmoor?"

"If you'd like to think so," Wren said with determined brightness and moved to pass them.

Connor stood aside with a polite bow, but Tyron stationed himself squarely in her path. "*Are* you?"

Wren crossed her arms. "Why should I go to Cantirmoor," she said, still firmly polite, "when my friend is in Senna Lirwan?" She tried once again to walk past them.

Tyron gaped. "You're not thinking of trying *alone?*"

Connor said seriously, "Perhaps you do not know that there is great danger awaiting unwary travelers to that realm—"

Wren whirled around to face them both. "How ready for danger are you, Tyron Prentice, when you aren't going to use your magic? And *you*, Your Highness. I do not want to speak with disrespect to Queen Nireth's son, but even though you are Tess's uncle, you aren't her friend. I *know* you never met her, so why are *you* going into great danger? For the reward? A job besides magic prentice, maybe?"

Connor's handsome features flushed.

"And," Wren went on ominously, "just how many adventures and great dangers have you faced, anyway? Either of you?"

Connor's smile was rueful. "None, it must be admitted, beyond what I've witnessed on the players' stage or read in my mother's library—"

"But he's been trained for it when it does happen," Tyron said quietly. "So have I, in a different manner. If I'm detected,

83

I *will* use magic—to get away if I can. You are right, we were going to send—to request, that is—you to return to Cantirmoor, not because we don't value all your help along the way until now, because we do, but because you haven't been trained to face any kind of danger and we were just thinking of your safety."

"Princess Teressa," Connor put in with his friendliest smile, "will want to see her friend whole and healthy when she does win free—"

"If there is anything," Wren spoke slowly and distinctly, "more red-nosed, flap-eared, fungus-grown *windbaggish* than people who bundle other people out of the way with rotten scrummage about 'keeping them safe,' just like flea-bitten hop-toad Keepers, I hope I never see it. I'm leaving. And I hope *you'll* be able to keep up, but don't try because I don't want to see you." Shoving angrily past Tyron, she stalked down the corridor.

Connor whispered, "Perhaps our suggestion about Halfrid and the Magic School should wait."

Tyron's face was as pale as Wren's was red. "How about if we leave at sunup tomorrow," he called after her. "Rain will be good and gone by then."

"If you would care to step into the quarters I am occupying, Young Mistress"—Connor bowed again, this time with princely flourish—"to consult the map with us and to debate the best route . . ."

Wren's steps slowed, then stopped. She turned and gulped. Neither boy blinked an eye, each seeming not to notice. Knuckling a fist quickly across her cheeks, she said, "Let me put my things away."

## Chapter Ten

They rode out the next morning into a clear, warm day, Connor having arranged for three horses. Wren was apprehensive at first, but said nothing as she watched the boys mount up. Then she copied their movements. By midmorning she felt she was as used to the horse as she was ever going to be.

After a long day's ride during which Connor spoke seldom and Tyron not at all, Wren wondered if the boys were angry that she had insisted on seeing the quest through to the end. They stopped for midday break under a shady grove of trees and shared out half the food the innkeeper had prepared for them while the horses drank in a nearby stream. Connor had also acquired a good supply of traveler's cakes from the rivertown magician, but they saved these for later.

Wren kept silent, looking about with her usual interest as they rode. The countryside was hillier, and on the eastern horizon the mountains slowly grew larger, more distinct, and more forbidding-looking.

By nightfall they rode by patches of dark forest. Electing to avoid these, they followed a ravine until they found a secluded gully, and there they camped for the night. After they'd cared for the horses and eaten the rest of the innkeeper's food, Connor unpacked his bedroll, gallantly offering it to Wren, but she politely refused.

Wren lay awake and watched ghost clouds passing silently

between her and the brilliant canopy of stars. The boys did not talk to each other any more than they did to her. After a time she heard Connor's breathing become slow and deep, but she saw Tyron sitting up, awake. Wondering if she should say something, she fell into a doze.

When she woke in the morning, Tyron was still sitting up. He shook his head violently and without saying a word began folding his cloak.

She looked around for Connor. He was standing a little distance away, tossing stale bits of leftover bread to an assortment of birds and whistling softly. One of the larger birds cawed and flapped its wings, then darted at the bread bits.

Tyron said, "Connor?"

Connor looked sharply. The birds swarmed skyward in alarm, flapping and chattering.

"Let's ride."

Connor nodded, rejoining them in a few swift strides.

As they mounted up, Connor asked, "Shall I ride to the nearest farmhouse and purchase provisions? I still have plenty of coins. Or shall we broach the traveler's cakes and trust to find more later?"

"I don't know . . ." Tyron started, looking around.

"Well, there's no need, Your Highness," Wren put in. "I saw any number of wild greens and fruits yesterday, and there's no reason to suppose there won't be more today. We won't have to see any people if you'll allow me to scout out food as we ride."

Which was exactly what happened. Wren found them some fine early berries and three different kinds of root vegetables, sweet after the spring rains. In the afternoon they passed someone's herd of cows, and Wren offered to milk one if a container could be found. Connor's saddlebags contained a waterskin and a basin that could be used for any number of purposes, including a rain hat. Telling them that the skin would be soured by milk, Wren took the basin off across the field and soon returned with fresh, warm, foamy milk, which they drank up at once.

When they camped that evening, Tyron squinted up through the gathering darkness at the towering, gloomy crags. "Another two days should see us at the mountains," he said, huddling into his cloak. He lay down on some long green grass, facing away, and fell asleep almost at once.

Lying silently on her patch of grass, Wren watched Connor, who was sitting with his back to a tree and looking up at the sky. Wren could see a faint gleam of starlight, blue and green, reflected in his eyes. Making a sudden decision, she sat up and scooted nearer to the tree so that their voices would not disturb Tyron.

Connor's head turned. "Still awake, Young Mistress?"

"Is it me that's making him glum, Your Highness? If so, maybe I *should* go on by myself."

"No, no, Young Mistress," Connor whispered. "Not at all."

"I wish you'd call me Wren," she muttered. "The other's for toffs and makes me feel like I'm wearing someone else's skin."

She couldn't see his grin, but she could hear it in his prompt response. "Then I shall try a second time to get you to use my name."

"But you're—"

"I'm the eighth child of a queen, but I have no land of my own, and further, I'm shortly to be thrown out of the Magic School. Connor'll do, I think."

"All right, then. You're Connor; I'm Wren. Besides, I was wondering how we'd curtsy and bow while climbing around in mountains. But something *is* wrong with Tyron. Don't tell me it's not."

"Well, I'm not the only one about to be thrown out of the Magic School. But to Tyron it matters."

"What? *Why?*" Wren hissed, then: "Oh yes—sneaking out." Indignantly she added, "Magic prenties get scuttled for *one sneak?*"

"The magicians were expressly forbidden by Halfrid to consult Idres Rhiscarlan. He didn't tell you?"

"He mentioned it in a general way."

"Then I suppose he did *not* tell you how much he stands to lose. It's not just the Magic School, though that is important to him. It's that he was selected last year to be Halfrid's heir."

Wren gasped. "Halfrid, the King's Magician? Tyron?" She remembered something now. "Idres called him Tyron ner-Halfrid. Is that what that means?"

There was a slight hesitation before Connor answered. "That's his new name," Connor said. Wren thought she heard faint regret in his quiet, pleasant voice, and she wished she could see his face to be sure. But then Connor chuckled very softly, and any regret was gone. "He's worked hard for that position, and in truth, he is the very best of us. Passed Basics younger than anyone else this decade, and with a flawless report. Seven languages, history knowledge as good as any of the heraldry prentices—we know this because we got in a—ah—discussion, with some at the Cantirmoor summer fair, and Tyron came off with the colors, so to speak."

"But that's horrible." Wren thought back over the events of the last days. "No wonder he's moody. So that's why he left the bag of books in the Free Vale, when he knew Halfrid was coming to fetch back the horse. Will he have to give up magic?"

"No. He knows enough to make his way in the world, but what he truly wants is the position he's earned. And he does love the learning. The rest of us groan at new lessons, and he joins in, for he's no prig. But for him the grousing never had much meaning. He often sneaked a candle into bed at night when he discovered some exciting old tome. Nearly set our dormitory ablaze a number of times until they made him vow not to do it again. He got a special dispensation for late reading in the library, instead."

"And all because he tried his own plan. If that isn't just like Keepers!" she added ominously.

"It's not just that. There is the matter of the *nature* of his plan."

"The—oh. Consulting that Idres monster," Wren said with distaste. "Why would he stake everything on her when 'everything' means so much?"

"I think 'twould be better that you ask him about this, as I was one of the ones most steadfastly against his idea. Some feel she's not to be trusted. When her family was murdered by the Lirwanis, she alone walked out untouched and went straight to Andreus to become his prentice. When King Verne went into Senna Lirwan later, after Andreus had taken his throne, he found Idres preparing to conquer some still-unchosen country, using Andreus's model."

"But didn't the King have something to do with her leaving that country and scorching Andreus the Worm as she went? Tyron told me that," Wren whispered, confused.

"That's true."

"Well, the King didn't give her a country, and she still hasn't got one. So maybe she changed her mind."

"That's what Tyron feels, but you see no one knows. And *because* no one knows and because of her name and her beginnings, Halfrid forbade us to communicate with her."

"What's that about her name? Do you mean it's not an accident that *Rhis*carlan sounds like *Rhis*adel, the King's and Tess's last name?" Wren asked.

He turned his face up toward the stars again. "A *very* long time ago, Meldrith was part of another, larger land. There was a terrible mage war, and much of the area was destroyed. People left, seeking more peaceful places to live. After a time this land was resettled and cleared of lawless types by a magician named Rhis. She ruled for long years, during the course of which she had four children. They were Adel, Carlan, Mordith, and Taris. Taris showed an ability for magic and learned from her mother; the others administered portions of the land. When Rhis died, the four took her name as part of their own and gave those compound names to their families. Descendants of one or other of those four have ruled here since."

"So then Idres is a kind of a cousin to Tess? So why—"

"Very long removed," Connor replied. "The Rhiscarlans

grew extremely powerful in the last century, and ambitious. They held the southlands; the Rhismordiths hold the north; the Rhisadels, the west. All three met to watch the east and Senna Lirwan, particularly in recent years."

"What about that last family? The . . . the Rhistaris?"

"They dwindled. Most of them inherited the talent for magic, and magicians don't tend to have large families—if any."

"I thought you said Andreus's rats attacked Idres's family's castle."

"They did, but there's more to that story. Perhaps Tyron should tell you what he knows. Anyway, Teressa is related to the Rhismordith family—her mother and Mistress Leila and all of my sibs had the Rhismordith duke for a father. Now her uncle Fortian Rhismordith is head of that family."

"You had a different father," Wren said. "That much I know—I just barely remember the country going into mourning after he died."

"Yes." He looked away for a moment. "To return to Tyron's plan and Halfrid, I do believe there were specific instructions to the magicians the night the Princess was taken." Now the regret was back in Connor's voice.

Wren nodded slowly in the darkness. "Sounds like Tyron wanted to give her a chance to make good. I *guess* I see it."

"Also, he has just as many qualms about me as he does about you. He feels it will be his fault if anything happens to me. That, too, is Tyron's nature. So when we do something to aid, he is grateful, but at the same time he blames himself for not having thought of it first."

"One thing anyone learns in a place like an orphanage," Wren said thoughtfully, "is that being alone makes allies more important."

"I came to much the same conclusion, living in a palace crowded with relatives, courtiers, and retainers," Connor's pleasant voice whispered back. "What we must do, I believe, is show Tyron the truth of this. Show him, not tell him. Shall we make a pact?"

"Sure." Wren started to reach toward Connor, then sat back abruptly. "Uh, how do toffs make a pact?"

"Hand in sign of honor, and vow spoken together. I always thought it rather dull. Possibly because, at least when we were small, my cousins and two of my next oldest sibs seldom remembered theirs past a day—"

"*Not* Mistress Leila."

"Oh, no. She was different, but she left to learn magic when I was very little. How's it done among your friends?"

"Scratch an eternal circle on each other's palm, press 'em together, and speak the vow. Some even scratch to raise blood, but I never saw how making a mess made people keep their word."

"Yours is a much better way," Connor said promptly. "Let's."

They made their pact and then decided to sleep. As Wren returned to her grassy spot and curled up in her cloak, her mind was busy with plans to aid Tyron in regaining his position— once Tess was free.

Tyron's spirits were again tense and morose when they set out the next day, and his conversation was still sporadic. But Wren, understanding the reason why, did not worry about him. She found plenty to occupy her mind in the increasingly wild country.

She not only found food, but she was also the first to recognize a sudden thudding underfoot as the approach of galloping riders. She and the boys guided their horses behind a large hedgerow just in time to see a raffish gang of men race by.

"Fine-looking fellows, eh?" Connor murmured softly.

"They look like robbers," Tyron said tersely. "As well we heard them first—I think it's also good we'll be giving up riding by tomorrow."

"Can't these lowland horses ride uphill?" Wren asked,

stretching her neck as she glowered up at the lofty peaks above. The closer they approached, the less inviting the mountains looked. "I guess I was hoping we'd not have to trudge straight up on foot."

"The road should be too steep by tomorrow night or the next day, and while we could hide ourselves if necessary with some haste, with horses we'd soon be seen," Tyron replied. "We'll have to leg it."

"Mountains," Wren said, sighing. She was remembering what climbing about in mountains was like. Then, remembering those riders, she pulled her knapsack up and transferred her pepper packet to one of her apron pockets.

"We'd do best to move on quickly, friends," Connor suggested.

"Certainly." Tyron agreed, frowning at the mountaintops.

Wren looked over at Connor, whose face was unwontedly serious as he scanned the gully beside them and a copse of dark firs ahead. Wren looked around as well, listening to the wind soughing in high boughs. She heard the scolding of some unseen birds; a closer one screeched suddenly, and Connor's head jerked around. As he scrutinized the rocky slope to their side, Wren did also. It was easy to imagine unseen things creeping up on them, and she shivered.

Tyron looked at Connor worriedly. "What is it? Hear something?"

"No, that's just it," Connor replied after a short pause, just as the three horses reached a narrow point in the trail. "I wondered what would make those riders run like that in this country, and then I realized we heard them pass on much quicker than we heard them coming—"

"*Hie!*" A sharp voice grated nastily, and four men jumped out in front of them.

# Chapter Eleven

𝒜 rough gloved hand snatched at Wren's bridle, jerking the horse's head down. The horse lurched sideways. She jumped free of the saddle and landed rolling.

Behind her she heard the sounds of desperate scuffling, and once the clang of metal. Connor's sword! But next came the sound of metal ringing on stone.

"Get the girl," a voice shouted. Steely fingers grabbed her arms and yanked her to her feet.

*So Connor was right. They saw our tracks and came back. Remember that,* a voice insisted inside her head. She blinked hard, trying to banish the dizziness that had come with the fall from the horse. *Get up,* the voice went on. *Think. Think. What would Eren Beyond-Stars do?*

The hands on her arms forced her around. She saw one ruffian holding their horses' reins. Another man sat on Connor's back as he bound some kind of thong around Connor's wrists. A third held Tyron against the ground as he kicked fiercely, trying to squirm free. The man holding him down snuffled evilly, obviously entertained by Tyron's futile struggles. At a barked word from the one holding the horses, though, he raised a big hand and smacked Tyron hard. Tyron lay still, blinking up and gasping.

The one with the horses put a hand on his sword hilt. He was tall and had an ugly grin on his bearded face. "Here," he said in Sirad, pronouncing the words in a way Wren had not heard before. "Let's not bother with the bravos. The lass will tell us what we want to know."

Connor stiffened suddenly, then made a tremendous effort to throw off his captor. The heavy man on his back clouted him hard across the back of his head. "Lie still," he snarled.

Gesturing toward Wren with his black glove, the leader said, "Now talk to us nice, little pippin, and you might be soon on your way. But if you don't talk, they will." He laughed harshly, joined by the others.

"I can think of a few things to get them talkin'," said a gloating voice behind Wren. "You might not like 'em, though." Once again, the others in the group seemed to find this hugely witty.

Wren's shoulders were starting to feel numb. *Act!* said the voice in her mind. She said, her voice sounding high and shaky, "Please let me go. My head hurts. I fell off my horse."

The leader looked at her scornfully and said with exaggerated politeness: "But you recall your name, Young Mistress?"

"Yes, I'm Eren of Grove Farm," she started. Then her mind went blank.

Abruptly the leader gestured, and the man behind her let go. He smiled nastily as he stepped over to stand beside the leader. Both boys were lying still. All four of the men were looking at her now, enjoying her fear; three of them stood close to one another, the one on Connor to her left.

Meanwhile, her tongue sat in her mouth like a dried-out potato and would not move. *All right. So my tongue refuses to produce any stories. Let's see if my hands can help out.* She knuckled her eyes and stumbled sideways, a step closer to the three men. Then, keeping her head hanging down and her shoulders hunched, she shoved her hands in her pockets. Connor's sword lay, she saw, by the third man's boot, but all these men had swords and knives at their belts.

Now that she had a plan, Wren found her voice. She took

a step closer toward the villains and said shakily, "We don't have any money, except what my grandmother gave us to stay at the inn. Why rob *us*?" She stood uncomfortably near the men, and her heart banged painfully against her ribs.

The leader laughed. "Full of questions, are you, Eren of Grove Farm? Supposing we hear some answers. Who are these heroes, and what inn were you heading for, so far from any town?"

"There must be an inn, or else we're lost!" Wren sucked in a breath and burst into loud, dramatic tears.

The leader said, "Shut up," and swung a fist toward her head. She jumped back, hand whipping out of her pocket. A yellow cloud of hot pepper flew straight into the ruffians' faces.

Howls of rage and pain came from all three men as they clawed at their eyes. The one on Connor leaped up. Wren threw pepper at him as well, but he flung an arm across his eyes and yanked out his knife. Wren jumped back—and the man went down heavily, his legs tangled in Connor's.

"Blade," Connor wheezed, rolling to his feet, his hands still tied behind him. Tyron was looking around wildly, so Wren snatched up Connor's sword.

Struggling to his knees, Tyron scrabbled shakily at a knife dropped by one of the men. He picked it up—but then Wren glimpsed him sinking back, watching helplessly. She sprang forward, and, between them, she and Connor felled the fourth man. Wren used the sword as a scythe at the man's legs, tripping him, then Connor deftly clipped him across the skull with a fast kick. The man slumped flat.

Meanwhile, the three pepper-blinded men reeled off the path entirely, cursing foully and rubbing at their eyes. The leader slipped and tumbled into a ditch.

"Horses," Connor between coughs called to Tyron.

Given a clear order at last, Tyron dashed at the mounts, catching the hanging reins. Connor placed one foot on a big boulder, then vaulted onto the back of his mount, which still had his gear attached to the saddle. Tyron tossed the horse's reins loosely over the saddle horn.

"Wow!" Wren exclaimed in admiration. "Can you teach me—"

"Let's be gone," Connor urged.

Wren tucked the sword awkwardly under her arm and snatched her knapsack from the ground where it had landed. Then she turned to Tyron.

"I'll hold the reins for you, and you go up on that boulder," Tyron wheezed, guiding Wren's horse next to the big stone. She scrambled into the saddle despite legs that seemed suddenly to have turned to water.

As Tyron mounted up, Connor, still with his wrists tied, kneed his horse into plunging straight at the mounts of the villains. "Run! Run!" he shouted, adding a strangled-sounding yell. The four riderless horses galloped off among the trees downslope and disappeared.

Connor led the way across the rocky terrain; the others rode in shaken silence behind. Wren was amazed at how Connor managed to ride his horse without hands. Her mind seemed unable to form a thought beyond that.


They rode for what seemed a long time, following no trail, until they splashed to a stop in a shallow stream.

As the horses put down their heads to drink, Connor turned to smile at his companions. "*Well* done, Wren."

"Yeah," Tyron added, his voice sounding high. "Wren, you were *right* about pepper being some kind of weapon. That was horrific!"

Wren laughed, glad she still could. "Great for bullies, pepper. And for some of the nastier small creatures you might meet in the mountains. Though I do wish I'd thought of a better tale to tell them. What *I* thought was knacky was the way you handled that last one of those toad-warts, Connor. *And*"—she pointed—"riding with no hands."

"This was something we had to practice round the training yard at home." Connor shrugged. "The trick is to guide with your knees and move with the horse. Though I must admit I'd never tried a gallop through woods before. As for the fight . . ." Connor shook his head ruefully. "I did badly. I was woefully out of practice, and we shouldn't have been taken so easily. Haven't done the shadow dance for days, and it showed. I thank you for preserving my sword."

"Oh." Wren looked down at the blade, which she had wedged across the saddle bow so she could clutch at the saddle with both hands. "Here—"

"I'll loose those." Tyron spoke in a more normal voice and edged his horse closer so he could cut the bonds from Connor's wrists. Connor jerked his hands free and rubbed the back of his head, wincing, before taking his sword from Wren and sliding it into its sheath. "Bad blow?" Tyron asked in concern.

"More to my pride." Connor shrugged. "I shall take care not to let that happen again."

"You did well," Tyron said. "Both of you. It was I who was entirely at fault, who did absolutely nothing—"

Wren and Connor turned to one another and grinned. Tyron stopped, looking unhappily at their faces.

Connor said, "You will pardon me for speaking bluntly, my finest of friends, but if you *dare* to take all the blame for yon encounter, then I shall personally bind you and toss you in the river."

"With pepper up your nose to keep you company," Wren added. "We're all to blame for being taken by surprise and for not doing what we would have liked. Still, we all got out alive. But now: *Who were they?* And what do we do to stay away from them?"

Tyron sighed, shoulders sagging. "I don't know. They could be anyone. Robbers . . ."

"They were looking for victims," Connor agreed, "but you'd think we'd be the sort to pass over. Of course we are getting close to the border."

"Baddiepeepers," Wren nodded sagely. "They looked and sounded just like you'd expect baddiepeepers to look and sound."

"*Baddiepeepers* is Wren talk for spies," Tyron put in.

"Unsavory fellows, certainly." Connor gazed around speculatively. "The thing is, we now have to abandon the regular road into the mountains. I suggest we also avoid any villages and farms as well. What say you?" He turned to Tyron.

Tyron shook his head violently. Then he gave a short sigh. "You're right. Avoid any signs of settlements. With Wren's help, we seem to be able to find things to eat and drink. Let's do that, riding as high up into the mountains as we can before we abandon the horses. We'll go the rest of the way on foot, as we'd planned. But we won't be following a road."

"There are lots of animal trails in our mountains, anyway," Wren said, starting suddenly to snicker and shake.

"That's what we'll have to find," Tyron murmured, studying Wren, who was now helplessly convulsed. "What is it?"

"The w-way they looked, d-dancing around . . . like d-drunken clowns . . ." Wren gasped, feeling tears mix into the laughter. "Oh!"

The others gave in suddenly to laughs as well, giddy with relief. At length they managed to fight their gusts back down to giggles.

When at last they were all breathless but normal again, Connor spoke. "Shall we use what's left of the day, then?"

They began to ride.


Leila sat in her sister's music room, looking around at the silent harp, the still lute and pipes. A servant had brought in tea and cakes, but Leila only toyed with them.

*I hate waiting*, she thought. *Most of the time I feel decades older than twenty-three, but now I feel ten again.*

The door opened softly, and her sister walked in, skirts whispering about her feet. Astren was dressed formally, as befitted a queen who had just attended a War Council of all the dukes, plus the company commanders from the distant countries who had come to help.

"Don't keep me in suspense. What did he decide?" Leila spoke before Astren could say anything.

Astren smiled tiredly. "He's given Halfrid a week to think of something else, it being a week that the Princess from Eth-Lamrec needs in order to get her army here. Then they will ride east to Senna Lirwan."

Leila sighed. "A week. I guess it's something. But it doesn't indicate much faith in us, does it?"

The Queen shook her head. "You don't understand how much pressure there is for war from *them*. Not Rollan, and not all of our own people. But some want to fight, for reasons ranging from the laudable one of getting rid of Andreus's threat once and for all, to the greedy one of carving up his kingdom should we manage to defeat him. Then there's that delegation from the last of the coastal city-states, eager to get allies. They know they can't keep Andreus off forever—the other five have all fallen—and they've promised that if we attack, they will launch all their allies' ships against Hroth Harbor, which Andreus has made a stronghold for his pirates."

"And if we win, what? Trade promises?"

"Tariff-free trade." The Queen lifted her hands.

"*If* we win, *if* we win. No one talks of the messy battles beforehand?"

The Queen shook her head. "You must not assume that Verne has no faith in Halfrid and you magicians. What no one else knows, and you are not to tell anyone, is that Verne sent a delay message to that princess from Eth-Lamrec."

"So we *can* have our week," Leila said, nodding.

"I know you have to return to your teaching," the Queen said calmly, "but as soon as you are free, will you take me to the Free Vale to talk to the Sendimeris twins?"

Leila stared at the Queen in silent surprise.

Connor took the lead. Scanning back and forth constantly, he led them very swiftly deep into a forest. At times shrubs and branches brushed the horses' sides, and the riders had to duck under others. Twice Connor stopped, dismounted, and requested Wren and Tyron to stay and listen while he did some scouting. Wren found that hard. She wanted to see *what* he was scouting, but memory of their earlier encounter made her reluctant to slow Connor up with her questions.

When they stopped for the last time that day, it was at a place selected by Connor. Swiftly and skillfully, Connor took care of his mount as Wren watched. Then, while Tyron slowly unsaddled his horse, Connor climbed up on a rock on the other side of their grove in order to coax a bird with bread crumbs. The bird was big and brown, with distinctive white bands on its wing tips and under its beak.

Wren turned her gaze from one boy to the other. Presently she asked Tyron, "Do you magic prenties keep pets?"

Tyron paused in rubbing his horse down. "What? Pets?" He waved impatiently at hovering flies. "No. What made you think of that?"

"Connor there. Thought I'd seen that brown bird before."

Tyron glanced briefly over his shoulder, then returned to his currying. "Just some plains bird. They all look alike. He's always throwing old bread to 'em. Makes friends with stray dogs and cats, too. And the palace horses—he just likes animals. Now, watch here."

"Something amiss?" Connor's pleasant voice came right behind them.

Wren felt a twinge of embarrassment, as if she'd been caught spying. She shrugged awkwardly, not wanting to say, *But I've heard that bird's voice before—just before the baddies attacked, and I think once before that.*

"Nothing wrong." Tyron made two last long rubs; then he thrust the cloth into Wren's hands. "Phew! Your turn."

Wren busied herself with her own horse as Tyron stood by with the much pleasanter task of directing Wren's inexpert movements.

Connor said, "Mind if I scout out once more before the light's gone? I'd like to be certain we won't be surprised again."

Tyron looked about in the deepening twilight. "Won't you get lost? You know we don't dare make a fire."

"I'll be fine."

Wren sighed. "I do wish you could teach me your woodcraft."

"Perhaps when we are not so hurried." Connor's tone was apologetic.

"Hah-hah," Tyron cut in.

"Sure." Wren laughed.

Soon Connor was lost among the shadows, and Tyron energetically resumed his spoken directions. When at last they were done, the horse cropped contentedly at long sweet grass, and Wren collapsed under some sheltering trees. Her arms and back ached. She looked around wearily, hearing nothing but the whisper of trees. Tyron was barely visible as he produced from his pack his somewhat bruised and flattened share of the fruit that Wren had found that morning.

"Today's morning feels like it was a week ago," Wren said tiredly as she bit into her own apple. Then, remembering last week, she added, "How about telling me something about magic learning?"

"What do you want to know?"

"If I can do more."

"Is *that* all?" Tyron joked. Then he looked considering. "Well . . . you did do the transportation spell, didn't you?"

"Yes. Took me to the school. Would it take me, say, to the palace if I did it now?"

"No. It would take you to the school, but if you *focused* on the palace, you might not end up anywhere. Ever."

"Ever?" Wren felt her stomach squeeze. "What's *focus*?"

"Well, it's seeing the place where you're going in your mind.

101

At the same time you say its designation words. There are places set up as designations, and people can transport to them, but you have to be careful."

"Mistress Leila told me it was dangerous. And Tess said it made her feel sick."

"Most people don't transport well."

"So you can only go to those special designation places?"

Tyron gave his head a shake. "If you know what you're doing, you can go anywhere. But you'd better be sure you know *exactly* what you're doing."

"And you can take people," Wren said, thinking rapidly. "Like Mistress Leila took Tess and me. Could we get into Andreus's palace and take Tess out again by magic?"

"Only if we're touching her," Tyron said. He grinned suddenly. "A certain amount of what we call object-contact magic is built into the transport spell, or you'd go and your clothes and shoes would remain behind." Tyron's voice and face took on what at first seemed an uncharacteristically serious tone. Watching, Wren realized then that he was slipping into a teaching manner. "To take someone along," he went on, "or even more difficult, to take someone who is holding a thing that you're also touching, requires both focus and emendation to the spell."

"You fix the spell so you take the person and the thing but not the floor?" Wren guessed.

Tyron grinned. "That's right. Though the floor—the building you're in or near—wouldn't go with you. The spell would just collapse. It takes some mighty spell-casting to move big things."

"Another question," Wren said, her curiosity about magic growing with each breath. "The way Tess was taken. Those palace people talked about illusions, and shape-changing wards. What's that?"

"Ask an easy one, why don't you?" Tyron groaned. "That's what we spend years learning. Here's the simple explanation. There are two kinds of magic. There's the easy kind, which is illusion. That's the most common kind. The play wizards use it, for instance, to make the audience see things during a play. Rains, or thunder, or whatever. It can be used to fool people who don't know how to see through illusions. Like you and the Princess that day. Then there's real magic, which moves or changes things. Spells were put over the palace ages ago to prevent someone from doing shape changes on themselves or someone else. Shape changes are especially tricky if you change someone's or something's form to another sort of being. Its nature might change as well."

"Can you show me an illusion?"

"A small one, I guess. I can't imagine it drawing traces *here*," Tyron muttered. Wren watched his fingers weave, and her ears caught the mutter of phrases under his breath. Then, suddenly, between his fingers was a soft green-glowing ball. He pulled a long shape from it, touched the ball, and the ball changed to a glowing purple rose before fading slowly into nothingness.

"I want to try that."

"Well you can't—" Tyron began, then stopped in amazement as Wren gestured, whispered, and a twin to his rose appeared in her hands. Hers lasted for only an instant before it disappeared. As she sighed in disappointment, he added grimly, "Of *course* you managed that *just* to make me out a fool."

Wren could hear the pleasure under his mock disgust. She laughed, then asked, "Why didn't mine stay?"

"Because you didn't hold the image, and I just realized that your being able to focus it in the first place means I've told you too much. No more questions until you can get to the school."

"So that's focus," she said. "Imagining a thing."

"*Seeing* it—" he began, then stopped himself, adding wryly, "and learning focus usually takes most of the first year of school."

"Well, I've had plenty of years' practice imagining I was somewhere else while I mixed clay and scrubbed floors." Wren stopped as her ears caught the faint crack of a twig.

"It is I," came Connor's voice. "There seems to be an excellent goat track not far from here. Should lead right up."

"And then?" Wren asked.

"What?" Tyron said as Connor murmured, "Your pardon?"

"Those are *high* mountains. We can't go up like this—we're not even slightly prepared. I lived in mountains when I was little, and even weather can be dangerous. How many weeks will a crossing take? And where will we get snow clothes for the peaks, because up there winter never really ends. Also, what's going to protect us against mountain creatures? That sword won't do much against a pack of timber wolves or, if we go *really* high, against the big night-flying gryphs. Or what if we find even *worse* things?"

"Well, there is a way . . ." Tyron began, then hesitated.

"People who keep secrets when everyone's in a mess together," Wren huffed, "are as welcome as itchwort in shoes."

Connor grinned. "True enough. One secret I think I can tell you: if we can get to the border, there is a tunnel route that will take us the rest of the way through the mountains."

"As for gryphs, if we travel during daylight, we'll be safe enough from them," Tyron added. "And I don't believe there are any timber wolves in these mountains—too rocky and not enough other sorts of life for them to prey on."

"What about chraucans?" Wren persisted. "They fly during the day, and they hate humans. And what will *we* do for food?"

"Chraucans don't *hate* humans," Connor spoke up. "They just don't have anything to do with them. But I've heard even the wildlife in these mountains will become unexpected allies of anyone who is against Andreus and his folk. Lirwani hunters are not well liked up there."

"And as for food—well, we have our cakes," Tyron said shortly. "We knew it wasn't going to be easy. So now the hard part is really beginning. Come on, let's sleep now so we can be on our way at first light."

He'd withdrawn into his worry knots again. Seeing this,

Wren felt badly about being the cause until she caught Connor's eye over Tyron's shoulder. He gave her a grin and raised his palm as a reminder of their pact. She sighed, resolving to talk less and watch more in the future.

Just about the time they settled down to sleep, on the other side of the mountains and across the bleak plains of Senna Lirwan, Teressa heard the clank of keys in the door to her cell.

"King wants you," she was addressed from without. "Double-quick."

Teressa was too proud to hide, or hang back, as she longed to do. Refusing to go meant she would be grabbed and shoved before one of these hateful guards. So she got up, straightened her back, and walked out.

*What now?* she thought as she followed the silent guard's heavy tread up the stairway to Andreus's tower. *More looking in that horrid stone that just makes me feel dizzy? At least I haven't eaten since noon in case it makes me sick again.*

But she was led through the wide, round room with its carved furniture and dark blue rugs to the balcony. There Andreus stood, to all appearances impervious to the unending cold that seemed to blight his country. Teressa hugged her arms as the guard stepped behind her and gave her a thrust between the shoulder blades to send her more quickly onto the balcony.

Torches on two poles streamed in the wind, casting uneven light across Andreus's features. He was probably somewhere about her parents' age, but he looked younger, with a round face, wide brown eyes like a spaniel's, and curling blond hair. He seemed about Aunt Leila's height and had the same sort of slight build, but she'd learned within the first couple of interviews that appearances could be deceiving.

*That spy, reporting. Why did he make me watch that?*

Teressa's mind unwillingly returned to the day a week ago, when she had been brought into Andreus's study. Three or four persons had been standing before the King, and one was speaking. A spy, she'd realized soon enough, giving a report. Andreus sat playing with a knife and smiling while the man had reported about Teressa's uncle, Prince Rollan, and his company being on their way to Meldrith. The spy had described Aunt Leila going back and forth from the palace to the school. Then he gave an account of the activities of Teressa's other relatives, ending with the youngest of the uncles, Connor, whom Teressa had never met.

The spy had finished his report by saying that they had lost track of the youngest prince on the road south. Andreus had still been smiling when he threw that knife suddenly, straight into the spy's heart. As the man fell dead, Andreus had addressed the others. "I said I want every member of that family watched and his or her movements reported. Are you capable of following orders?"

*They were as frightened as I was. How he smiled, then sent me away with no further words. I hate this, I hate this . . .*

"Come here," he said now. "What? Still sullen? Now, look at that." He lifted a hand and pointed to a faint green-yellow glow that outlined the distant mountains. "Don't you think that an inspiring sight?"

She swallowed. When she had to be near Andreus, her throat was always dry. "It looks like magic."

"Would you like to learn that? Perhaps I'll teach you one day. Most useful." His odd voice, which always reminded Teressa of knives and swords, sounded truly pleased.

Teressa shook her wind-lashed hair back from her face and silently studied the steady glow. It was a weird, glimmering light; it made the mountains look unreal.

"Aren't you curious what it's for?" Andreus spoke at her shoulder. "How can I inspire a sense of adventure in that lumpish brain of yours, girl?" He laughed. "What you see there is a magic trap. A splendid one, protecting my entire mountain border."

"A light is a protection?" Teressa said slowly.

"The light is only visible to us here in Edrann. If my spell is tampered with from the other side, the light will alter—or disappear. A great deal of effort went into that, but it was well worth it. Just today I received the first report of the trap's efficacy. Some stupid shepherd blundered into it. The sheep made it through the magic—bleating, though, bleating plaintively. But the man bounced as though lightning had struck. How I wish I could have known and thus could have witnessed my success myself. No matter—"

"You mean your spell kills people?" Horror chilled her insides colder than this wintry wind ever could.

He laughed in delight. "Kills people? Of course, my reluctant pupil, my spell kills people. Out there in your sunny Cantirmoor, perhaps even this very day, your diligent father has called together his War Council. They will decide of course that if I act once, I shall do so again, and they are right. They will assure one another that I am in a bad strategic position, faced with war on the east as well as on the west, and that is right, too. Or would be, were I as stupid as both my eastern and western neighbors, content to sit and regard the mountains as enough protection for my borders."

"Warrie beasts," Teressa whispered, now shivering uncontrollably. "You said before that you'd set warries loose in the mountains."

"Had I mentioned them to you? Yes, I do recall. Well, I've released warries more for sport. They'd enjoy hunting down and feasting on any stray parties of heroes, I feel sure. But in my border spell we have an excellent protection against large armed companies. Just think: the war parties divide and ride up in . . . say . . . three groups, in order to cross at those three low points easily visible to us now, the idea—a good one in theory—being to converge from three directions on us here in Edrann. But they reach the summit, and—" He clapped his hands once, sharply. "Gone. But," he said with a laugh, "the finest part is this: their horses continue on over the border, and my men herd them up. You know we've a shortage of good mounts. They don't seem to like our climate. Well? What do you say?" He took hold of Teressa's chin, forcing her head up.

*Don't think of the border. Don't think of Papa. Think of a plan. You have to do something.* She kept her cold face stony as he studied her intently. Then he released her and once again gave her that hateful smile. "What? You don't appreciate the magnitude of my plans? Think of the game, girl, think of the game!"

Teressa's teeth were chattering. She said nothing, but inwardly she braced herself. Twice before he'd struck suddenly, knocking her down for not paying attention to her lesson, he'd said.

But now he only shrugged with exaggerated disappointment. "First, I fear, I must endeavor to teach you a sense of humor," he said. "That, and a little endurance. You've been overindulged."

Tess coughed—and deep inside some of the stone-cold bleakness eased a little: she had an idea. Not much of one, but at least it gave her something to try. She coughed again, more loudly, as the guard took her away to lock her back in her cell.

# Chapter Twelve

Connor's goat track proved to be a good route to follow for some distance, and they rode steadily upward. Conversation was sporadic; all three watched carefully about them. The steep slopes stretching overhead seemed eerie. Wren wondered if the curious atmosphere she sensed, a sort of unpleasant *waiting*, was a threat, her hunger, or just a bad feeling about climbing in the mountains again after so many years. Whatever it was, she felt uncomfortable and kept her eyes moving from one rocky scree to the next shadowy gully in case more ruffians were lying in wait.

They stopped at midday on a high, wind-scoured cliff, wedging themselves into a rocky crevice while overhead a short, fierce storm thundered by.

Rain slashed at the mountainside, obscuring the far slopes and making little brown streams tumble down the rocks on either side of their shallow shelter. Purple lightning intermittently flashed from peak to peak. Moving farther into the crevice, Wren discovered a large, musty-smelling nest.

When the rain slackened, they continued on, but before long saw more ugly gray-green clouds tower threateningly high beyond the mountaintops.

"The horses seem nervous, my friend," Connor finally said after Tyron gazed up and winced for the third time.

"Then we'd best let them go. They'll find shelter before we

will," Tyron said with sudden decision, throwing his leg over and jumping down.

Hastily they unpacked the saddle pads and Connor's more elaborate equipage. Connor divided his gear, saving out only food, the water bag, and his cloak. The rest of the tack was dragged into a shrub-shaded crevice a little ways from the trail. Tyron and Wren did this work while Connor knelt on the trail, fashioning his saddlebag into a knapsack.

"What a waste of good tack," Tyron said with regret as they piled branches and dirt over the gear.

"Can't be helped," Wren answered practically. "What ruffles me is that from here on up it's going to be harder to find things to eat."

"I've got about eight days' worth of cakes here. A trifle dry, but I've heard they're good for a month." Connor patted his bag.

They began moving up the muddy trail in silence. Wren rubbed her arms, then swung them; she did not want to put on her cape until night. It was only going to get colder, and she had no more clothes.

After a time they stopped so that Connor could refill the water bag from a large, rushing stream. Wren waited nearby, hopping in place to stay warm as she darted distrustful looks at the deepening shadows that were starting to close in on them.

But then as they started up the trail again, mud clinging to their feet and to Wren's skirts, Connor said in a low and dramatic voice:

> " 'Here I lie, wounded, cold and alone,
> In this damp fortress of solid stone' "

Wren gave a gasp of pleasure. "That's from our—Tess's and my—favorite play, *The Quest of Eren Beyond-Stars*."

Connor grinned. " '*Beset not by monsters, brigands or beasts*' "

" '*But by darkness and silence and memories of feasts,*' " Wren finished with low-voiced enthusiasm.

Behind her, Tyron snorted. "If she talked to herself like

that, no wonder she escaped—they wanted to be rid of her."

Connor laughed. "Quiet, O enemy of poets. You know that play, eh?"

"Tess and I acted it often, under our secret tree."

"Two of my cousins and I used to do it as well. How about this one . . ."

Connor went on to try some more quotations. Some of the plays Wren knew, but most she did not; her sole source of plays had been Tess's one book. But she listened with enthusiasm and pleasure as he repeated the most extravagantly bombastic lines, lowering his voice sinisterly for villains, sniveling whinily for traitors, or squeaking in an impossibly high voice for certain of the female characters.

From time to time Tyron added a caustic comment about what had *really* happened, according to the historical records. Wren enjoyed these interruptions. She loved history as well as stories, and she could appreciate that Tyron had no use for the exaggeration of plays. He didn't say anything belittling about people who liked them, just made comments about the exact facts of a well-known situation. Or about how the facts were not really known and the playwright had surmised how it had gone.

It was so much fun, she scarcely noticed how the trail narrowed steadily and also got steeper. Their pace slowed, but they kept winding their way upward.

Twice Tyron, who walked in front, called a halt so they could search each branching of the trail. Some of the paths they chose were narrower than goat tracks, only as wide as a human foot.

Again they found a stream rushing and tumbling down the rocks and got a good drink. This time Wren washed her face and hands in the shockingly cold water.

Just before sunset Wren and Connor started acting their way through *The Quest of Eren Beyond-Stars*, Wren saying her heroine's lines with great energy and feeling, and Connor doing

111

the rest of the parts in a variety of voices and accents. Tyron listened in silence, looking at the same time for a likely spot for them to spend the night.

"Something with at least one solid wall to lean against," he muttered out loud as he peered ahead in the long mountain shadows. Wren handed him the water bag and he drank thirstily. Passing it back to Connor, he continued: "It'll be dark soon, and we won't see any cliff edges. The rocks we sit down on we'll have to sleep on."

" '*My quest carries me far, from a world with silver sun*'— what?" Wren stopped, tapping Tyron on the shoulder. They were walking in single file, Tyron leading and Connor last.

"I was just muttering to myself. I think—"

Tyron stopped speaking when from far below them came a long, echoing cry. Another followed, starting low and rising to a screech that made Wren press her back against a stone outcropping.

Both boys stood still and unbreathing as the last fearsome echoes died away. Silence followed.

Wren whispered, "What was that?"

"Warrie beasts," Connor said in a low voice.

Tyron's shoulders hunched tightly. "Right. Of course they *might* just be after . . ."

"Found our track," Connor answered softly.

"Warries . . . they're like wolves, aren't they? But they run on two legs, and they—"

"Hunt and eat humans," Tyron finished grimly.

"I thought they didn't live anywhere near this part of the world," Wren said, suddenly feeling cold again.

"Andreus," Tyron said shortly.

"I'd heard rumors about the possibility that he'd brought some here and turned them loose in the mountains, but I didn't want to believe it," Connor murmured. "We'd better move."

Wren clenched her teeth as Tyron turned about, put his head down, and started stalking at a vigorous pace up the trail.

No one said anything for a long time. Wren was soon panting. Behind her she heard Connor's breathing, short and harsh, and she knew he must be looking continually this way and that. The last red rim of the sun disappeared behind them—not that Wren dared to glance back—and there were no more warm splashes of golden light. The blue shadows began melting into darkness.

Tyron kept up the fast pace even after Wren heard his breath beginning to wheeze. She was on the point of asking if they might stop and just listen when the sound came again: a long, wavering cry trembling on the air and growing closer.

"Hunting cry," Tyron gasped. "That's got to be. Described it perfectly . . . in the records . . ."

"That's it. Look." Connor pointed above them as rocks skittered down and tapped the narrow path about them. Up the steep slope, a frightened shape blurred past. "Goat," he said. "They know. Everything alive is on the run now."

"The warries . . . eat goats. . . ?" Wren coughed as Tyron started up the trail again.

"Anything." Tyron jerked around briefly. "S'long as they can chase it first."

"Tyron," Connor murmured, "do you see that cliff on that next slope?"

Tyron turned his head sharply and scanned the trail ahead. Without abating his pace, he glanced back and said abruptly, "Chraucan nest?"

"I think so," Connor said.

"But what good will that do? I don't think chraucans will scare off warries. I don't know if even gryphs would scare off warries."

"Shall we try? At least in a chraucan cave, we might be able to fight these creatures better."

"With our luck both sets of creatures will attack us." Tyron coughed hoarsely, and as if in answer, the warries' hunting cry came again, closer still.

"Let's run," Connor said, taking Wren's hand. He started ahead, pulling Wren so that she could move faster. She did not protest; that cry made the back of her spine ache as though a thousand stinger bees crawled on her.

113

They ran uphill for what seemed an agonizingly long while and soon were stumbling over shadow-hidden rocks. One by one they fell, tumbling to knees and elbows, but the other two always helped the stumbler up. They ran on.

Suddenly Tyron gave a cry. "Here! Over here!"

He began scrambling sideways across the cliff face. Gasping out loud, he pushed with his hands at rocks to speed himself on. Connor still held Wren's hand, keeping her from falling headlong in the darkness.

Behind them, they heard the faint thump-thump of feet and the snuffling and wordless chattering of eerie voices.

Tyron cried thinly, "We're . . . nearly . . . there . . ."

Suddenly Connor dropped Wren's hand, lunged, and caught Tyron's tunic hem. "Allow me, please."

Tyron whirled about, mouth open. "What? Don't be a fool—"

Connor gasped urgently. "Those chraucans will have heard the warries as well and might want to escape. Maybe they'll take us—I've heard of it. Or they might try to drive us off their cliff, in which case it's better if only one of us finds out first. Here—take this." He drew his sword and handed it to Tyron, who let the point drop as though he had not the strength to hold it. "I shall be fast."

Tyron stared after Connor, looking too dazed to respond.

Wren heard the shuffling coming closer and thought: *Eren would make a plan to save her friends. Now . . . what . . . what . . .* "OH!"

She felt the cold mountain wind scour across the back of her neck as she ran a few feet farther down the trail toward their hunters. Her fingers plunged into her apron pockets.

"Wren—don't—" Tyron gasped.

"Just here. Now watch," she hissed, and opened her hands.

A puff of wind took the yellow powder in a cloud back down the trail. A moment later she sent another cloud, the last of her pepper. A few seconds later she and Tyron heard howls and yelps of anger and pain.

114

*"Come now!"* Connor's voice shouted from the gloom above, and Tyron and Wren ran with a speed lent by fright.

A moment or two later they stumbled onto a wide cliff.

"What is it? What is that funny noise?" Wren shuddered as she registered a strange, croaking noise, an inhuman *Chrauc! Chra-a-a-auc!* "More warries?" She thought she heard Connor's voice as well, but she could not be sure.

Suddenly she heard a distinct cry from Connor: "Hurry!" And, in clear triumph, "We're going chraucan-backing." He appeared a moment later, laughing breathlessly, and he plucked his sword from Tyron's hands, jamming it in its sheath. "Come!"

The Queen moved with seeming tranquility through her day, a smile affixed to her mouth. She said nothing to anyone about her appointment with her sister. When the King left her to go have supper with the various commanders at the garrison, she dismissed her maidservants and dressed herself in one of her formal gowns in the Rhisadel colors. Slipping on a plain cloak with a hood, she went out.

Leila was waiting near the designation room. No one else was about. The servants were used to seeing Leila and the magicians come and go; no one suspected that anything was amiss.

Leila also wore a dark cloak. She looked amused and faintly perplexed as she greeted her sister. "Sure you want to do this, Astren?"

"Do you think those famed wizards constitute a danger?" The Queen felt the anger she had fought for days seeping into her voice.

Leila said promptly, "Not the least bit. But you might come out with more questions than when you went in."

"Let us go."

"Verne know?" Leila took her hand.

"No. No one. If it's a mistake, it will be mine alone," Astren replied, shut her eyes, and held her breath.

115

When the lurching dizziness faded, she opened her eyes to see before her a small, round cottage. It sat in the late afternoon shadows, looking peaceful in the midst of its little garden. Astren stood where she was, reflecting that she had seen many such cottages but had never been inside one.

Leila was looking at her, waiting.

"I'm recovered." The Queen breathed deeply. "How you can bear that, I'll never understand."

Leila smiled briefly but then said, "Shall I wait without?"

The Queen made a face at her sister. "Don't be absurd."

They walked together up the short path to the door. Before they reached it, the door opened, and a white-bearded old man said pleasantly, "Good day, good day. Come within, and welcome. You will forgive my sister for not immediately speaking?"

As the Queen followed him in, she thought: *No bowing or titles, but he knows who I am.* She sat down on the chair that Master Gastarth had courteously indicated. There at one side of the hearth sat a tiny old woman, head sunk on her breast and hands folded gently in her lap. Her breathing under the snowy apron was gentle and even, and the Queen assumed she was asleep.

The old man offered drink and food. After politely refusing them, the Queen folded one hand over the other in her velvet-clad lap and said directly, "From what I can understand, none of our magicians want to approach you and risk offending you with questions, but the life of my daughter is in the balance."

"Ask us whatever you wish, my child." Master Gastarth's slow, rumbling voice was mild.

"Very well, then. *Are* you the Sendimeris twins?"

He smiled gently. "While we are here, we are Selshaf and Gastarth. But it is true that Halfrid once knew us by other names and faces."

Queen Astren made a slight gesture of impatience. "Perhaps *names* are not as important as *purpose*. Are you manipulating things—events, people—from a distance? If so, to what purpose? And if not, then why did you hold Halfrid back and allow those children to pursue a dangerous and impossible course?"

"We manipulate no one," Master Gastarth replied, "and those children would have been difficult to stop. Outside of one other person, they have the best chance of entering Andreus's lands."

"And then? What then?" the Queen cried.

In her corner, the Mistress looked up briefly. Her glance was not without sympathy, but almost immediately her chin sank again.

Astren saw Leila frown slightly at her, but she went on. "They are on their own in Senna Lirwan—"

"They are still in Meldrith, though very near Andreus's border," Master Gastarth interrupted mildly. He looked at his sister again. She nodded once, eyes still closed.

"So they are near it, while all the magicians sit in Cantirmoor—or here—and wait. And you say you do not want Verne to go to war?"

"Those young people have unexpected resources within and aid without," Master Gastarth said in his tranquil voice. Then he paused and looked over a third time at his sister at her place by the hearth. She did not move.

"Aid? What aid? You're *here* . . . You've been here for six years, doing *nothing* while Andreus by his threats held us from seeing our child and while he conquered nearly all of the eastern coast!"

The Mistress opened her eyes again. "Our concern has not been so much with Andreus," she said apologetically, "as with the one who tutored him." She stood up and gave her skirts a little shake. "You will pardon us a moment? We will bring out something hot to drink."

The Queen watched as the old people moved into the kitchen area; then she turned to face her sister. "You were right," she murmured. "I've more questions now than when I first entered. But there's a sense . . ." She stopped, gazing thoughtfully at the rings on her hands. "I can't explain it. I feel a sense of reassurance, though I've heard no words of pledge."

"I'll tell you what frightens *me*," Leila said, "and that's that I never gave a thought to who—or *what*—might have taught our busy friend in Senna Lirwan his tricks." She looked up as the Master and Mistress came back in, each carrying a tray.

"*Outside of one other person*, you just said. You mean Idres Rhiscarlan? Halfrid has forbidden the magicians to speak with her, but the King and I are not bound by his sanctions. Perhaps I should go and beg for her help."

"Ah, but she is not in the Haven," Mistress Selshaf murmured, setting her tray carefully on the hearth.

"She's gone?" Leila asked in dismay.

"We come and go without hindrance; that is our rule here," Master Gastarth answered. "Shall we have some hot cider? So good on chill nights."

"And it will be chill on the mountain," the Mistress said, smiling, her eyes almost merry. "I fear we must soon leave as we have a task awaiting us there. Andreus seems to have placed an ugly spell over his border, a very deadly one, which we feel we should lift. Our timing must be carefully managed, though, because our action will bring him immediately to investigate, and we don't wish him to find anyone in view. Would you like to come with us and witness, I wonder?"

There was no sign of the Princess of Siradayel or the disguised mistress of deportment, the Queen thought as she glanced at her sister's smiling face. At the prospect of observing the powerful magicians at work, Leila looked fourteen again, and happy. The Queen reached to accept a steaming cup.


"Here—quickly. Before they leave," Connor cried.

Wren felt his strong fingers grip her wrist, and he pulled her over the lip of a huge cliff. Behind him stood three tall birds. Their necks were very long; the small heads turning this way and that were a full two handspans higher than Connor. At the base of the long necks their broad bodies were covered with dully iridescent purplish feathers. Or rather, Wren noticed distractedly, two birds were purple and one was silvery gray.

Connor turned and vaulted onto the back of the nearest

bird. It sidled forward a step or two, ruffling its feathers and calling out in a strange, whimpering voice.

"I've never heard of chraucans doing this." Tyron thrust both hands through his hair, making it stand up crazily. "Never." He threw himself across the back of a second bird and looked astonished when it allowed him to remain.

All three chraucans sidled closer to the edge of their wide ledge, their skinny legs bending backward and their toes clicking on the stone.

"Hurry, Wren," Connor called.

Beyond the rocks Wren heard the warries' voices, and she flung herself up on the last bird's broad back. The bird stepped forward, clumsily jolting her. Quickly she grabbed hold of its neck, crouching forward a little to do so. The great wings fluffed out, and she tucked her feet up against the tendons that joined the wings to the back.

"*Chra-a-a-auc!*" The bird croaked, fluffing its wings again, which jammed Wren's feet more tightly into its wing pits. It moved forward, and Wren gave a shout of exhilaration and fear as the bird dove off the edge of the cliff.

"*Yeeeeee-ayy!*" Connor shouted as his bird took off.

"*Oo-ooo-oo,*" Tyron hooted.

Behind them, warries swarmed onto the cliff, screaming and leaping angrily.

Wren's chraucan spread its wings, and the bird leveled smoothly. Wind tore fiercely across Wren's face, and her eyes squinted against it. Glancing back to the ledge, she saw the jumping gray shapes of the man-eating warrie beasts at the very edge of the cliff. Scraps of wind carried the chittering voices to her, and she tightened her grip on the base of the bird's neck. Then the bird began to climb into the clouds, its body jerking up and down as the great wings flapped. Wren gritted her teeth, thinking: *Don't scream and don't stiffen. A pirate queen would think of the near escape and laugh.*

Well, she might not be able to laugh, but she did try to feel the movement of the bird's body beneath her, as she had with the horse. The feathers were soft, and her feet stayed securely in the wing pits.

Somewhere in the fog, she heard Connor laughing joyously. Fainter was Tyron's shout: "Do you think we could get them to fly to the bridge?"

"I should think they know—where else would humans want to go?" came Connor's answer, against the strong wind.

Tyron's chraucan let out a piercing shriek, and all three birds veered and flapped again to build speed. Then suddenly they broke free of the clouds into a burst of golden-bright light.

"Oh!" Wren cried in awe.

The sky was a benign blue dome over them, diamond-brilliant. At the west sat the sun, a smiling round ball of molten gold. The horizon stretched away immeasurably, with clouds forming a glowing cottony floor, pierced by snow-gleaming mountain peaks.

The birds kept climbing, veering around rocky spires and flying along huge crevasses whose depths faded away in distant gloom. Every now and then Wren spotted their shadows on the cloud floor or stretching for an instant over the gray face of a stone cliff. The flight was so beautiful, so unlike anything she had ever imagined, that she did not notice her hands and feet and nose going numb in the icy air.

Connor's bird soared, circled, and dove majestically. Once, as he neared the chraucan carrying Wren, she saw a big grin of pure enjoyment on his face. Tyron, though, seemed to be holding on as tightly as she was, and he squinted downward with careful attention.

Just as suddenly as the flight had begun, the birds banked around a long gray slope and dropped rapidly. Wren felt her stomach curling. The bird slowed, drifting, and came gently to another wide ledge. Here was evidence of human work—part of the rock had been smoothed upward into a wall.

The birds landed running, and Wren was bounced alarmingly. She discovered then that her numb hands were no longer able to grasp. She fell off and rolled up against the stone.

Sitting up somewhat dazedly, she began to rub her hands

together, working her toes as well. The boys got off their birds, and the chraucans promptly took flight again.

Tyron swooped down on Wren and hugged her fiercely. "You and that pepper."

Connor was still laughing with joy. "Close one, eh, my friends? I don't mind admitting that those warrie voices will haunt my dreams for some time to come."

"At least we'll be alive to have nightmares," Wren said, standing up slowly. Her hands and feet were still cold, and one of her arms ached where Tyron had squashed it wrong against her body, but she felt like laughing and dancing. The escape—the flight— If they could get this far, she knew they *would* win Tess free. "Wish there was some way to thank those birds. Why did they help us?" she said, her teeth chattering slightly.

"They're against the baddies, who shoot them for sport," Connor said, wiping his hair off his forehead and squinting into the windy sky.

"Where'd you hear that?" Tyron was wringing his hands vigorously. "I didn't see that in any of the books. But then none of the books that mentioned chraucans had been written since Andreus took his throne."

"Around." Connor shrugged. "I must say, I don't care for the look of *this*."

"I guess the birds feel the border spells." Tyron nodded thoughtfully. "My book did say that they never cross over."

"Cross over?" Wren said.

"Yes. Below that bridge there—that's the border between Senna Lirwan and Meldrith." He pointed over the edge of their cliff, and wind sheered coldly across Wren's face as she stared down into the deepest chasm she had ever seen in her life. Spanning the chasm was a bridge. Over that wide distance, the bridge looked fragile and insubstantial. Above, the sky was as stone-dark gray as the rocks around them, and below the wind moaned through the gaps.

"That chasm runs through most of these mountains," Tyron went on. "According to the books, it was caused by a terrible quake long ago, set off after an especially monstrous mage war.

121

I guess the bridge was put up then by our own magicians—at any rate, few know of it. Halfrid crossed it himself many years ago and said it was still undiscovered by the Lirwanis. I doubt anyone's been over it since."

"Sure no roads around," Wren muttered, teeth chattering loudly.

"Hey-ho," Tyron exclaimed happily. "That's another thing. That ride has saved us days of floundering about in these mountains. Anyway, supposedly Andreus doesn't know about this bridge, but his creatures might."

"What, more warries?" Wren shivered.

"I don't think so, not this high. Nothing lives easily up here. Nothing that moves on foot, that is, which is why the bridge was put there." Tyron slapped his hands together.

"There are, however, gryphs," Connor murmured.

"Right. They attack anything that moves, but they usually hunt at night, which is soon. Let's warm up our hands—mine are too numb to grip—then get ourselves across quickly."

The icy wind defeated their attempts to try to warm up, and Wren found that she could not get her cloak to wrap around her properly, so she stuffed it back into her pack. Looking down again, she saw that the gloom below was darkening steadily; nightfall came suddenly this high.

Presently Tyron stopped breathing on his fingers, flexed them once or twice, then spoke. "Well, shall we get it over with?"

"You mean, get *us* over." Connor laughed. "Come. I shall go first, and you are not to notice my shudders of cowardice."

They moved down toward the waiting bridge.


"*Now,*" Mistress Selshaf spoke softly.

She stood and held out her hands. Her brother faced her. They took one each of the sisters' hands.

The Queen winced, bracing herself for the dizzying wrench of transfer. Warm hands on either side squeezed hers comfortingly. When the hands let go, she felt sudden cool, pine-scented wind. Opening her eyes, she looked up in wonder at the brilliant canopy of stars, as if someone had set jewels afire and scattered them across the sky. They were now standing high on a mountain peak. She felt no trace of dizziness from the transfer.

The old people were still facing one another. They stretched out their hands toward one another until their fingers nearly touched. The Mistress sang on a low note, no words that Astren could make out, but there was a curious compulsion to the tone. With no warning, a fire burst into existence on the ground.

The Queen stood back in alarm. The Sendimeris's faces were lit warmly, showing calm expressions.

"Come closer. This is just to keep you from taking chill in this air."

As Queen Astren stepped forward slowly, her sister stretched her hands over the fire, eyes gleaming in the firelight with scarce-contained excitement.

The Queen held out her hands to the warm blaze, watching the twins stand still as stone. She caught a glitter of blue and silver on the old lady's breast, tiny reflections of the stars, and she realized that the woman was not resting but was staring down into a scrying stone.

Mistress Selshaf raised her hands slowly, then said, "Begin." The word was nearly carried away by the wind.

Master Gastarth turned to face outward. Stepping to the very edge of the cliff, his beard blowing back over his shoulders, he brought his hands up and clapped them.

Thunder cracked the peace of the sky. Underfoot the mountain trembled. Master Gastarth's hands were now apart and facing out; lightning sprang from them, yellow, white, sunbright, and jewel-red. Spears of light shot out across the black chasm, leaping into the sky. Again, in echo, bright lightning danced upward, sent by his sister. Joining, the lights found a target unseen and flashed—blindingly—from horizon to horizon. Just for an instant.

Then the light was gone, and once again the sky was benign and star-jeweled.

"There. That was quite pretty, don't you think?" Mistress Selshaf said, lowering her hands.

"It will give Andreus something to puzzle out." The Master chuckled comfortably.

"You might assure your husband that a wait will do no harm, my dear." The Mistress took the Queen's hand and patted it kindly. "But I understand his impatience. You might also ask our friend Halfrid to ride with him if he goes."

"Andreus is a clever young man," the Master said.

The Mistress nodded and smiled, eyes gleaming with kindness and good humor in the light of the fire. She reached to take the sisters' hands once more, saying, "Yes, indeed. There's a bit of work ahead for us all, and not a great measure of time to accomplish it in . . ."

Magic overtook them again, smooth and fast. The Queen found this much more endurable. But instead of appearing once more in the Haven, the sisters found themselves alone at the palace designation.

Queen Astren put a hand to her head.

"Dizzy?" Leila asked.

"No, I'm *not*, amazingly. But I . . ." she stopped.

Leila nodded, one of her eyebrows slanting steeply. "I agree. I don't know *what* to think. And neither will Halfrid when I tell him that I strongly suspect those two removed that border trap just in time for Tyron, Wren, and Connor to cross."

The Queen drew a deep breath. "So she *wasn't* sleeping. She was watching them all the time? In one of those magic stones you people use?"

Leila nodded slowly.

"Then she's watching over them. I'll feel so much better, knowing that. But why didn't she tell us directly?"

Leila looked rueful. "Probably because she knew her watchfulness was about to end. No doubt it was relatively easy for her to see them while they walked in this land. But I don't think she can see them past Andreus's border."

124

## Chapter Thirteen

The bridge stretched over the chasm, suspended by braided cable, the cables fitting so smoothly into the rock walls that Wren figured magic had done the work. The cable rails were about chest high for Wren and nearly as thick as her waist. As she and the boys moved cautiously down to the platform at the edge of the bridge, she saw that the floor of the bridge was made of many slats of wood and was too narrow for two to go across abreast.

Connor stepped out first, moving as if he'd just discovered someone had slipped eggs into his boots. Wren went after him, reaching her hands to either side and gripping the thick, icy-cold cables before shifting her weight to the next step. Behind her, Tyron stepped silently and carefully.

The bridge had looked stationary, but as they got closer to the center, Wren found that it jiggled with their movements and swung a little in the wind. Her stomach curled even more tightly, and she tried a step with her eyes shut. That was scarier.

"Shall we talk?" she asked nervously, trying not to think of what was below her—or rather, what was not.

"A poem, do you think?" Connor called out ahead. "My oldest sister wrote a fine one, about the freedom of the wind—ahem."

"Oooh." Wren sighed as the wind made the bridge sway. She clenched at the cables, feet braced, until the movement subsided a little. "Sorry, Connor, but wind is *not* a good subject right now."

"Faster we go, quicker we're across," Tyron said stiffly from close behind.

"Tyron," she said hoarsely. "You've never said anything about *your* family . . ."

"Mmm," came his indistinct mumble.

"You would not know this, Wren," Connor said jovially, "but we never ask a serious wizard such a question. Might jeopardize the innocent."

"But what happens—oh, I see. You don't tell your friends anything, but if enemies ask, then it's the 'old grandmother on the farm' routine. Except, what about Mistress Leila? She's a serious wizard, yet everyone knows her in Cantirmoor."

"It's different for those royal types," Tyron said. "Everyone already knows who they are anyway. And if they *do* want to live secretly, then they leave and use a different name. No one knew who Mistress Leila was—or that she knew magic—in your village, did they?"

"True. So can you still go home?" Wren asked. "I mean, if there is one to go to?"

"Sure," Tyron said awkwardly. "You just tell nosy villagers that you travel as a caravan escort or whatever. Most magicians still learn another 'respectable' trade. Makes the stories easier—"

"Ho," Connor called in warning. "Danger ahead—"

Wren squinted up in the direction he was looking in and saw two dark specks against the night sky. Tears blurred her vision from the icy strength of the wind. She let go of the cable with one hand and wiped her eyes impatiently. The specks grew bigger with frightening speed.

"Gryphs." Tyron groaned. "Lie flat."

"They'll pluck us off if they see us," Connor began. "I think we'll have a better chance if I try to ward them while you two run—"

"*Down*, Connor," Tyron yelled.

Then both boys froze as a moment of blinding light made it impossible to see anything at all.

Wren shut her eyes and pressed her head against her arm, her hands clinging to the cable. Overhead she heard the flap of great wings, but the sound passed very swiftly.

Connor gasped. "What was *that?*"

"Magic. Had to be. Felt like a *big* spell," Tyron replied, shaky-voiced. "Whatever it was, those gryphs are flying like crazy in that direction."

"Then let's get going before they come back to investigate here," Wren said.

Connor led the way, calling after another dozen steps or so, "Halfway. We are now in Senna Lirwan, my comrades."

Wren kept her eyes on the wooden slats as she placed one foot, then the next, then the first, on and on till the bridge's end. At last Tyron, the last to step from the swaying bridge to the rocky cliff opposite, let out an explosive sigh of relief.

"Hoo! Now, let's hope that the baddies haven't found the bridge, so maybe we can find a few moments of peace in the refugee tunnel."

"I shall go first," Connor stated promptly. "Can you find our access way?"

"It's near, according to Idres."

They stood in a huddle close to the cliff wall on the Lirwani side of the border as Tyron leaned out and scanned around. They could no longer see the distant and deadly gryphs, but Wren imagined she felt their presence. She was afraid that, at any moment, they'd appear above the rocks, swooping, shrieking, and tearing.

*Tess is here.* The thought was like a stone inside her. *We're just at the border of this awful country, and already it's scary. But we're coming, Tess. We're coming to get you out.*

"Ah, there. I see the sign."

Tyron dashed around a rock and scrambled into a steep-walled crevice. He traced a sign with one finger on a knobby outcropping of stone, then all three watched as the smooth rock face flickered out of sight and left them staring into a black hole.

"This part of the rock is illusion," Tyron whispered.

Connor's sword made a metallic hissing noise as he drew it and stepped into the blackness. Tyron moved in next to Wren, then turned and did something in the darkness. She heard the rustle of his clothes.

"There. Sealed," he said, breathing a sigh.

Little sounds seemed overloud in the complete darkness. Wren felt her eyes widening, but still she could see nothing. She heard the boys' breathing, distinct as the soft hiss of their clothes as they moved.

"Take hands," Connor murmured. "Which way, O sagacious one?"

"This tunnel is supposed to be narrow and shortly will give onto a cavern, lit by glow moss. There doesn't seem to be anyone here, does there?" Tyron raised his voice slightly. "I don't see how anyone could have found the bridge from the other way. It's only reachable by a really horrid trail marked carefully by an oak sign. Unless Andreus has those gryphs spying."

"You mean, carrying baddiepeepers about on their backs? Or the gryphs themselves do the spying?" Wren asked.

"Gryphs don't carry humans," Connor responded. "They prefer to eat them if sheep and goats are in short supply. But they will spy about, in a limited sort of way, for someone who's trained them. I wonder if they would recognize a construct like a bridge as being something to fly home and squawk about? They might if they saw humans on it."

"Right, and they saw us. As plain as bugs on glass. But they also saw that flash and went dusting off to nose it out. Maybe they can't hold two separate thoughts in their nasty bird brains," Tyron said firmly. "Let's hope that they forget *us*. The thing is, we can't worry about that now. And speaking of light . . ."

"If you're right about the tunnel, this darkness won't last much longer," Connor replied.

"Chlonger, longer, onger." A sudden ghostly echo came back.

"Cavern ahead," Tyron said. Wren could almost hear his grin, and his fingers jerked in hers.

Out of the darkness there came a soft greenish glow. Connor, who had been edging forward without lifting his feet, now stepped more quickly, pulling the others along.

They emerged in a large grotto. Wren thought that a small village could probably fit into the enormous cavern. Strange, luminescent green moss grew up the curving walls in increasing clumps. As the ceiling was completely covered with it, the entire cavern glowed.

"Wow!" Wren said breathlessly.

Connor resheathed his weapon, the sound hissing through the still, cool air of the cavern. Pulling out the water bag, he unstopped it and each of them took a long drink. As he replaced it in his knapsack, he said, "And now?"

"Bear left. Search for a flower sign, and follow the tunnel leftways."

Connor shook his head slowly. "You know my luck with those signs," he whispered with cheerful regret.

"I tell you, don't even look, but *feel* for them first. It's so easy if you know there is one."

"So says Tyron!"

"Feel with your fingers?" Wren put in curiously.

"Feel with your . . . oh, inner senses. Remember how the border into the Free Vale felt?"

"Ugh!"

"I mean, the sense—"

"What *that* felt like," she said, "was worms crawling through my brain. No thanks for more of that."

Connor laughed in agreement.

Tyron sighed. "Why am I surrounded with bread-heads?" he asked the glowing ceiling. "You'd think someone . . ." He stopped and turned his head this way and that, frowning.

"What is it?" Wren whispered. That familiar claw was grabbing her insides again.

"Someone else in here?"

Out came Connor's sword again. They stood quietly, each scrutinizing the rough cavern walls, floor, and then the various dark openings in the rock of the cavern walls. Nothing.

Tyron shook his head. "Baddies would drop on us like stone if they'd found us."

"My thought exactly," Connor agreed.

"Weird. Must've been those warries and gryphs unsettling me. Shall we get out of here?"

"I'm with you." Connor made a graceful bow.

Tyron walked on in silence. Presently he said, "This way."

Wren looked at the narrow opening that they were entering. It looked exactly like all the others. As Tyron passed, he touched the wall. Wren, glancing back at the spot where his fingers had made contact, thought it was indistinguishable from the rest of the rock.

This tunnel wound downward abruptly, then opened into another cavern, also lit by softly glowing green mosses and some dull bluish gray moss as well.

The still air smelled of ancient stone, and for a long time the only sound they heard was the noise of their walking and breathing, and the creak of leather as Connor—whose hand rested firmly on the hilt of his sword—looked this way and that.

They moved steadily downward and came to a cavern with a rushing dark river winding along its floor. The trail brought them right to its edge. Bending down to drink, they found the water was numbingly cold but very good. Connor refilled their water bag again.

They walked until Tyron said, "I think I'd like to eat something."

Connor instantly pulled his pack off his back. As he brought out an oatcake, dry and bent as it was, Wren said, "That thing looks great, so I must be starved."

"I shall be glad to join you," Connor said.

They sat down near some stalagmites marked with blackly glittering gemstones and ate in silence. After a while Tyron mused, "I wonder how long we've been walking. Impossible to judge time here."

"I don't know, but it feels good to be sitting down," Wren said. "And if it feels good to be sitting on damp stone, I *must* be tired."

Almost as soon as they had wrapped themselves up and pillowed their heads on their knapsacks, all three were asleep.

Wren's dreams scattered when she heard Tyron snort, sit up, and say sharply, "Who's there?"

Her eyes opened in time to see Connor fling off his bedroll and rise to his feet, sword out, all in one smooth motion. Despite his grimy velvet tunic and the red curls ruffled wildly all over his head, he suddenly looked dangerous.

Wren held her breath, listening.

Nothing, beyond the steady, mournful *drip-drip* of distant water.

Tyron let out a whooshing sigh. "Sorry, Connor. Maybe it was just a weird dream, but I was so *sure* there was someone watching us."

Wren rubbed her eyes and yawned. "Hope not. But—what for, if someone is? I mean if he's a baddiepeeper, why not just pounce on us and throw us in a dungeon? And if it's someone on our side, maybe someone else who wants to rescue Tess, then why not join us?"

Connor had moved a ways off and was swinging his sword back and forth, back and forth, passing it from hand to hand at the top of his swing.

Tyron yawned. "Shall we regard this as the breakfast hour? I believe I've slept long enough."

He pulled Connor's bag over and brought out a cake for each of them, laying Connor's cake on top of the bag. Then, hunching over, hair in his eyes, he stared intently at his lap. Wren turned to watch Connor, who was now moving the sword smoothly through a variety of motions, as if fighting an invisible foe.

"What's he doing?" Wren whispered.

Tyron blinked and looked up. "Shadow dance," he said briefly. "It's a kind of practice." As Wren opened her mouth to speak, he added with a sudden grin, "Yes, you could learn it, too, but you have to know something about sword fighting first, and you won't get that from me. I hate those clumsy, dangerous things."

Glancing back at Connor, Wren thought that in his hands the sword did not look clumsy, but she said nothing as she bit into her dry and chewy oatcake.

Presently Connor rejoined them, his brow now wet but his usual smile in place.

"Tired?" Wren asked.

"Not at all," Connor replied. "Thank you." He stopped and picked up his cake and pack. "I can eat as we walk."

Wren said, "You know what really gets me curious are these signs, leading us through the caverns. Do you think I could learn them?"

Tyron considered. "You are so good with the scrying, I'd think you could. And I don't think teaching you this would put you into any danger. Shall we try, then? Next one."

"That'd be great." Wren clapped her hands.

The sound echoed uncannily, like the crackling of ghostly sticks.

Connor murmured, "Strange, this place."

"At least we aren't being rained on. Though maybe some rain would beat the nasty mud out of this dress." Wren looked down in disgust at her clothes. The apron, once white, was stained with dirt and with the juices of the fruits that she had gathered and carried when they were riding along the southern border of Meldrith. The seams of her clothes made her skin itch.

"Perhaps you could rinse your things out in one of those streams," Tyron suggested.

Knowledgeable after years of helping in the laundry rooms of two orphanages, Wren shook her head. "No soap, no wringer, and in here, without sun and wind, it would take three days to dry anything."

Tyron grinned. "One thing about these brown togs is the dirt doesn't show."

"Don't you feel it?" Wren made a face.

"I might if I had to put a dirty one on," Tyron said, "but

132

now that it's already on, I don't much mind. Same with the hose." He looked down at his brown woolen hose, now bagging at knees and ankles.

"Your tunic is hemmed at the knee, so it doesn't pick up half the trail as these long skirts do." Wren sighed. "Is that why the girls at your school wear the same sort of tunics?"

Tyron shrugged. "I never thought much about it, I guess." Then he squinted intently down the cavern. "Did you hear . . . no. I won't worry about it any more. That's—"

"*I* hear it," Connor murmured.

A distant hissing noise, too uneven to be water, came to all their ears. As it got louder, they noted an odd, dry quality to the hiss.

"A serpent!" Tyron choked. "Let's hide." He led the way to a large stalagmite about twenty feet behind them. Wren followed closely.

As soon as they reached the safety of the stone, Wren noticed that she and Tyron were alone.

"Connor," Tyron cried, but Connor, who was now on the other side of the cavern, sword out, motioned Tyron to stay back, then disappeared through an archway.

The hissing got louder, breaking at intervals.

Wren crouched into a ball. Next to her, Tyron was breathing hard. When he essayed another cautious peek, he sighed in relief. "It's going away."

They peered around the stone where the glisten of scales shone through an archway across the cavern. The segment they saw must have been as round as Tyron was tall. The hiss diminished slowly as the writhing serpent wound away, its body getting smaller and smaller until the tail disappeared altogether. But they waited until the hissing noise was also gone. Wren noticed her knees felt shaky when she got up, and Tyron was making an awful face.

Connor reappeared right then, looking just as usual.

"No signs of battle," Tyron spoke up, still sounding nervous.

"Or nasty, squelching *sounds* of battle," Wren added.

Connor grinned. "It was just an old serpent," he said. "No real danger. Or not much, anyway."

Tyron put his hands on his hips. "But how did you *know* that? Aaagh, Connor. I nearly died from fright when I looked up and saw you weren't with us. Don't *do* that."

"I think if we face danger, we've got to do it together," Wren added. "Or run together," she amended.

Connor's expression was odd as he looked at his dusty boot tops. "Your pardon," he said finally. "I did not intend to frighten you on my behalf—"

"Well you did."

"I do feel that your part of our expedition is as wizard, and there you must take the lead. But my part is as escort." He patted his sword. "Defense."

"No it's not," Wren said roundly, "because all that leaves is baggage, and I won't be that. Shall we make a pact about sticking together?"

"As you wish." Connor held out his hands. "I am very sorry if I've caused you alarm."

"Oh, let's go on," Tyron said, with a rueful laugh. "I suppose you can't *help* doing heroic deeds. You've read too many of those plays. It's addled your brain. Come on, Wren, let's get back to those signs."

"All right," Wren agreed, but her ears were still open to both boys, and she caught the faintest whisper from Connor, "He was so old. And I had always wanted to meet one."

## Chapter Fourteen

*T*hey penetrated farther into the caverns, Wren looking around with interest. She wondered if they would always hear such things as serpents before the serpents heard them. Beside her, Connor walked with his head down. He appeared to be lost in thought. A little ways ahead, Tyron was studying the archways closely, and Wren hurried to catch up.

"Who laid the signs down? Halfrid? The ones who made the bridge?"

"They're *much* older than old Halfrid," Tyron said. "Probably the bridge-makers—"

"Not wishing to contradict," Connor interjected apologetically, "but I heard that they go back a lot farther in time than the mage war."

"That may be true," Tyron said. "I'll find out later. Anyway, the signs were put here centuries ago, according to Idres. She didn't tell me any more than that, just how to follow them. And she mentioned a couple of the landmarks we'd see along the way, so we'd know we hadn't gone astray. Here."

They had come to the end of that particular cavern, and Tyron stopped at a smallish archway. "Shut your eyes."

Wren did.

"Now, turn your face slowly side to side and listen with your mind, the way you did when you looked into my crystal and the window."

"What should I listen *for?* I—oh." Wren stopped, staring, then squeezed her eyes closed again. "Lost it. Wait. Wait." She frowned in concentration, eyes still shut, then edged forward slowly. Her fingers reached and touched on a vein of dark stone in the archway wall. Opening her eyes, she caught a very faint bluish glow on the stone. "In my mind, this is the color of periwinkles, and it's shaped like two spiky leaves with a kind of lily sprouting between."

Tyron grinned. "That's it. That's great. I've just *got* to take—" The other two watched as all the laughter faded out of Tyron's face. "That is," he corrected himself, "Connor, you'll have to take her to the school."

"They'll be scuttling me as well," Connor said gently.

"Yes, but *I* won't go back to let them do it." Tyron's face was tight. "Wren, try sign-sensing as we walk." He started forward.

They walked for a long time, through several large caverns and down old tunnels. They stopped in the middle of one with a stream of icy water to eat, drink, and rest a bit, then went on.

Their path led steadily downward, which made it easy to keep up a smart pace, though after a while everyone complained of aching knees and thighs.

Once they stopped and slept. When one woke, the whisper of that person's movements brought the other two to wakefulness. When they got up, Connor did his shadow dance while Wren and Tyron ate their cakes and talked about history and travel. She found that he knew something about countries that had been on the very edge of the old map at Three Groves—and that talking about these things, rather than about the Magic School or affairs in Cantirmoor, was easier for him.

Three more times they walked, stopped, and slept in the long series of caves. Always they walked downhill. Wren soon caught on to the sign sensing, and she made the discovery that many of the archways and caverns had different magical markers. A variety of colors and images glowed softly in her mind, but she avoided those and stayed with the lavender-blue lilies.

She began to wonder where those other signs led, but she

hesitated to ask anything that might get Tyron brooding again. Finally the question was answered in a totally unexpected way.

They were walking along as usual when Tyron suddenly stopped and gazed upward, exclaiming in surprise and amazement.

Hereto, the ceilings had been well grown over with the familiar glow moss, usually green, sometimes bluish, or even a soft pink. Tyron was now staring at a segment of carving in the ceiling of the tunnel. It went for a ways, then broke off at the end of the cavern. Wren's glance fell to the jumble of rock at the base of the cavern wall.

"That *must* be old," Connor said mildly. "Whatever cataclysm broke this up was ancient. The stone fall is also moss-covered."

Tyron paid no attention. His eyes went back up. The carving was a long strip, bordered by diamond shapes. Between the borders were various stylized birds, curly lines, and dots.

"It's pretty," Wren said, then looked more closely. "That's some kind of writing, isn't it?"

"Iyon Daiyin. It's *got* to be," Tyron whispered reverently.

Connor shifted, one of his boots scraping on stone. "Oh, you don't know that. We need to go on."

"I wish—oh." Tyron groaned. "I don't dare do a lift spell. *How* I'd love to get closer."

"Can you read it?" Wren asked.

"N-no," Tyron said with regret and longing; then he pointed. "See? That looks there like an old *thoth* letter, and there might be a *tsar* . . ." He sighed shortly. "Well, if Halfrid was ever in here, he saw it, and it's in the records somewhere. You can learn more about it, Wren, if you ask him."

"I'd prefer to put even more space between us and our serpent friend," Connor suggested.

Wren protested, "But we haven't seen him for three or four sleeps."

Connor shook his head. "But he might have a family nearby."

"I suppose you're right." Tyron jerked his head down, as

if tearing his gaze from the segment of ancient carving. "This must have been one of the Iyon Daiyin access ways . . ."

"I was told," Wren said tentatively, "that the Iyon Daiyin were just stories, that they were never real. Stories to scare children, though I was never scared—not even by the child-stealing ones. I thought it would be fun to fly away to their mountains or to Starborn Island. Better than washing dishes and pulling weeds, anyway."

"They were real," Tyron said with conviction. "There may even be some left, in another part of the world. They weren't monsters, or spirits, even. They were a race of people, some say from another world, who were born with certain magical abilities. Halfrid told me once that some of them intermixed with some of our people and that a few of their magical traits will show up unexpectedly even today. In the past, there were those who did not like this, and . . ."

"The children were killed." Connor's voice echoed with matter-of-fact calm. "The child-stealing stories came out of the fact that the Iyon Daiyin used to rescue children who were born with their traits."

"That's what Halfrid said." Tyron turned to Connor. "You've been asking him about them, too? I wish I'd known you were interested."

Connor just shrugged, smiling. "Is anyone ready for another cake?" he asked.

But Wren was not done yet. "*Why* were the children killed? Were the traits nasty?"

"Not," Tyron said, "according to Halfrid. He meant to bring me some of the old records. They're so old that they are kept in the heraldry archives, but he didn't remember. He said that people were frightened by the children because they could do some amazing things. There are those who don't like others to have access to powers that they don't have."

"Or maybe it was just that they were different," Connor said softly.

Wren hugged herself. "Iyon Daiyin. Real. Oh." She spun around. "I do hope you are right about the Magic School because it would be so horrid to go back to Three Groves, where every time I stop to think about magic, and history, and ancient carvings, a Keeper will shout, 'Wre-en.' " Her voice went high and nasal, and Tyron and Connor laughed. " 'Wre-en, get back to those carrots!' "

Connor said, still chuckling, "Let us go on, shall we?"

They walked on for a long time. They found more of the carving in a cavern just off a steaming hot spring. Tyron expressed a desire to go exploring in the other caves, but Connor demurred. Politely, of course, but firmly.

"Why?" Tyron threw up his hands, excited by the prospect of more discoveries. "We won't get lost—not when there are two of us who can read the flower signs."

Connor said gently, "I am thinking about how impossible it is for us to know how much time we are spending here, how many serpents possibly patrol this part of the cavern, and that Princess Teressa awaits."

"Urk." Tyron stopped short. "You're *right*." He winced in embarrassment. "How could I have . . ." He left the sentence dangling.

Nothing more was said about the carvings, but when they agreed that they were hungry and tired and should stop to sleep, Tyron stayed sitting with his back to a stone. Wren, wrapped in her grimy but warm cloak, waited in silence, not quite asleep. As soon as Connor's breathing deepened, Tyron got up and moved away quietly. Wren struggled with two strong but conflicting urges. She wanted to get up and follow Tyron, but it felt so good to lie there, resting.

*Maybe he'll find something, and maybe he won't. We can look if we make it back this way. Meanwhile, Connor's right. Tess waits, and I know I'm going to need all my wits about me to be any good at all at rescuing her.*

She closed her eyes and fell asleep instantly.

"It was the most amazing thing," Tyron told them later as they walked along. He couldn't sleep and had gotten up to explore, coming upon an archway with carving all around it and eight signs up the left side.

"When I went through, I saw a huge lake. The water was still and ink-black. I felt it, and it was nearly icy. But *that* wasn't the discovery. Above the lake the ceiling was smooth and covered with a fresco. The gold paint still gleamed faintly, and the blues were strong, some of the reds as well. The rest of the colors had faded, but I could still see that it was meant to picture the night sky. Stars were painted, though not in any constellations I know. Maybe that sky was fanciful. Anyway, all around the rim were distant painted forests, and mountains, and birds in flight. I'm sure it was meant to make the cavern resemble a valley somewhere on the surface."

"Where did the light come from?" Wren asked.

"That's what's really odd. Bluish light, and from no discernible source. There was some glow moss in spots over the fresco, and on the walls, but that wasn't the light. It had to have been some sort of magic spell, left all these centuries. Potent indeed."

Connor said almost nothing as Tyron went on marveling aloud about the lake cavern and the people who had made the paintings and carvings. Wren listened with interest, but her thoughts kept returning to Tess.

"Look there!" Tyron cried.

They peered through a narrow opening in the wall into another large cavern with a singular feature: two enormous stalactites, covered with a yellow-gold glow moss.

"Idres said I'd recognize them when I saw them, and she was right. We're almost finished with these mountains."

"Then may I suggest we discuss our plan of action?" Connor said. "And anything else Idres might have told you about, especially if you think you may go off on your own again."

"When we stop to camp." Tyron waved a hand. He was still excited by his discoveries, so excited he didn't hear the uncharacteristic edge to Connor's polite voice.

But Wren noticed.

When they decided to find a place to camp, Wren put in her preference for one of the caverns with running water.

"I like the pleasant sound, and it's also nice to get a fresh drink as soon as I wake. After all," she added, "it's the only fresh thing we can get."

Both boys laughed at this crack, for the oatcakes were not getting tastier with the passage of time. They wrapped up in their cloaks and lay down. But this time it was Wren who remained open-eyed while the others dropped off to sleep.

*Almost through the mountains,* she told herself. *According to the cakes we've eaten up, it's been many days. Maybe while we're hidden safe in these caves, I should try to think to Tess again.*

She got up noiselessly and moved to the side of the dark, rushing water. Kneeling, she looked down into its night-black depths. *Why does it always have to be glass or water?* She shrugged.

Emptying her mind of any other thoughts except of Tess, Wren stared at the water. She felt almost as if her mind had dropped into it, sinking. But before she could register vertigo, there were sudden strange, flickering images—Three Groves, Mistress Leila reading from a book, and then . . .

*Is that you, Wren?*

*Yes! I'm trying this again. We're coming to get you, Tess, but I have to know where you are.*

*Oh, Wren—*

Wren felt Tess's fear for her, and beneath that, her fears for herself and her yearning to escape.

*Don't worry, we'll think of some good way to get you out, but I have to know where you are. Quick, in case that nasty Andreus hears this again.*

*Wren, I don't know where I am. I'm in a dark room, as punishment for running away. I nearly made it, too.*

*You ran away?* Wren's delight carried clearly to Tess.

141

At once Tess's thought was stronger, and now sent back a glimmering of laughter, as bright in mind as the gleam of gold in candlelight. *You know what Eren Beyond-Stars did, in that play—*

*Pretended she was deadly sick.*

*And it worked. At least, it almost worked. But I got caught—oh, Wren, he was so angry about that. And about the dissolving of this horrid border spell he's made to kill anyone crossing into this country. How did you manage that? Oh, but after he talked about that, I had to watch them kill the guard I fooled, and then he hit me and hit me . . .*

Teressa's remembered pain and terror came clearly to Wren, who began to feel the warning throb in her head.

*What a slimeslug! We just have to get you out, and soon. Tess, I think I'd better go. So you don't know where you are?*

*I was in the capital fortress, and may be still. They made me ride back blindfolded. Wren—*

Wren felt it distinctly then, another thought, in question to itself, *Wren?* Not at all like Tess's voice in her mind—a sharper, darker voice.

It was questioning her identity. As she realized this, sudden fright made her break the contact, and she sat up, her eyes opening. Then she fell backward dizzily.

*Oh, I do hope that wasn't a mistake,* she thought as she crawled back to the others and wrapped tightly in her cloak. *Though it was well worth it just to hear Tess and catch that laugh. I think it did her some good.*

Since she had no concrete information on Tess's whereabouts to offer, she decided not to mention the contact to the boys when they woke.

By the time they emerged from the caves at last into a bleak, cloudy, and desolate land, she had forgotten everything about the contact except Tess's laugh. No reason to share that. It had simply been an exchange between friends.

## Chapter Fifteen

*T*hin, steely fingers dug painfully into Teressa's shoulders.

"Who is Wren?" Andreus repeated in a deceptively gentle voice.

Teressa's eyes swam with tears of pain and fear, making the torches behind his head fuse into streams of molten fire. Anything was better than looking into his face.

"I won't tell you," she said again through gritted teeth.

Her cheek stung where he had slapped her the first time, and now she braced for the second blow. Instead he abruptly shoved her so that she stumbled back and landed in a chair.

"Pity. I could use someone who can scry so steadily despite my deflections. I wonder if this is the same person who ripped apart my border spell last week. Impressive magic knowledge indeed, and all the more imperative we bring her here as our guest. A physical description will suffice."

Teressa could not hold back the sobs that shook her. She covered her face with her hands. "No . . . no."

The fingers grabbed her again, forcing her head up. "You are going to have to learn that when I have a use for loyalty, *I* will ask for it. Until then I am only interested in obedience. You have just condemned your Wren to death."

He let go. Unfriendly hands yanked her to her feet and out of the room. She was locked again in the cell.

"This is it," Tyron said when they entered the last tunnel. "She said it would be dark, like the entry tunnel near the bridge. Wren, would you like to find the last sign?"

They felt their way along the tunnel, and Wren easily sensed the last glowing lily sign.

None of them had any idea how long they had been in the caves; time felt as if it had stopped. When they'd first wakened, and after Connor had done his shadow dance, they'd discussed Tyron's plan for sneaking across the plains and getting into the citadel through a secret entrance that Idres had told him about. But just in case the entrance might no longer still be good, Tyron had another plan.

"We can use being prentice age as a sort of disguise and just walk into the city looking for work."

"I like simplicity," said Connor.

Wren agreed. Overcomplicated plans always made her nervous.

Now Tyron made the rock illusion vanish, and they looked at a gray-lit landscape. The outside light seemed glare-bright to their eyes, and the wind that came in to ruffle their clothes felt chilly. One by one they went out; then Tyron sealed the tunnel again.

They started picking their way down a rubble-strewn incline to the rocky trail below.

"Here's where we find out if the gryphs were spies and the biddie-baddies are on the prowl," Tyron said.

"Biddies don't prowl," Wren said.

"They cackle," Connor agreed, with an instructive air.

"Baddies on the cackle," Tyron said slowly, then nodded. "I like the sound of it. Perhaps we should think of something as suitable for old Andreus, the evil king."

"Instead of *King* Andreus, we could call him something insulting . . ." Wren began.

"Something with the same initial sound," Connor put in consideringly, eyes half closed and nose elevated, like a good cook sniffing a new soup.

"Angleworm Andreus," Wren suggested. She loved word games of any kind. "Or Anchor-nosed Andreus."

"Aguewort Andreus," Connor countered promptly.

"Abominable Andreus," Wren fired back.

They were thus getting started in a contest when they rounded another rock-strewn slope and six men gripping drawn swords converged on them.

One of them said something that Wren didn't understand, and she felt a sharp pang of regret that they'd never had the time to give her the language spell. Tyron seemed to understand the soldier, though, and shot a curious look at Wren before Connor ripped his sword free and ran forward to attack.

Of course Connor was outmatched, but he did not slow as he charged the soldiers, yelling, "Run! Run!"

Wren watched as two much taller men raised their weapons to fend off Connor's fierce attack. Two more moved purposefully on Tyron, and two started her way. She backed slowly, her hands plunging into her apron pockets, to find—nothing. Then she remembered having used the last of the pepper on the warries. She stumbled over a rock and fell to the ground.

Raising his hands, Tyron froze, then shut his eyes in intense concentration. "A spell . . . a spell . . ." he muttered.

Wren yelped, "Call the rest of them," and watched with a fierce surge of pride as Tyron caught her idea and his fingers wove rapidly. Off to one side shadowy figures moved, and Tyron's two men turned toward the illusory foes. A moment later so did one of Connor's, but he turned back and waved angrily, shouting at his allies.

As Wren's two converged grimly on her, she got to her knees. When one man bent to pick her up, her fists swung upward and released handfuls of dirt straight at their faces.

The nearer one jerked away, cursing. Wren rolled in the other direction. Her fingers closed around a good-sized pebble, which she threw at the second man, who did not seem to be at all bothered by the dirt. The pebble struck his helm with a *thunk*, but he paid no attention.

"Tyron—" Wren yelped, trying to dodge grasping hands. She was hampered by her skirts.

"Ahh," Connor gasped, as his sword was twisted violently from his grasp. He stumbled and landed in the dust, and then, just before reaching fingers could grab him, something astonishing happened. The six soldiers vanished, and on the ground six tiny blue lizards writhed crazily.

"Was that you?" Wren gaped at Tyron in admiration.

"No," Tyron said flatly. "I couldn't do anything. No *real* magic, remember? And their leader saw through my illusion immediately." His head jerked up. "Connor? If that was you, I take back everything I've said about your magic."

Connor just shook his head, trying to recover his breath. "I wish," he gasped out. Laughing a little, he added, "The only time I ever succeeded in such a spell . . . I was trying to do something entirely different."

"Then it's *very* strange," Tyron said. "Let's get away from them."

Wren and the boys backed away from the scurrying lizards, and Connor picked up his sword, resheathing it. Tyron looked up, scanning the barren hills either side of them.

"Whoever did that doesn't want to be known," he said. "Let's put some distance between us and this place." Then, with a concerned glance at Connor, "Are you all right?"

Connor's pleasant face was pale, but he nodded firmly. "A bit of a blow across the back, that's all. I think my pride smarts more. I suspect they had orders to disarm and secure, or we would have been hash in no time."

"Some time, anyway," Tyron emended. He added wryly, "That's what you said after our tangle with those baddiepeepers in the forest. Only *you* would feel discouraged at not defeating grown men!"

Connor shrugged, smiling slightly. Then he turned to Wren. "The dirt was fast thinking, like the pepper."

"You get used to fast thinking when you live in a village with a lot of rowdy boys. The dirt gives you a chance to run and hide, if you're lucky. But there's not much around here to hide behind."

Tyron looked up at the barren hills again. "Weird," he said. "*Some*one did that spell. And another thing..." He looked perplexed now. "Just before they attacked, one of them said, 'Here's a girl. Grab 'em.' Like they were *looking* for a girl."

"Arglebargle." Wren winced. "Maybe they were. And *if* they were, maybe it was my fault."

As the others listened in silence, she told them about the scrying contact she had made with Tess and the third entity that she'd sensed, and why she had decided not to mention it when they woke.

Tyron shook his head slowly as Wren talked. "You probably caught her asleep. Dreaming. That would explain those images of your Three Groves before she *heard* you." He frowned. "But why did you do it? I thought we were agreed you wouldn't because it was too dangerous. I told you Andreus is crafty with that kind of thing."

"*We* weren't agreed," Wren said. "*I* didn't agree to anything. It's just that you told me not to, and that was supposed to be that." As she spoke, she sounded merely pettish in her own ears. Face hot, she added, "I didn't think you meant danger to us all. I thought you meant just to me. And it was worth it," she said stoutly, "to hear Tess laugh. She needed to know that help was coming."

"But it was *you* who said that the three of us had to do things together."

"Defense things. This was different—I was trying to find my *friend*."

Connor had been silent throughout this exchange, watching the ground thoughtfully.

Hesitating, Tyron said glumly, "Done is done. No use in arguing." He scratched at his head violently. "But *now*, what do we do? My plan for entering the city as prentices looking for work is blown in the wind."

He was trying not to be angry, but he was anyway. Wren

could hear it in his voice, which quivered on the last word. Connor walked along, still silent, his face solemn.

Wren was also silent, feeling angry and ashamed. Inside, she thought of lots to say in her defense ("Even if I had told you, those men still would have heard us and pounced." And, "As for no more scrying, you should have made it clearer. How was I supposed to know?"). But her own sense of honesty just kept repeating: *We're in worse trouble now, and it's all my fault.*

They walked in silence as the shadows deepened and merged, until Connor and Tyron found a well-shadowed gorge for their camp. Connor made certain that their tracks were thoroughly obliterated.

When they sat down to eat at last, Wren still felt sore in spirit. Connor remained exactly as polite and gracious as ever, except there were no jokes, and Tyron addressed her only when he had to, and then in a short voice. When Connor dug low in his pack and pulled out the inevitable cakes, the boys exchanged a brief glance—very brief and very expressionless. But Wren's feelings boiled over.

"Very well. If you want to talk privately, please feel free. I'll go see the view." She added stonily, "And I *won't* leave a trail. *If* you can believe me."

On that unfair note, she stamped up the trail. Behind her she heard a sudden movement, then silence. Before she was quite out of earshot Connor murmured, "Let her walk it off, my friend."

Wren stalked away.

She was not able to keep up the smart pace for long. Descending darkness blotted out more and more of the rough landscape. The hills here looked as if they had been broken up by a giant hand and scattered about in pieces. She looked this way and that for slinking baddies or dangerous animals, but she knew that there was little to feed the latter, and as for the former, they would have as much trouble seeing her as she would them—unless they advertised their presence by carrying torches.

So she slowed. Besides, she did not want to get lost. Checking every so often, she made certain that she could still see the outline of the hill above their gorge.

Some of the stones were strange. In the rapidly waning light, she could just about make out long stripes of different colors marbling them. She touched one long slab that could almost have been some kind of wall.

*"Connor's right,"* she thought grimly. *"I guess I did need to cool off. Well, if Tyron has cooled off, maybe he can tell me something about this country."*

She turned around, realizing as she did that she was hungry and thirsty.

"Ugh," she muttered softly. "Oatcakes. I think at this point I'd rather have sticky, nasty, cold Three Groves rice meal, even the runny kind that always seemed to appear when Zanna couldn't cheat her way out of helping in the kitchen. At least rice meal's wet . . ."

*Wet.* She lifted her head, hearing now the splash of a stream that, before, she had been too angry to notice. Turning again carefully so that she did not lose sight of her landmark, she began to walk in the direction of the sound.

She found it very quickly and knelt down on a rock to scoop water into her hands. When she brought it to her mouth, she felt a brief sensation in her mind, a little like the cave signs and a little like the scrying, but stranger. Another time, that strangeness might have served as a warning; the results of her last scrying, flooding uncomfortably into her mind, caused her to dismiss both memory and reaction.

She drank once and dipped her hands in again. The aftertaste reminded her of rusty metal, but she was thirsty, so she drank once more. The dank taste made her decide against a third.

Halfway back to the gorge, she thought she saw serpents crawling over the hills toward her. She lifted her feet—or tried—in order to run, but discovered that she had turned to stone . . .

She tried to yell *"Serpents,"* but her voice was gone.

So was her body.

Dark winds tore at her and pushed at her, sending her spinning crazily toward the stars. She tried to fling out her arms and drift, as she remembered the chraucans doing, but then she saw the stone walls of a castle . . .

*She was inside.*

*A room, with three long slit windows, showing darkness outside. Table and chairs in the room, tall chairs, with carving across the backs, and a dark blue carpet on the stone ground.*

*Sitting, reading a big book, was a man. About Connor's height, if as tall. Round face, blond hair, brown eyes . . .*

*Nasty, triumphant smile.*

*"Wren," he says. "Aren't you? Did you find one of my little traps? Incautious for a valiant hero, don't you think?"*

*Wren couldn't speak.*

*"Shall we summon your physical self?" the man said, closed the book, and laid it carefully aside. Wren watched, without being able to move or talk. A ruby in a gold ring glittered on one of his fingers. She watched it closely—and thought suddenly of Tyron. The man began speaking in a soft voice.*

*Couldn't hear . . . Couldn't hear . . .*

*"Wren?"*

*It was Tyron, calling. But so far off? She turned toward the dark windows, trying to hear . . .*

*"WREN?"*

*Feeling torn apart and cast into the winds . . .*

*And nothing.*

Halfrid watched from his tent as chaos slowly formed into a camp. The worst of the swarm took place directly before the royal pavilions. Dukes, local and foreign, splendidly decked to the knees and anonymously mud-coated below, strode back and forth issuing orders to their own men and arguing with Verne's stewards. Servitors and foot soldiers struggled with gear, horses, and tents. Between them dodged the green-tunicked messengers, with the adroitness of long-time running.

Beside Halfrid lurked a young magic student named Standis, plain in his Magic School brown tunic and hose. He stared out in obvious longing at the excitement and botheration of an army settling down for the night. Halfrid felt again the strong twinge of regret and worry that heralded any reminders of Tyron. He had brought Standis as his aide, Standis being the senior prentice in the field-experience group, but Halfrid wished that Tyron were here. *If nothing else, we would laugh about the squabbling of the would-be heroes.*

A familiar voice outside the tent startled the chief magician. "Well, tell Fortian to place his tents to the west of Scardru then." King Verne strode in, looking impatient.

Standis bounced to his feet and bowed. The King gave him a preoccupied smile, then turned to Halfrid. "You look calm and assured."

"We've just the two of us to organize and very little equipment," Halfrid replied, pulling forward his own padded folding chair.

The King sat down heavily. Over his dark head Halfrid flicked a look of dismissal at Standis, who stared back uncomprehending. Halfrid could not prevent the thought: *Tyron would have disappeared in a wink.* But he resolutely put it aside.

"Standis, fetch two glasses of wine, please."

"Sir? We haven't any wine." Standis's honest face was confused. "Shall I go to the cook tent? I don't think they're quite set up yet."

"Yes. The cook tent. They'll find the wine." Halfrid smiled, and Standis bowed once more before disappearing.

Now Verne frowned. He gestured Halfrid to the other chair, and Halfrid lowered himself carefully into the spindly folding chair meant for his prentice. As he did, he glanced outside the tent and was reassured at the sight of Steward Helmburi's beanpole figure and long, mournful nose. Helmburi stood just out of earshot, still directing the ordering of camp. He could judge by one look when the King wanted to be approached and when he wished to be left alone. Halfrid could rely on him to delay Standis if the boy returned too quickly.

The King spoke. "At this rate, it will take us a week to reach the mountains."

"The rain, sire." Halfrid stated the obvious in a regretful tone.

Verne managed to look amused. "Yours was the single voice against this expedition, yet you've been the only one since we set out not to goad me with constant complaints."

Halfrid spread his hands.

"How much of that serenity is assumed?" the King asked abruptly. "Do you, for example, ever give a thought to that boy you'd told me last year is to succeed you?"

Halfrid did not hide his surprise. "I think of Tyron often."

"But you let him run off without lifting a hand to stop him."

*Ah. It's not Tyron, it's his daughter he's worried about. But he won't say it out loud. What he wants to hear is how well we've trained Tyron because then he can be assured that Leila did the same with Teressa.*

Halfrid said carefully, "It is not our way to force our students to go or stay. Tyron felt that his quest was more important to him than my prohibitions. I had to let him go, but a day does not pass by during which I do not think of him at least once. I believe I will see him return to Cantirmoor—if he chooses."

The King grunted, staring out at the colorful city of tents with its streaming, many-hued pennants. After a pause he said, "He's related to our fourth royal family, the Rhiscarlans, is he not?"

*Now how did he know that?* "It's true, though there has been no public acknowledgment by either Idres or Tyron, and I know he had not met her previously."

"He would gain nothing by seeing her reestablished in the Rhiscarlan lands and title."

"Nothing beyond a sense of justice having been done. His mother is a cousin out of the line of inheritance. There is an emotional bond, though. Idres did save this cousin when Andreus's men destroyed the Rhiscarlan fortress, and she saw her safely into hiding. Very few people know about that."

The King grunted again. "A strong-willed boy, but impractical. Accompanied by young Connor, who's a dreamer, and by a child from a Siradi orphanage."

"They both have certain abilities, though perhaps the girl doesn't know hers yet," Halfrid said even more carefully. "Leila had intended to bring her to us in the course of things."

The King looked up, smiling. "You're hedging." His hands came down on his knees with a decisive slap. "I'll take that wine."

And sure enough, though he could not have heard that remark, Helmburi turned and gestured to Standis, who waited with his two brimming goblets just beyond Verne's line of vision. As Halfrid watched his prentice walk slowly and carefully over the churned-up ground, the King murmured, "Fortian was hinting that I might do well to choose another heir and abandon Teressa to her fate."

Halfrid was startled into betraying his dismay and revulsion. But the King, watching him intently, seemed to find that reaction pleasing.

"I want my daughter back, Halfrid," he said quietly, and looked up and smiled as Standis handed him the goblet.


Wren woke slowly. Her head hurt, and the rest of her felt stiff and strange. She lay without moving, feeling a cool breeze ruffling across her face.

The breeze smelled interesting. Plants. Water. Dirt of different kinds. People.

*People?* She remembered Tyron and Connor, but her head still hurt too much for her to move it just yet. She was glad to lie absolutely still, with gray light warming her eyelids.

*How did I get back to camp?* she thought.

She registered voices then.

A low voice, a woman's voice? ". . . fools never posted a guard while you slept."

Connor said, with stiff politeness, "The fault for that rests with me, Mistress."

"With us all," came Tyron's voice, sounding tired. "I did think of it once or twice, but I never believed anyone was going to sneak up on us and pounce, not when we'd seen so few people."

"You were fools not to realize that those rangers came from somewhere, and you didn't look for their horses," the woman's soft voice went on relentlessly.

"All right," Tyron said curtly. "You've saved us—Wren twice—and we're grateful. But using that as an invitation to jaw us down is a dismal trick."

"It's not a trick," the woman replied, cool and amused. "You are learning. If you wish to make a career of valiant heroism, and not merely end as valiant but foolish martyrs, then you must think of these things."

*Valiant heroism.*

That man. He'd said that.

Wren remembered it, and now she recognized the woman's voice. Idres Rhiscarlan.

Wren sat up and abruptly made another discovery. She was no longer a girl in grimy borrowed clothes, her hair too long unwashed, and packed dirt beneath her nails.

She was now a dog.

# Chapter Sixteen

*What?* she meant to say, but it came out as a peculiar growl. She saw three heads turn toward her.

The two boys jumped at the sound of her voice.

Idres merely smiled slightly. "Welcome back," she said.

Tyron scrambled up and came over, looking anxiously into Wren's face. "Can you understand me, Wren? We had to do it. You drank from a poisoned stream—I'm so *sorry* I forgot to warn you about those—and Andreus almost got you. We were able to call your mind back, but he was about to get your body, and we had to do something hasty."

*That man I saw was Andreus?* Wren tried to say, but what came out were yaps and a funny bark.

Tyron sat back on his heels. Both legs of his hose, Wren noticed distractedly, had holes in the knees.

"Can she understand us?" Tyron's face was a strange mixture of worry and relief and question.

Behind him, Connor started to say something, stopped, and coughed behind his hand.

"We don't know yet," Idres said coolly, "if her mind *did* come back. Wren"—now the dark eyes were looking directly at Wren's face—"if you understand us, nod."

Wren moved her muzzle down and up. The action felt strange to her new neck.

"Very well, then. She is here in mind. I gave her a language spell as I made the change. She will understand any language she hears until she is returned to her natural form. This was done for two reasons."

Now Idres once again spoke to Wren directly. "You were not merely altered in form with an illusion spell; you have been changed into a dog, just like our lizard friends. They can be changed back if, by the time they crawl to Edrann to their master, they don't forget that they were once men. The same is true for you. I cannot change you back because if I do such powerful magic again, it will bring Andreus at once. As it is, we are in danger. He knows a magician is in the country, but that can't be helped. Meanwhile, there is always the danger that you will become accustomed to your new form and that you will forget the old. As time goes on, this danger increases. I gave you the language spell partly so that you can stay near humans, hear them speak, and remember—if you wish—their ways. My second reason was that because you will be able to understand anyone you encounter, it will be easier for you to make your way back to Cantirmoor. There Halfrid can restore you to your natural form."

"You keyed it generally?" Tyron began with interest.

"Any magician can reverse the spell," Idres said. "Do you understand, Wren?"

Once again Wren dipped her head.

"Then I suggest that you get started on your journey. You will find that you have a dog's speed, but still the way is long, and you will not be able to cross the mountains with the chraucans."

*NOT WITHOUT TESS!* Wren tried to shout the words. Her voice yowled and growled.

"What's the matter?" Tyron reached toward her head as if to give her a comforting pat, then snatched his hand back hastily.

"It would be my guess," Connor said tentatively, "that she wishes to carry on with our quest."

Idres's answer was short. "Don't be stupid, child. You

156

are useless here, and I tell you that time is dangerous for you."

Wren's reply came out as a growl, but what she *tried* to say was, "Rather be stupid than a fungus-tongued traitor to a best friend."

Tyron sighed. Connor's face was a study; he turned his back on them all, took out his sword, and began polishing it with an edge of his cloak.

"Well, she's not leaving," Tyron said, turning to Idres, "and I won't be part of driving her away. We'll manage, thank you."

Idres ignored the hint in the last statement. "How did you propose getting into Edrann?" she inquired.

Tyron's sigh was short and exasperated. "Does it matter?"

"Do not test my patience any further, boy. Answer me. After all, you tried to draw me into this madness, did you not?"

Tyron's cheeks were crimson by now, but he said steadily, "You told me about those two secret tunnels in Andreus's citadel. And you warned me that they might since have been found and turned into magic traps. I'm sure I could sense something like that. So I planned to find both of these tunnel entrances and try them under cover of darkness. Failing them, we'd enter the town during market hours as itinerant prenties looking for work."

"Nobody ever enters Edrann without specific business," Idres said, still with that same deadly calm. "Each citizen is identified, and the rare tradespeople who bring business to Edrann carry special identification. Anyone who would be mad enough to try to enter that fortress as a beggar or peddler or work-seeker gets thrown instantly into the dungeon and is questioned closely. Often enough such persons are never seen again."

Tyron shook his head slowly. "I couldn't know that. There's nothing written in the school reference books about modern Edrann, just where it lies on the map, when it was built and by whom, and so on." He seemed to struggle silently; then his head jerked up. "We'll find a way. See if we don't."

"I have no respect at all for courage born of ignorance,"

Idres said. "But then I did not expect you to come this far. When you approached me in the Free Vale, I told you as much as I did, believing that it would discourage you from making the attempt."

"Yet you've been watching out for us," Tyron said. "That was *you* I sensed, soon as we crossed the border."

Idres nodded. "It was I, watching and following you across that bridge. You planned badly, boy. Look at you. Half starved, and out of food, I would wager. Where did you think you would find it in *this* land?"

Connor said politely, "You'll pardon me, I trust, if I remind you that that is our concern?"

Idres gave a short, soft laugh. "So you still wish to persist in this quest of yours?"

Silence answered her.

Wren, bursting to have her voice heard yet frustrated because no one would understand, felt hot all over. Her mouth opened. The cool air now felt good. As she began to pant gently, a sound escaped her. It sounded very much like "Aaargh."

"So that flash of magic was you, too?" asked Tyron. "It drew off some gryphs just when we were crossing the bridge."

"It was not. I assume it was Andreus, attacking someone in the far north. Did you not sense that it was a very powerful spell indeed? And who else could have dared be so open?"

Tyron looked rueful. "I didn't know what to think. I was just desperately glad to see those gryphs flap by harmlessly overhead."

Idres dusted her fingers. "Very well. I have done my best to dissuade you, though perhaps"—she gave a sudden, rather wintry smile—"what I've done is to merely make you stubborn. What is important is this: nothing you have faced yet is as dangerous as the prospect of going into Andreus's citadel. He knows someone has entered his kingdom and that that someone did magic last night. I was able to ward off the general tracer magic, but he's only going to increase it. You can see, no doubt, the evidence of heavy protection magic in the air."

"Tainted," Tyron said slowly. "Like the land."

"The land is blighted mostly because of experiments made by its ambitious and impatient master. He has tried to get crops ready for harvest in a month so that the rest of the year his men might be better employed as soldiers."

Wren saw Tyron's jaw drop.

"That is only one example," Idres went on. "Yes, I know this goes directly against what your Cantirmoor school calls the Twelve Natural Laws. You spend the better part of your early years learning a sense of balance between nature and magic. When to act and when it is better not to."

She looked at Tyron directly now, smiling faintly. "What actions aid all, and what actions are trespass. You are taught to consider, as far as you are able, the consequences of your actions. Not so with those like Andreus. There are no limits to his ambition. For him, *right* is his wishes, and *wrong* is anyone who dares to cross him."

The boys listened intently. At last Tyron said, "I think I understand. We have to forget our rules when trying to figure what he'll do. Honor, and fairness, and so on."

"That for a start." Idres looked aside, touching a dust-covered lump of canvas. "What is this? I sense magic within."

"That's Wren's knapsack," Tyron said. "I found it after you did the spell and brought it back. These cloaks we were given are somewhat dirty, but they're still good."

Idres looked in the knapsack and let out a startled exclamation. What she pulled out was not the gray-brown cloak that Master Gastarth had given to Wren, but the beautiful fringed scarf from his sister.

"Where did you get this?" Idres demanded.

"Mistress Selshaf gave it to Wren." Tyron shrugged. "Wren said she was not going to wear it while adventuring because it'd get ruined, and she meant to give it to the Princess as soon as she was free. Guess Teressa likes pretty things."

"Mistress Selshaf," Idres said softly, then looked up. "She did not tell you what it is for?"

"What it's for?" Tyron repeated. "You mean, there're magical properties to it?"

Idres smiled ironically at the beautiful scarf in her hands. "There are indeed. And the fact that she did not see fit to tell you means that . . ."

She broke off, and instead flung the scarf over her head, tying the ends loosely under her chin. Then, as Wren and the boys watched in amazement, her features altered slowly into an ugly parody of her own face. Then they altered again, this time forming an ordinary female face that did not at all resemble Idres.

"Disguise illusion." Tyron exclaimed. Then he looked puzzled. "But why would Wren need that? It's not as if anyone knows who she is."

All of Idres's irony was back as her features resumed their natural form, but now it was not directed at the boys. "The scarf wasn't meant for Wren. It was meant for me."

The boys looked stunned, but Wren growled, frustrated at not being able to talk.

"Come." Idres got to her feet and brushed her dark-colored skirts off with her hands. "Those men will be missed if they do not report back to their garrison within two days. And, as the outposts communicate with Andreus by magical means, he will know almost immediately that something has happened to them. When he links their disappearance to the magic of last night, he will probably wish to lead the hunt himself."

"Then let's get as much distance between them and us as possible," Tyron said.

Wren heard the distinct *crunch-crunch* of Tyron's scroungy sandals in the dirt, and the heavy rustle of his worn old tunic as he moved. As he and the others picked up their belongings, and Idres packing Wren's knapsack inside her own large one, Wren tipped her head and looked down at herself.

Long, thin dog legs stretched out before her, covered with short, wiry fur that was exactly the same color as her hair had been.

*I'm a stripy dog*, she thought. *Just as funny-looking as I was as a girl.* Her body was short, and she had a long, plumed tail. When she heard a sudden noise behind, her ears flipped up and turned.

Laughing inside, Wren thought: *Well, there may be danger, as she says, but the fact is that being a dog is fun.*

She trotted around in a circle, experimenting with the way her new body moved, then ran a little distance ahead. Moving so quickly while being close to the ground was very strange, and the way everything smelled so strong was distracting. *Nothing smells bad, either,* she thought. *Even this patch of aguewort here. It's all interesting.*

Behind her, the boys talked in low voices as they walked. After a short, exploratory excursion, Wren ran back to listen.

Tyron gave her that funny look of mixed regret and curiosity. "Hi, there, Wren. I wish you could say how you feel about all this."

*I've always loved dogs. While I never thought I'd become one, I don't mind,* she barked back. By now she knew that words were not going to come, but she hated not to say *anything.*

Tyron sighed. "I can't tell what she means."

"She's fine." Connor smiled down at Wren. From her new position, he seemed to be as tall as a house.

"I hope so," Tyron said dubiously.

"I know something about dogs," Connor said. And as Tyron's expression did not change, he added, "Frightened and miserable dogs do not, for example, wag their tails and prick their ears up."

*Right!* Wren yapped.

Tyron ran a hand through his shaggy, wild hair, then dropped his hand. "I wish . . ." He looked at Wren, then at Idres, and frowned at his feet.

Connor said gently, "We made our mistakes together, all three of us. Not just you. But we are still alive, and we have learned."

"That is the first bit of wisdom I've heard out of you, Prince of Siradayel," Idres murmured.

Straightening up, Tyron said, "All right. I'm being a hen.

I can see you all think it. Idres, why did Mistress Selshaf want you to come to Senna Lirwan? And how did she know you would?"

"I don't know. Personal questions are seldom asked in the Haven, and Selshaf and Gastarth have not offered any information about themselves beyond their names. I never paid any attention to them, but the fact that they know a great deal of magic I've heard mentioned by others in the Haven."

"Have they *done* any?"

"No, but they've received some unusual visitors," Idres said.

Tyron had been frowning. Now he said, "I *knew* it. I knew it wasn't an accident that Wren and I met them first that night. But if so—if they wanted you to join us—why not just tell us?"

Idres's dark eyes were distinctly mocking. "You ask that after years at the School? You—me—perhaps all of us are being tested. And that is an invasion of my freedom that I strenuously resent."

No one made an answer to this statement. After a moment or two, Idres laughed softly, adding, "Though there are worse things, which is why I am going on anyway. I thought you might need some fresher and more varied food." She indicated her heavy knapsack. "So I prepared for it. Why don't we stop, eat, and discuss the best way to approach Edrann."

Teressa leaned her palms against the damp, gritty stone wall and twisted her neck until her ear rested on her shoulder. Her eyes turned up—and she could just barely glimpse an edge of the sun through the narrow slit window high on the adjacent wall. The sun looked weak and pale, half hidden behind gray clouds, but it was there. She stared at it, enjoying the faint warmth on her face. The glare made her eyes water a little, but that felt good, too.

When the last glow had moved westward, leaving a gray sky only a few shades lighter than the gray of the stone walls surrounding her, she turned away and climbed off the wooden table.

Dropping heavily onto her cot, she fought against a sudden spring of tears. No. She *wouldn't* give in. She wouldn't blub. But it was hard.

She pulled the mildewed blanket over her and shut her eyes. Her forehead still throbbed from the fall she'd taken a while ago, just before the guard pushed her back into this cell. She sniffed. At least that rotten Andreus hadn't been able to make her look into the glass ball and call to Wren. Teressa smiled just a little, remembering how mad he'd been when he discovered that she'd kept her eyes shut. Then, of course, he'd knocked her down, and she smacked her head on a chair leg.

*And then I pretended I was so dizzy I couldn't see straight*, she thought grimly. *Well, Wren, I always thought you'd be the actor, not I. But it seems to work—and I enjoy fooling him.*

Except he always won. After any encounter, back she came to this awful cell. If he was mad enough, she didn't get anything to eat for a day. To teach her manners, he said.

She pressed her hand against her growling stomach. *I won't give up.* What was it Wren always used to moan loudly when they were stuck with an exceptionally boring chore at Three Groves? She'd quote from the play she loved, about the off-world visitor Eren Beyond-Stars:

" 'Here I lie, wounded, cold and alone,
In this damp fortress of solid stone' "

Teressa choked on a laugh. *It's true. Wren said it to be silly, but it's true here—and it still seems silly.* Teressa felt the sting of tears again, but this time she knew they were laughter. She sat up, smiling at the stone walls. *I'll make a game of it.* She tried to recall as much of the play as she could as daylight slowly faded and left her sitting in the dark.

## Chapter Seventeen

*I*dres and the two boys walked steadily all day, moving northward through the hills. Mindful of Idres's warning, Wren at first trotted near them, listening to their rare exchanges of words.

Edrann lay to the northwest, but Idres and Connor both agreed that walking in the hills rather than descending down to the flat plains that stretched directly to the east of them now would afford them at least a little protection from roaming patrols.

"You mean, Andreus has parties of soldiers just riding around, looking for any rescuers who might come along?" Tyron asked after one of these discussions. "How many soldiers does he have?"

"A great many. And, yes, the patrols do ride around, but that has been a fact of life here for many years. They don't just look out for foreigners who might be foolish enough to try and come over the border; they also look for citizens who might not be in their designated places, or might be doing something outside the exceedingly strict laws."

"Or running away?" Tyron made a face.

"That, too."

"What a life!" Tyron exclaimed. "But all this dusty walking's making me thirsty. Let's look for a stream."

Eventually, they found two. The first time, as they approached, Idres said nothing. It was Tyron who ran to the water's edge, knelt down with palms above it, then looked up and frowned.

"Tainted. Magic."

Idres nodded in slow approval.

The second stream was also magic-poisoned, this time with a very powerful spell. Wren sniffed at each, finding that the warning she felt in her head was stronger even than the signs had been in the caverns.

As the day drew toward its end and everyone got thirstier, Connor shared a sip with each from the little bit of stale water remaining in his water bag.

"There's a possibility," Idres said, "that all the waterways between here and Edrann will be tainted. The Lirwani patrols have an antidote for themselves, so they can use these streams safely."

Wren then got an idea: she'd run in the opposite direction, to try to find some water. She was not able to tell them her idea, of course, so she just turned and raced off.

She ran westward and before too long found a fast-running stream in a deep gully. Sniffing carefully, all she could smell or sense were minerals in the water. Otherwise it was perfectly clean. She drank, then lay down to wait for reactions. When nothing happened, she raced to the east again.

She tracked her companions easily, but once she found them, she wondered how she was to get what she wanted? Barking, *Water! I found safe water*, at Connor, she jumped and brushed her nose against his knapsack.

"What is it, Wren?" he murmured. Kneeling down, he opened his kit. She closed her teeth around the water bag and shook it. "You've found us some water, eh?"

"Now, how did you figure that out?" Tyron's admiring voice was the last thing Wren heard as she ran west again, the water bag in her teeth.

When she found the stream again, she worried the stopper out of the bag, and it dangled on its cord. Then she held the bag in the water by pressing her paws on it. When it was as full as it would get, she hauled it out. There was no way to get the stopper in again, so she just closed her teeth around the neck of the bag. Lifting her head high, she started back.

All three of them praised her when she appeared with the water. Taking the bag into his hands, Tyron did his magic sensing.

"It's safe," he said finally. Then he took a long drink and passed it to Idres. "You know, I wonder if animals can scry."

"Animals?" Idres repeated, handing the water bag to Connor.

"Dogs. Wren," Tyron said, pointing. "She seems to be able to find untainted water."

"Probably by sniffing out the poisons," Idres said. "The local animals are already doing as much, or there wouldn't *be* any local animals. But what's this about scrying?"

"She does it," Tyron said, his brown eyes shining with excitement. "Not just in my scry glass. She scried the Princess in a window, and then again in the river in the cave."

"So that's how Andreus knew about your coming," Idres murmured. "I wondered if he'd known something about you before the episode with the lizards. What else has Wren tried?"

"She made an illusion—on one demonstration. It didn't last, but *still*," Tyron said proudly. "And she sensed the lily signs in the caverns. She's got amazing magical potential. Both Connor and I think so."

Idres pursed her lips, looking interested. "It seems, if we win free from this adventure of yours, you should take her straightaway to Halfrid." She added, "But if you're looking for her magical aid now, you'll be disappointed. Many powerful magicians ended illustrious careers by forgetting that in taking animal shapes, they lay aside their powers as well as most of their human traits."

Wren yipped, *I won't forget!* and she hoped she'd remember.

When they stopped to eat, Wren realized suddenly that her search did not have to stop with water. The food in Idres's sack might very well be all the humans would get until their quest was over. Those dried meat strips had tasted good last night, but now Wren knew she should find her own food.

When darkness fell, Wren discovered that her night vision was sharp and clear. Colors and shapes were not as distinct as human sight, but her sense of smell was sharp enough to enable her to sniff things long before she saw them.

Since she was not tired, after the others bedded down, she ran off and did some exploring. Little existed on the barren hills, but she did meet a few other creatures. They seemed to know at once that there was something odd about her. She smelled their fear—and curiosity. Once she came across some wild dogs. The pups were friendly enough, but the mother was suspicious and chased Wren off.

Later that evening she heard the howling of distant wolves, which made the hairs along her back lift. Nearby, she smelled a whiff of rabbits' greater fear, though she could not see their holes. Then, she caught another smell that made her decide against sniffing the rabbits out: horses and riders.

*A patrol.*

Running across the rocky ground, backtracking the scent of her own trail, she finally spotted her companions. Idres and Connor were asleep, and Tyron sat, ostensibly on guard, with his head on his knees. She bounded into the camp, breath rasping and tongue lolling.

*They're coming. Lirwani soldiers,* she barked, and three heads popped up.

Connor surprised everyone by saying sharply, "Patrol."

They grabbed their gear and marched higher on the rocky hill. Hiding in a pile of rubble, they lay silently. Wren tried to still her breathing as the distant rumble of hooves steadily approached.

The Lirwanis rode at a distance from one another, each scanning the ground between them. Since the hillock that Wren

167

and her friends lay on was covered with loose stone, as long as no one moved, the horsemen would not ride up close.

The soldiers drew closer . . . came abreast . . . then, still at a steady pace, passed by.

When the last sounds of their presence died away, Idres said softly, "That was not a patrol, it was a search party. Apparently Andreus has added up a girl named Wren, who could scry the Princess and escape one of his spells, to a missing patrol, and come up with a search. And"—she looked at each of them in turn—"if he exerts himself to that extent, he will not stop until he finds someone. This is our last opportunity to turn back."

Peering through the darkness, Wren saw Tyron hunched into his familiar knotty ball. Connor's usually pleasant face looked carved from stone as he gazed off across the ugly dark-shrouded hills.

Wren did not have to think. Somewhere on the other side of those hills Tess lay in prison, and Wren was going to get her out. That was that. Meanwhile, something more immediate impressed itself on her mind. She had not forgotten Connor's *Patrol* a little while ago. And she remembered other incidents: Connor's voice with the chraucans, his comment about meeting the serpent, the brown bird back in Meldrith whose voice she had thought she'd recognized . . .

A sound escaped her, a little whine. Connor looked up, and Wren gazed into his face.

*Tell Idres we all want to go on*, she yapped.

Tyron's head jerked around. "What's wrong? Wren? Is there danger? I *wish* we knew what she was saying."

Connor studied Wren silently, his eyes two dark shadows. Wren could not see his expression, but she sensed his sadness.

*Why not tell him? He's your friend*, she yipped.

"Connor? Why is she barking like that? Does she have a stone in her paw? What—what is it?" Tyron now looked at Connor, his voice tentative. "What's wrong? Something's wrong. I can see it."

Connor sighed. "She wants to go on, of course. Tyron, I'm *sorry* I never told you. One learns very early not to trust others easily. By the time I trusted you enough to want to tell you, I knew you well enough to realize you'd be hurt that I hadn't trusted you earlier. It was easier to say nothing."

"What?" Tyron groaned. "I don't *understand!*"

"Simply put, I seem to have been born with the knack of comprehending—as much as a human can—the thoughts of animals. Ah, and the speech of birds."

"So that's how you find things out," Tyron said.

"I usually have to touch animals to hear their thoughts, but Wren, being human, projects her thoughts quite clearly when she tries to speak." His pleasant voice sounded sad. "My father told me before he died that several of his family had been born with this particular Iyon Daiyin trait. Some of them had been exiled or killed for having had it, and I was never to trust anyone with the secret. I wanted to tell you—many times."

Tyron said briskly, "I'm just glad we know now, at least."

Idres smiled.


Dawn came, cold and bleak, several hours later. They walked steadily northward, picking their way over the treacherous shale-strewn ground. Once more, just before first light, they had to hide from a patrol, and again Wren heard it first. This one came from the south.

No one said anything immediately, but after a glaring gray noon hour arrived, they stumbled across a canyon caused by a long-ago quake and decided that this would be a splendid place for a few hours' rest. Wren stretched out on a flat rock above them, where she could see beyond but still hear the conversation below.

After food had been divided and consumed, Tyron turned abruptly to Idres and said, "Why did you change your mind? I don't see *you* turning back, yet you said you'd never help King Verne."

"Nor am I," came her wry voice. "As you rightly pointed out, this matter concerns his daughter. I realized I couldn't tolerate the prospect of sitting by while Andreus used a child in his vengeance games. I long to tell him just what I think of him—*after* I spring her." She finished on an acid note that caused Tyron to choke on a laugh.

Idres went on, "I came because I'm fairly certain I can still get in and out of Senna Lirwan at will, and I'd love to point this out to Andreus. If I thought it a hopeless quest, I would have stayed in the Haven. I haven't the sense of 'honor' that binds the rest of you. Most of the time, such 'honor' is merely a preoccupation with how others think of you. I act to suit myself—that much I learned from Andreus."

Tyron exchanged a look with Connor, then said impetuously, "When Andreus first got you, I know that nearly everyone in your family had been killed. But still you helped my mother escape. *No one* but us knows that. And I think *that's* honorable." He watched her with covert intensity as he spoke.

Idres smiled suddenly. "No. Not honorable. I saved her because I liked her. I knew I could get one person out beside myself, and in my critical childish eyes the rest of the family really deserved what they got. What you don't know is that the attack on the Rhiscarlan fortress was not engineered by Andreus directly. It was set up by my uncle, the one who had been teaching me magic on the sly. The Rhiscarlan fortress was not an easy place to get into, which is why everyone has assumed—correctly—that inside treachery was responsible."

Connor sat up straight. "Then you were *not* responsible? Report has it that you were—that you went immediately from the burning ruins to Andreus in Edrann."

"I had ambition, but not to replace my father," Idres replied. "It was knowledge I was after, and at that time I did not know about the existence of the Magic School. Well, I was younger than any of you when all this happened, and my uncle had always told me that Andreus knew more magic than anyone. So when Andreus caught up with me, I thought it proper and reasonable to go with him." Idres put back her hood and gave the boys a wintry smile. "There was little talk in my childhood about 'good' or 'right.' Just—'power,' and what it could accomplish if one worked hard to acquire it."

Tyron rested his chin on his knees, his grubby, foxlike features radiating curiosity. "What was it *like*, with Andreus?"

Idres shrugged. "What's study like anywhere? He gave me books and treated me well enough. I had already mastered the Basics, as you call them, and under his tutelage learned rapidly. I enjoyed power. Growing up with ambition around me, I fitted very well into what of his life he allowed me to see. It was a strange existence, but I did not dislike it. I had my books, after all. And he promised I would soon rule my own country. Thus passed seven years—until Verne came."

Wren asked, *What really happened when Tess's father came?* As usual she was surprised when the sound came out yaps and barks.

The others laughed, then Connor translated.

"Here's where your King Verne's sense of honor benefited me—he's told no one my part in the story's ending, but in truth I don't come off very well. We were all young then," she went on. "Andreus was new to his throne. You know all about how he took it, too. It was an act of bravery and perhaps of madness on Verne's part to disguise himself and come into the kingdom on his own. He is, as I am sure you've heard, good with weapons, and using that skill he worked his way into the castle guard."

Idres paused and smiled a little. "You've probably heard that—while he was in Edrann, living right under Andreus's nose—he talked me into abandoning Andreus and joining his side, thus earning Andreus's enmity forever. What you don't know is how ridiculously easy he must have found it. I'd never had a friend, you see. Startled one night by questions from the night guard in the library, I was soon in the habit of discourse with him. From there I came gradually to look forward to our talks, friend to friend. It made me angry, very angry, for a long time afterward, when I understood how I'd been used. Now . . . I have learned tolerance, perhaps."

"But, where's the problem? After you left the country with

him, he and Halfrid would have welcomed you at the school. I know *that* much. But you refused," Tyron burst out.

"What Verne never told anyone was that, heady with my very first friendship, I flattered myself into thinking it returned—no, that's not quite fair. He would have remained friendly. What I thought, at the time, was that we made a splendid couple, he and I. And I tried to convince him of it. His heart was already given, and there was an angry scene on my part. He knew very well what a dangerous enemy I could have been. But he held firm to his vows, which at that time were secret."

Idres turned to survey Connor with her dark eyes. "You probably also don't know that your mother, Queen Nerith, had far more ambitious plans for Princess Astren than to waste her on quiet, neighborly Meldrith. One of the younger daughters—Lusra, I recall—was deemed suitable for Verne—"

"My sister Lusra?" Connor murmured, making a nauseated face. "Horrible thought."

Idres looked amused. "You'll note that Verne prevailed there as well. Anyway, now you know that my mysterious exile to the Haven was nothing more than petty spite on my part, and sentimental dashed hopes, though why I should be confessing all this to you now, I hardly know. Danger breeds confessions, I suppose." She laughed wryly. "Since then, of course, I've been learning magic on my own."

"I know some of the things you did to Andreus's magical protections when you left," Tyron said slowly. "I'm sure Andreus remembers as well."

"Perhaps," Idres said unemotionally. "But I resent his using a child, as he used me, in his game of power and vengeance. And that's enough talk, don't you think? We'll be worthless if we don't rest awhile. The dangers we've already passed, I'm afraid, are going to be nothing to what lies ahead."

♛

*Chapter Eighteen*

*R*acing through tall, harsh grasses the next day, Wren sniffed the wind, enjoying her keen sense of smell. Twice she caught faint drifts of wolf scent, and three times she perceived approaching patrols.

*Patrol from the north*, or, *Patrol from the southeast*, she'd bark at Connor, and he promptly repeated it to the others. Then off she'd go, stretching her legs out into her fastest run.

She found water again and meat for herself and was having a race across the flat bed of a dried lake with some wild dog pups, enjoying the pursuit, when she scented another patrol, this one carrying with it the distinct smell of angry dogs. Running parallel until she could spy on them from a vantage downwind, she saw chained hounds sniffing at the ground, soldiers holding fast to their leashes.

Crawling backward so that they could not catch her scent, she ran straight to Connor: *Tracking dogs. Coming from the south*.

Connor relayed the news, and Tyron cried, "Give Wren your shirt."

Connor looked surprised, then laughed. "Oh, well thought. Can you make a false trail, Honored Mistress?" He bowed to Wren.

*Hurry*, she yapped.

Connor took off his tunic and shirt, then replaced his tunic.

Tyron, who had no extra clothes to spare, rubbed Connor's shirt over his own face and hair and dropped it down to Wren.

"Does that smell like us?" he asked her.

She barked a *Yes* and picked up the shirt with her teeth. When she reached a place she thought might intersect the path of the coming patrol, she dropped the shirt and began dragging it by one sleeve. At first she tripped over it, until she figured out how to run with the shirt directly under her, and then she created a zigzag trail to another deep quake chasm. There she dropped the shirt over the edge. Running back, she saw the patrol had just begun following her trail.

She dodged the patrol and circled around to her companions, hardly out of breath. Interrupting them, she barked triumphantly: *Headed them off. I'm hungry now.* She was going to leave again to hunt for food when she caught a frowning glance from Idres. The frown was slight, and Idres said nothing, but Wren's mind suddenly filled with images from her day as a dog. She realized that today she'd had less interest in the talk between her slow-walking human friends than the trail scent and the chase.

She trotted near to Connor and yelped: *Do I seem less a girl and more a dog?*

"I can still hear your human thoughts," he said.

Now that she was close, she could see that his face was grimy and his expression tense and tired underneath the amiable demeanor.

"Continue to think about human beings, Wren. Don't give in to every strong animal impulse," Idres added. "Follow us."


The sun sank behind the western bank of clouds, and deepening shadows confused the landscape ahead. Still, they did not stop walking. Idres shared out food from her pack, and they ate as they went.

Now that she had slowed, Wren felt the effects of so much running. She was tired, and again and again had to resist the temptation to flop down and sleep. She wondered whether more running would make the tiredness disappear, but found that she just could not get started. It was hard to listen to the others with even part of her attention.

When Idres finally suggested that they stop the night and that she'd take first guard herself, Wren happily dropped in the dirt. The two boys wrapped themselves tiredly in their cloaks.

Wren woke to the shivery sound of howling wolves. And, from much closer, the belling of hounds on the scent.

Idres said sharply, "They've tracked us."

Fighting back a whine of terror, Wren shook herself awake as Tyron sat up groggily.

"Magic," he said thickly. "Lizards again . . ."

"Andreus will trace us in a moment. Do you think he is not prepared for just that?" Idres's tone was calm as always, but her voice sounded dry-throated and raspy.

"They are too close to outrun," Connor put in. "I believe we shall have to hide and ambush them."

"And take their horses," Idres agreed. "That is our last chance."

"What you're saying is, we're walking into a trap," Tyron burst out.

"Yes." Idres nodded in the darkness, pulling a long knife from her pack. Its blade gleamed with an edge of reflected moonlight from the clouds overhead. "I thought you had realized that long ago."

"Let's find a gully, create a trail along the bottom, and station ourselves high on either side. We can swoop down at the same moment," Connor said.

"Good."

Tyron shook his head slowly. "A trap . . . a trap," he muttered.

"How else can we get into Edrann?" Idres asked with slightly malicious amusement.

They had no more time for conversation. Finding a likely spot, Connor and Tyron crouched down on one side, Idres on the other. After a moment's hesitation, Wren joined Idres.

When the patrol arrived in full cry, horses pounding, dogs

baying, and weapons clanking, Connor and Idres moved swiftly, each spotting and pouncing on one rider. Tyron yelled crazily, brandishing a stick, and was felled by a blow from a mailed fist. He rolled over and over and lay still. Wren raced down among the horses, teeth bared, which sent three of the enemy horses bucking and shying.

The track hounds howled and yapped in a frenzy of anger, but as they were attached to the horses' saddles by chains, they could not get near Wren. Instead, they added to the confusion by plunging and snarling at every creature that moved. Two riders were thrown free, and in the resultant chaos, Idres and Connor felled two more of them. Connor was fighting desperately against a third soldier, who was backing him steadily toward a ditch, when Wren leaped on the soldier from behind, knocking him off balance.

"Unfair," Connor called breathlessly as he reversed his blade and stunned the fellow with his hilt.

Idres silently and efficiently took care of her foe, with a combination of dirt in the eyes and her knife. Then: "Mount up," she said.

Tyron sat up groggily. Wren nuzzled him and licked his face. *Wake up. Get on a horse*, she barked, trying to get his attention.

Connor appeared and gave Tyron a hand up; then Connor leaped on the plunging horse behind him. As they wheeled the horse about, Idres said harshly, "Listen!"

They heard the sound of hooves.

"The clacks of doom," Connor murmured, irrepressible to the last.

"Silence," Idres hissed. She twisted about, her fingers clawing through her bag. "Remember: *I am Wren.* All the magic was mine." Hastily she tied the scarf about her head. "If you play stupid, he will not put a magical binder on you. As for the Princess—"

She broke off as the reinforcements fell upon them.

This fight was short and grim. The patrol separated, half swooping on Idres and half circling Connor and Tyron. Wren tried her barking trick again, but this time it did not work. One soldier took a swift, hissing slice at her with his swordblade, and she retreated.

Idres, Connor, and Tyron were disarmed and tied with ropes, then each was seated in front of a Lirwani soldier. Another soldier gathered the reins of the riderless horses, and the cavalcade set off at a gallop. They left their dead and wounded lying on the ground behind them.

Realizing that no one knew who she was, Wren followed silently. The tracking hounds, still chained to saddles, bayed crazily until one of the soldiers gave a short command and a handler swiped viciously at the dogs with a whip. They ran more quietly after that, continuing on through the night. At last, unable to keep up with the horses, Wren dropped back, slowed to a lagging trot, and then finally dropped dizzily into unconsciousness.


The ride seemed to last forever.

Tyron's head ached, and one of his eyes had swelled nearly closed. His stomach was horridly queasy. Looking over at Idres and Connor from time to time, he was silently amazed to see them both managing to sit tall and proud. Somehow that only made him feel more dismal.

They stopped briefly at a garrison. After the three had been gloated over for what seemed half the night, a larger troop of Lirwani soldiers joined them for the ride to Edrann. This trip involved several stops, during which Tyron and his companions were twice allowed a swallow of water and once a tough crust of bread to chew on, but no chance to rest. Another company of Lirwanis replaced the first one, and they rode on.

Exhaustion and chill added themselves to Tyron's soreness. By the time they clattered into the steep-walled courtyard in Edrann's central fortress, Tyron was so weary and stiff that he was not able to stand up when the soldiers pulled him off the horse.

The Lirwanis seemed to find his stiffness funny, laughing

coarsely as the leader cuffed him and shoved him forward. Being forced to move restored his ability to stand. Tyron saw that Connor also staggered and Idres as well, for she pitched heavily against Tyron.

He felt her mouth by his ear: "Free her and get out." Then someone pulled them apart and marched them up a great many stairs to a tower room.

Neither Idres nor Connor was near him on the long walk, and Tyron used the time to try to breathe slowly and deeply and to collect his thoughts.

On entering the room, Tyron gained a hazy impression of nice furniture and a dark blue carpet before his eyes found a large scrying stone on a stand before two long windows. The stone was a perfect sphere of silvery crystal. He sensed magic in it. A great quantity of magic. A terrible compulsion to look into it stole over him, and he fought the urge. *I can't let them see I know what it is.* He felt the weird inner pull of the sphere even after he turned his head away. Then a hand shoved him into place between Idres and Connor.

Idres still wore the scarf on her head, the pretty colors and dancing fringe looking incongruous in this somber room.

A man came through a far archway. He was about Connor's height, with mild-looking brown eyes and a mouth with sarcasm-hardened corners. Tyron knew him for Andreus and disliked him instantly.

Andreus gave Tyron and Connor only the briefest of glances. His attention was bent on Idres. Tyron sneaked a hasty glance sideways: Idres had assumed an illusory face resembling Wren's.

Putting out a hand, Andreus snatched the scarf from Idres's head. Her long black braid swung over her shoulder, and her own face now stared back at him with cool detachment.

"Idres," Andreus said, addressing her in Lirwani. "Once you followed a fool out of here, and now you've led two back. Who *are* these?"

"Useful urchins from a small village."

"Where Verne hid the girl, perhaps? I take it *you* are her friend, Wren. That would explain the magic certainly. A delightfully unexpected surprise. Tell me, does Verne know? I hope not. So much more fun this way. But why did you not simply come to me?"

"One of the many tiresome things about you," Idres replied calmly, "was your humility. I see you haven't changed."

Andreus turned, smiling, to Tyron.

Idres spoke again. "That one is a cut-purse, and the other has a way with horses. They don't speak Lirwani."

Tyron tried to look uncomprehending. He let his gaze wander to Connor, in whose dark gray eyes fatigue and noncomprehension were clear. Connor really *didn't* understand Lirwani, and it showed in his face.

Idres went on, "If you let them go, they'll find their way back to prey on the respectable citizens of Meldrith."

"Perhaps, perhaps," Andreus said with amusement. "We shall see. But—later. Take them out, would you?" He gestured to one of the guards flanking Tyron. "I wish to continue this long-deferred interview, Idres. Please, do sit down. I might mention that this room is warded against any spell-making but my own, though you are welcome to experiment . . ."

Rough hands pulled Tyron and Connor from the room. The last thing Tyron saw was Andreus picking up a knife and leaning over, with an air of mock hospitality, to cut the cord from Idres's wrists.

Then he and Connor were marched back down the stairs and thrust into a small, bare stone cell. A Lirwani guard followed them in and cut their hands free, taking the cord fragments with him.

As soon as the door was shut, Connor murmured hoarsely, "So much for untying ourselves and garroting one of 'em when they return. What happened in that tower room?" After Tyron told him, Connor said only, "What do you suggest we do now?"

Tyron sagged down onto the cold stone floor and put his head in his hands. "I wish I knew."

When Wren at last woke up, it was to confusion, discomfort, and hazy thoughts. *Thirst . . . hunger . . . more sleep.* She opened her eyes without lifting her head. A dusty road stretched ahead of her in the gray dawn light. *Not familiar in look or smell.* Thirst and hunger again crowded into her mind, but with them came a scrap of memory. Just a scrap—of carrying a water bag in her teeth. That was enough, though. She thought about that water bag and remembered Idres and Connor and Tyron, and then she remembered what had happened last night.

*I'm Wren. I'm a girl named Wren, orphan, lives at Three Groves, and ohhh . . . my body hurts so much.* She lay without moving, scared by the effort it had taken to regain her memory, and wondering what she should do.

Thinking of Three Groves brought more memories. Suddenly she saw Zanna's sour face and heard Zanna's nasty voice, "Wren? Turned into a dog? *Just* what you'd expect. That striped hair, and so clumsy . . ."

The thought of Zanna made Wren laugh. The sound came out more as a sneeze, but it worked. Rising to her feet, she moved forward a few steps. As she did, she noticed that it got easier. *Maybe this is the kind of soreness I used to get when I practiced acrobatics too long,* she thought, and sped up a bit.

She saw that she was in the middle of a field of tall stickleweeds. Stretching in a trail before her lay the hoofprints of the horses, as well as the horses' heavy scent, leading to the east. *I seem to have fallen asleep right on the trail,* she thought. *What could be easier? Lead on, prints!*

She trotted forward a few steps, sniffing the air. As she sorted the many different smells, she thought: *Will I be able to sniff out danger this well when I'm a girl again?*

Then she remembered how she'd felt when she first woke up. *I didn't wake up as Wren, I woke up as a dog. That's what Idres meant when she warned me. Will it get harder each day?* Wren imagined waking up one day and racing off on dog pursuits without remembering she'd ever been a person.

*It would be easy*, she thought, shivering. She sat down, looking back toward the looming mountains in the west. *I told them I didn't mind being a dog, but nobody seemed real happy. Now I think I know why.* Idres had told her to go back to Cantirmoor as fast as she could. The magicians there could change her back.

Wren looked east again at the prints leading off across the bleak plains. *I don't know how far it is to Edrann or how long it will take me to get there.* She looked west again. *How long would that way take? Would it be too late if I went to get Halfrid's help?* She remembered why Halfrid couldn't come to her. Andreus had lots of magic waiting should the King's Magician try sticking a toe inside Senna Lirwan's border.

*Nobody's coming—except us. Us?* She remembered Tyron, Connor, and Idres being carried away by the Lirwanis. *Except me. It's up to me.*

She began to run. Slowly at first, for she was cold and sore, and her hunger and thirst had not abated. But as she ran, warmth coursed through her and even thinking seemed to come clearer. She thought about magical signs, and also about those silent signs that Tyron had shown her when they first set out from the Free Vale. She reflected on all she'd learned about history, and about the chraucans and that beautiful flight. She thought about Tess, and all the good times they'd had together in Three Groves. And she thought about how happy Tess had been to be united with her parents at last.

*I can't go back. Not without trying. If I become a real dog on the way—well, there are worse things. And one worse thing would be turning into a girl again, safe in Meldrith, and knowing I'd left Tess behind.*

She ran faster still, until the tall grasses flashed by her in a blur.

Eventually the field met up with a road, and the hoof prints and scent turned to follow it. The road led on and crossed a river. This water was not tainted. She lapped up a good, satisfying draught and then set out again, remembering, always remembering.

181

Before long she saw her first signs of Lirwani civilization, a walled town with tilled fields beyond. Occasional traffic along the road, mostly soldiers, made her leave the road and run alongside it. She was seen once or twice, but no one paid any attention to her, except for a troop of soldiers sitting beside a fence, who shied a few pebbles at her.

Presently she saw that the road ran directly to a large out-post built of heavy stone. The doors stood wide open. Wren hung back, watching traffic come and go. Timing her approach for when there were several horses and a cart or two passing one another in the gate, she slipped in. Straight ahead she spied a long, low guardhouse, with some open windows. She veered near these, listening, and almost immediately she overheard an unseen soldier telling someone else that the prisoners had been sent directly along to Edrann, and so these lucky fellows should be expecting their bonus by week's end. This news was met by a hearty cheer. She slunk away.

She no longer had a trail to follow, but she already knew that Edrann lay eastward. *All I have to do is find a big, walled fortress, gloomy and forbidding, with no one allowed to enter or leave without being checked*, she thought grimly. *Inside it, Tess is waiting. And Tyron, and Connor, and old Idres.*

She took a quick trip back to the rear of the guardhouse, where she had seen some roasted meat cooling on a rack. Leaping up, she snatched a whole chicken and streaked off, leaving a yelling guard behind her.


The boys sat undisturbed in their cell. Darkness came and, with it, the chill of night. No one offered them any food or water. Their packs were gone, of course, but Connor's tunic pockets produced a few fragments of a long-stale oatcake, and also a short candle and a sparker.

They shared the crumbs, and Tyron joked halfheartedly about trying to attack the Lirwani guards with the candle and the tiny metal sparker.

"Nothing to burn, though." He finally sighed, and silence fell.

Tyron had sunk into an uncomfortable doze when the sounds of boots and keys announced the arrival of the guards. He couldn't see Connor in the utter darkness, but he wasn't surprised when the light of the guard's torch revealed Connor standing ready to attack. The guards found this funny, and Tyron was glad that Connor could not understand the remarks that they made in Lirwani as they shoved the boys out of the cell.

Four armed guards took them back up the stairs to the tower room, where Andreus waited alone, sitting at ease in a carved chair and drinking wine from a golden goblet. On the other side of the room faint lights winked eerily in the dark scry stone. Idres was nowhere in sight.

Andreus addressed them in Sirad. "Tell me about yourselves."

Tyron glanced quickly at Connor, who stood stiff and grimfaced. Connor was as filthy as Tyron, with dirty hair hanging in his eyes and bruises adding color to the mud on what flesh was visible. Connor's once fine gray tunic was not only grimy but also slashed here and there from his sword battles, and of course his shirt was gone. To Tyron's eyes, though, his friend's posture looked suspiciously princely, and so he said hastily before Connor could speak, "Wren promised us a huge reward."

"A reward?" Andreus repeated mildly. "For what service?"

"Get into a castle. Steal someone."

"Someone being Teressa Rhisadel?"

Tyron shrugged, wondering desperately what to say next. "You know her, apparently."

Tyron shrugged again, wishing he knew how to lie well. Andreus seemed to be assuming from Idres's statement earlier that Connor and Tyron came from the village where Teressa had been hidden. Tyron had actually never met the Princess. Should he say he knew her, or would that be a mistake?

Recalling Wren's description of village life, he said, "Toffs aren't allowed to play with us much." He went on quickly, adapting Wren's stories to create a confusing picture of maybe having known Princess Teressa and maybe not.

Andreus listened without commenting, drinking from his wine from time to time. Tyron was just beginning to enjoy spinning out these lies about pot-making, weeding, and village games, when Andreus interrupted suddenly.

"Would you know her on sight?" He looked at Connor. Tyron opened his mouth to speak, but Andreus gestured for him to remain silent.

"He doesn't talk much," Tyron said after a moment.

"He will if I desire it," Andreus replied, with just enough edge to his voice to make his meaning very plain. Enjoyment now completely gone, Tyron fell silent.

"Well, horse-coper? Would you know Teressa Rhisadel on sight?"

"No," Connor said shortly.

Tyron added, with as much indifference as he could muster, "We'll see her, maybe?"

"Maybe," Andreus said, and laughed.

Tyron mistrusted that sound.

Andreus waved lazily at the guards, and the boys were taken out.

As soon as they were alone, Tyron collapsed against the wall and sighed. "Rot. I never thought that lying could be an art, and now I wish I had it. Did I make things better or worse? I was hoping he might be hinted into putting us together with the Princess, and then . . ." Tyron slapped his hands together lightly. "Out we go."

Connor shook his head. "Do you think he's that stupid?"

Tyron grimaced. "Well, there's *one* thing in our favor. He believed all that village-idiot foolery enough not to suspect that I have magic. These cells are not warded against magic. I've got my chance to do one spell—more would bring him in a flash, because there are tracers everywhere. But just one transportation spell could get us all out."

"*If* we are together," Connor repeated soberly. "What about an object-contact spell?" His voice changed to meditative. "Would a wall work? Suppose we are in the next cell over from the Princess?"

"Can't focus a wall," Tyron answered. "Maybe a better magician than I could mentally separate out one stone—*if* the Princess and we were to locate and touch both sides of the same stone. Otherwise it has to be an object separate from anything else for object contact to work. Anyway, we seem to have the time to wait for a chance, and I won't give up hope. I keep thinking about Wren. I hope she's halfway to Cantirmoor by now. I think Halfrid's going to like her. She's smart and stout-hearted, and maybe she will take my place as Halfrid's heir. I'd like that, I think."

Connor said, "She makes a splendid dog, but she'll make a better magician."

They slept then and woke at dawn when a guard came around with a bucket of none-too-clean water and a dipper.

Feeling lightheaded and reckless, Tyron took a drink, and then addressed the guard in Sirad. "We could use a blanket and hot food, my man."

He was surprised when the man uttered a short laugh and said, "Waste."

"It wouldn't be a waste to us."

The guard thought that funny enough to repeat in Lirwani to his two companions waiting at the door. They guffawed noisily. As the first guard plunked the ladle back into his bucket, he smiled cruelly at Tyron. Speaking in Sirad, he said plainly, "After tomorrow, even to you because you'll be dead."

The door slammed on his laughter.

# Chapter Nineteen

*W*hen Wren emerged from a thinning forest of scrubby but hardy oak, she saw the citadel. Edrann was a city of stone, built upon a hill. The countryside immediately surrounding it had been cleared of any growth so that the posted guards on the high towers could, no doubt, see for long distances. No army could enter that place by surprise, but Wren hoped a single dog might have a chance.

Returning to the cover of the oak forest, she lay near a shallow, poisoned stream to wait for nightfall. Listening to the sound of running water was difficult, for she seemed always to be thirsty, so she tried to keep her mind on good memories. *Remember what Idres said.* She thought back longingly to the easy days of games, songs, and plays under the spreading branches of the Secret Tree. *It's probably worse for Tess.*

As soon as night fell, she left, staying well away from roads. Once she heard wolves, but the pack ran toward the forest that she had just left. She kept head and tail low as she raced on.

When she neared the citadel, the straight stone walls loomed like threatening thunderclouds overhead. She slowed to a creeping pace, hoping that the tall grasses that she tried to stay in would not move too much and give her away. She felt exposed, like a fly crawling up a glass window. Occasional drifts of wind brought down comments exchanged by the guards walking back and forth, back and forth, on the battlements way above her.

When at last she reached the walls, she moved cautiously along them as close as she could while still keeping within the old weeds and sparse shrubs that had been allowed to grow there. A road, flat and smooth, lay directly adjacent to the huge dark stones of the walls. This Wren was afraid to step onto. She smelled wrongness on it and thought that some kind of magical trap awaited the unwary spy.

Working her way slowly toward the main entrance, she found that the big main gate, larger than the entire house at Three Groves, was closed. A road lay directly before it, leading away into the darkness. Like the wall road, this one made her afraid to set a paw onto it. Something about it felt wrong.

So she turned and worked her way slowly in the other direction, scanning the walls for any kind of way in. This took her much of the night, and she found nothing. Giving up when she was once again in sight of the main gate, she crawled beneath some strong-smelling itchwort leaves and tried to sleep.

Idres ordered the silent guard at the door to fetch something hot to drink. To her surprise he went at once, to be promptly replaced at the door by another fellow. It still amused Andreus to pretend that he was welcoming back a long-lost colleague. *Let him.* Idres would take comfortable surroundings as long as they were offered.

And she needed them. Despite the nice furniture in this room, the heavy ward magic made her feel enervated, as though she had just recovered from a terrible illness. Movement cost extra effort, and it was very hard to think.

And that was really all she had to do, between interviews with her former tutor. Think—and remember. She ignored the heaviness, which dragged at her limbs whenever she moved, and stood to look out of the slit window. The years had not improved the countryside in Senna Lirwan. She found herself pitying the citizens who, fifteen years ago, she had scorned as cowards and dolts. They had not asked for this master, and they were not able to get rid of him.

She turned away restlessly and sat down again. The guard returned then, with chocolate. It was good chocolate—evidence of Andreus's successful conquest of the harbor of South Hroth and his control of trade there—but she drank it without enjoyment.

*That foolish boy.* She thought of Tyron, thrust away the thought—then, with determination, brought it back again.

"Idiot," she said softly. It did not help.

She had been surprised and angered when he had appeared that rainy night in the Haven, begging for her help. The next day's interview had been worse. And it had been worse, she admitted to herself now, because he had *not* claimed blood kinship or reminded her about her having saved his mother. The same unquestioning honesty and goodwill that had made that one cousin special now shone in the boy's eyes. He had no motives beyond an urge to see justice done and a genuine desire to help.

She had decided long ago to live alone, without the terrible bindings of kinship or friendship. One could do one's work without being pestered by what others perceived as duty. She had not felt those awful ties since setting up the solitary house in the Haven. For many years that life had suited her well.

Then this boy came.

After his visit, thinking about him and about Verne and his daughter had awakened all the old feelings she had thought gone. Foremost, of course, was anger. Anger was always easiest. She thought it would be satisfying to snap her fingers in Andreus's face by rescuing the girl. Then she would disappear again and dismiss them all from her mind.

*I could get out on my own,* she thought now, looking about that room. *It will not be easy, but he has been master here too long. If I am patient, there will be a slip. All it will take is an instant, and I can be gone.*

*But . . . curse all feelings anyway!* Idres railed resentfully against the old, hurtful emotions. *What is love or loyalty, really, but an excuse for the weak to put bonds on the strong?*

She laughed softly and humorlessly to herself. She could think thoughts like that all day and night, but the fact remained that even if she saw a chance to leave right now, she would not take it. Not unless, somehow, those two boys could be included. And Teressa.

"I promised Teressa an execution," Andreus had gloated pleasantly last night. "That was before I knew that *you* were her Wren. No matter. Those two boys will serve me just as well. Why did you disguise yourself and follow the child to her hidden village, by the way? Did you form an abduction plot of your own? Tell me."

"You're a fool," Idres had said. "She doesn't know those boys. She won't know who you're having executed or why."

"Ah, but she's Verne's daughter. Don't try to tell me she will not be affected. Really, a salutary lesson in many respects, don't you think?"

*A lesson to me, he means. As in who's master,* Idres thought grimly. *I don't want to see either of those boys die, but there is nothing I can do to stop it. He will not let me out of this room by tomorrow.*

She formed a fist and struck it softly against the arm of her chair.

*Curse all feelings anyway!*

The girl was sitting somewhere in this fortress, unaware of anything that was going on; the boys were sitting somewhere else, facing execution on the morrow, Tyron knowing quite well that he could get himself out. Idres knew equally well that he wouldn't do it. *Loyalty again. Foolishness. Then here am I, caught like a fly in honey.*

*And Wren, out in the western mountains no doubt.*

Idres's mind called up images of Wren running back and forth, plumed tail high and bright little eyes watching eagerly. She remembered when Wren first woke to discover that she was a dog. *That child certainly has pluck.* She remembered Wren's reaction to Idres's instructions for making her way west over the mountains . . . the long, wordless howl.

*Loyalty, and friendship.*

Wren was not a prisoner, she was free. She had not turned back after the disaster that changed her shape into an animal's. *She probably has not turned back now.*

Idres rubbed her hands together slowly, then laid them in her lap. For the first time in a life of thirty years, she experienced the birth of hope.

Just before dawn Wren heard a terrible shrieking, graunching noise and poked her nose up cautiously. The gate opened slowly. As she watched, four columns of mounted soldiers emerged riding at a gallop, dark blue pennants flying at head and foot of the columns. She watched as they disappeared from sight and sound, trying not to sneeze from their dust. Behind, the gate did not close. As light strengthened, she saw that armed guards stood at either side of the gate. No one entered or left.

Full morning grayed the skies before a caravan of covered carts approached slowly from the south. Wren counted at least a dozen carts, could smell their individual loads. When they neared the gate, the line halted, and two men at the front dismounted from their ponies, approaching the armed guards. They each held papers in their hands. The soldiers looked, waved, and the men turned back to their waiting ponies. Then, with shouts and cracking whips over the dusty, tired-looking draught beasts, the carts began moving . . .

*And I'll not get another chance like this*, Wren thought.

Belly-crawling through the brush, she eased right up next to the road and sniffed cautiously. She sensed that the spell on the road was no longer active. So, as a great, creaking cart rumbled close, she slipped beneath and trotted slowly along with the cart as cover. Looking from side to side, she saw human feet, horses' hooves, and once a pack of track hounds being exercised. She smelled their suddenly sharp excitement. Some of these barked at her, but their collars were jerked, and they fell silent.

The cart seemed to groan as it started up a narrow street paved with uneven cobblestones.

She was in.

After the guards left, their laughter echoing coldly down the stone corridors, Connor turned and stood for a long time facing the tiny windows high up on the wall. Tyron could not see his expression. Finally Connor spoke.

"You've got to leave, Tyron. It is your responsibility. You must return to Cantirmoor and tell the King what's happened here—"

"And you?" Tyron interrupted.

"One of us should remain, in case an opportunity presents itself."

"Don't say it," Tyron answered, his voice high and thin. Ever since he was little, he had hated how his voice always betrayed his emotions, but now he did not care. "I won't leave. I won't do it, no matter how many reasons you think up. Not alone."

"I will not leave without the Princess," Connor responded softly, but with absolute conviction. "Perhaps we'll find a way to get all three of us into transport range. Let us think about that, then."

But all Tyron could think was: *I've failed everyone, Halfrid included.*

Wren thought her pounding heart was going to burst as she walked at a slow, steady pace under the cart. Her legs shivered, but she kept her eyes moving steadily from side to side, back and forth, trying to spot or sniff danger before it found her.

The cart creaked slowly up the steep street. Wren eased closer to one side when she saw that there were narrow, dark gaps between some of the stone houses. At a moment when she thought she was safe, she emerged and dashed toward one of those gaps. She heard a surprised shout, "Hey! Whose dog is that?"

The driver of the cart jumped down and aimed a kick at her ribs with his heavy boot. She splashed hard into the foul-smelling water running in the gutter at the side of the street and let out a pained yip. The man cursed and jumped back to avoid the gutter water. She scrambled to her feet and escaped into the narrow alley.

Up two more streets, and she began to get an idea of the construction of the city. The houses were built in rings around the huge central edifice, which had to be King Andreus's castle. Walls went out from the castle to the outer walls at intervals, like the spokes of a wheel. Arches in those walls connected the streets—but with drawn iron-fanged gates that could be lowered quickly to trap anyone being chased. Wren looked up at the castle again.

*That is where Andreus lives*, she thought. *And it's also got to be where the others are kept. He wouldn't trust anyone else.*

There was no way to know for sure until she got in to see for herself.


High in the mountains near the border of Senna Lirwan, Halfrid watched the lackeys swiftly striking and packing all the camp equipment. The King waited only for word from his scouts; then he planned to ride to the attack. A mood of grim preoccupation seemed to have overtaken everyone in the army, from the quarrelsome Duke Fortian down to young Standis.

Thinking the boy's name made Halfrid turn his head to see how his own packing was going. A deep flicker in the crystal sphere set in the darkest corner of the tent drew his eyes from Standis's sturdy brown hands.

"What's this?" he murmured, moving over to the contact sphere.

He frowned, gazing down into it. Despite his being the

King's most experienced magician, his talents did not lie in the direction of scrying, much less scry contact, and his bringing of the sphere had been only to please Falstan, who felt that Standis needed to keep up his nightly practice with the glass.

Deep in the sphere colors swirled and coalesced. Behind Halfrid, small rustles and clunks indicated Standis was still packing. Halfrid crouched down before the stone, touching it, and putting all his focus into the crystal.

At once he saw a perfect image of the old man who called himself Master Gastarth. Halfrid bit back an exclamation of pleasure, realizing ruefully that his first clear contact was entirely due to the strength of the old wizard's magic, and not at all his own. Then the pink mouth in the snowy beard moved, and Halfrid cleared his mind in order to receive the words.

*Young Verne leaves for the border soon, I suspect.* The wizard's thought was clear and mild. *It would be very helpful to everyone if you could fashion some kind of fiery diversion when you do reach the border. Even illusions will suffice—so long as the range is extensive. May we ask that of you?*

Halfrid gazed into his scrying stone for a moment, his mind blank with surprise. Then a thousand questions streamed into it. He tried to still his thoughts, but some of them must have leaked through, for Gastarth's image in the stone smiled suddenly.

*If all goes well, you will be hearing sundry explanations of what has happened, soon. But first—*

*I'll help you in any way I can.* Halfrid carefully framed the words in his mind. *Though it would help me to know what precisely is needed.*

*As dramatic a display as you can dream up.* Gastarth winked, and his image flickered out, leaving an empty crystal.

With a sigh, Halfrid straightened up. Standis was just returning from carrying another load to their packhorse. He passed politely by his master, clearly unaware of anything unusual going on.

Halfrid moved away and stood near the door of the tent,

193

absently scanning the peaks and thinking over the scry-stone conversation. He was still standing at the opening to the tent when a green-coated boy dashed up breathlessly.

"Sir. Master Halfrid. You're to come at once—King's command."

Halfrid slipped his tired feet into his riding boots and followed the messenger through the crowds of laboring soldiers, nobles, and servitors to the King's pavilion. There were the two mud-splashed, exhausted scouts who had been sent ahead into the mountains two days earlier.

As Halfrid approached, Verne said to the waiting Helmburi, "Get them food and drink." The steward led the scouts away, and the King turned to Halfrid. "Andreus dispatched troops from the outposts on all three passes. Weather permitting, we'll meet them within a matter of hours." He paused, his eyes narrowing consideringly. "This is it. We may be facing battle soon. Do you ride with us?"

Halfrid looked up at the mountains again, then turned to smile at the King. "Will you allow me to try some mischief of my own before you attack? If I'm right, you and your allies will be saved a great deal of effort."

The King returned his smile briefly. "Get your bag of tricks packed and mount up."


Wren had nearly completed a circuit of the city when she saw what seemed to be her one chance.

Some of the houses were tall, with steep roofs. While none of the houses at any time touched against the castle, several had been built close to the spoke walls connecting the castle to the outer walls. Wren saw guards walking along the tops of these. Along one wall Wren spotted a narrow ledge, high up, where apparently someone had added height. The roof of a house stood near that wall at the outer end.

The house next door's roof was slightly lower, and the one next to it lower still, for the houses sat on a sloping hill. At the far end Wren saw a low shed.

She followed her trail carefully with her eyes and decided that she would have to try it. Then she turned away and wondered if she dared take the chance to look for something to eat. She was afraid to give notice of her presence by starting a chase. But after a quick, unproductive search, she decided against food. Water was easier. She sniffed out a rain barrel and got her last drink before she crept under a stairway to wait for nightfall.

When the sun was gone, bells clanged at intervals throughout the city. The traffic of the city stopped abruptly. Wren heard men's voices echoing up and down the streets: "Curfew. *Currrr-few.*"

First she heard hasty steps, then fewer, furtive ones, and last the slams of doors and windows. After a long period of quiet, she decided it was time to move.

Getting onto the roofs was the easy part. She tried to keep her toenails from clicking loudly on the hard slats as she moved up, then down, then up, then down. When at last she reached the wall, she saw that the ledge was very narrow.

A narrow ledge, and below a very long drop. A human could not have walked along here. Maybe a dog would not be able to either.

She stepped out onto the ledge, one of her sides pressed hard against the stone wall. A cold breeze sprang from nowhere. Now it seemed to pluck at her, trying to make her slip and plunge to the cobblestones below.

*This is an angry city. Even the wind is vengeful.*

*Don't think, and DON'T LOOK.*

*Farther . . . farther . . . oh no. The stone here is crumbling.*

*One paw, then the next. Then the next—tail, stay still.*

Suddenly she heard noise above, a clanking and clattering, guards walking on the wall. She froze into a semblance of the stone around her and listened to the steps approach, draw nigh, pass.

She moved on.

*There's the castle, and the battlement . . . Closer. Closer. Close. One paw, then the next, then the—*

Sudden relief made her bones feel watery as she slipped

195

onto the wide stone battlement of the castle itself. Poking her muzzle out, she sniffed. Man smells, but none near. Skulking down onto the walkway, she cowered along the wall. Then she saw a narrow doorway.

Slinking into it, she stared with growing dismay down a huge stairwell. From each level—and she could not immediately count the levels—halls led off in all directions. This castle was *huge*. How would she be able to find anyone?

As it turned out, instinct solved the problem.

She was still looking about when something wonderful forced its way into her awareness. *Food*. The aroma of stewed mutton made her mouth water. Licking her chops, she felt irresistibly drawn toward that smell as if a magical magnet of astounding strength had been employed.

She sneaked down a narrow, steep stone stairway and trotted cautiously along a torch-lit hall. Ahead a sudden sound of laughter echoed. *Men. Don't give in to every impulse*, she was thinking desperately, when she heard something that drove the thought of the stew right out of her mind.

"Well, that smells better than what *we* got tonight."

A harsh laugh in answer and, "It seems Her Gracious Highness is getting coddled again."

"A whip across the shoulders is what I'd advise. She'd learn obedience mighty quick."

The second voice replied, with heavy sarcasm, "Did you want me to pass your advice along to *him*?"

"No no, blast you, Sorus. I was joking you, of course."

"Then you might let me by some time this night so's I can finish my duties."

"Yes, and help yourself to the better morsels on the prisoners' plates."

Now Wren was crouching in a shadowy doorway, and when the soldier carrying the tray stamped by heavily, she slipped behind him and followed silently all the way down the long hall.

At the end another guard stood outside a door. Wren hid

in an adjacent archway as, with a great clanking of keys, the door guard opened the door, holding it open while his companion carried the tray in. Wren crept shivering, belly to the ground, just behind his heels.

*I hope it's Tess*, Wren thought, taking a quick glance upward. In the wavering light of two sputtering, streaming candles sitting on a rough table, she recognized Teressa. The Princess sat on the far side of the room, arms crossed, looking pale and cold. Neither of the two men ever looked down at the floor.

Wren snaked into a shadowy corner as the guard set the tray on the table with a thud.

"There you be, Your High and Mightiness," the soldier said. "And I'm to tell you that you'll get some fine entertainment tomorrow. An execution. Seems there was two village buffoons trying to get to you. King figures it's only fair that you watch." Laughing loudly, he retreated and the door swung shut. *Clank. Clunk.*

They were alone at last.

Wren poked her head out from her corner to see Teressa cover her face with her hands. No sound escaped, but Teressa's thin shoulders shook in the fitful light.

Trotting over, Wren nuzzled her friend's arm.

"Uh?" Teressa sat up with a gasp; then her tearstained face lit with delight. "A dog? How did *you* get in here?" Her voice dropped to a whisper as she glanced fearfully at the door. "Don't bark." Teressa touched Wren's nose with a finger. "Can you understand me?"

Wren stared at her friend in silent sadness. Teressa's face looked thin and shadowed, her lovely hair matted and dirty. Her once fine dress was worn and every bit as grimy as Tyron's and Connor's clothing. The room was bare of anything but one narrow cot with a thin blanket, and the table with the tray and candles. Two other trays covered with bits of dried food sat under the table. Apparently the guards were not very good about taking away dirty dishes.

Wren opened her mouth, then closed it again quickly. She

knew what kinds of noises came out, and what if that big-nosed guard outside the door heard? In one wall she saw a bare fireplace, cold and dark, with ash on the grate. Moving to it, she traced a paw slowly through the ash. Her leg did not want to move smoothly in order to form letters, so she needed to try several times.

Puzzled, Teressa followed her and crouched down next to her, watching. She did not interrupt until the wavery letters for Wren's name lay in the ash.

Then Teressa looked up with huge eyes. "You? *Wren?*"

Wren dipped her head in a nod.

"Oh. Oh, Wren . . ." Teressa flung her arms around Wren and hugged her tightly, pressing her cheek against Wren's muzzle. "I've wondered so long. What happened? But, you can't talk. Oh, Wren, I'm so glad to see you, but *not* here. And not as a dog! And now, this talk about executions. Did—did someone come with you, is that it? And get caught? Those two people the guard just mentioned?"

Wren nodded.

Teressa's eyes filled with tears again. "That it should happen on my account! I'm sorry I asked you in those dreams to come. I did not think of the danger to you until *he* came and started pestering me about you. But I told him nothing. How did you do that? How did you become a dog? Oh no, you can't talk . . . and I, I . . ." Teressa's voice went shaky. She squeezed her eyes shut, trying to regain control. Finally she opened her eyes again and whispered, "What can we do?"

Wren licked her chops again. The smell of Teressa's dinner filled the room, and Wren's dog instincts clamored strongly for food.

Teressa smiled tremulously. "You wouldn't be hungry, would you?"

A little whine, just a tiny one, escaped Wren.

"Well, that's *one* thing I can do." Teressa leaped up and brought the tray to the floor. "I never have any appetite, but sometimes I eat the food, just to pass the time. You have no idea—being scared and bored by turns. Now, you eat this, and I'll enjoy it for the first time since I was brought here, just by watching you."

Wren needed no further invitation. Shoving her muzzle into the bowl, she ate the plain, heavy stew, then licked the bowl clean. She even ate the dried greens on the other plate. Teressa poured some water from the jug on the table into the stew bowl, and Wren lapped that up as well.

When she was done, Teressa said slowly, "I wish . . . I wish I could at least find out who they are and send a message that I'm truly sorry. But I cannot get out of this room. There is always someone outside the door, which is locked all the time, and this window is too narrow." She glanced up at the slit-window.

Wren looked up as well. *Too narrow for a human*, she thought. *But not for me.*

Dragging the blanket over, Wren lay down on it, then pointed her muzzle at the window.

"What is it? Are you cold? Is that it?"

Wren shook her head, ears flapping. She pointed her nose at the window, then at the blanket.

Teressa drew in a deep breath. "What? You mean, lower you through the window? With the blanket?"

Wren nodded.

Teressa frowned, thinking rapidly. "Why not? That is, if you can bear being lowered through a window with such a long drop. If those prisoners are anywhere, they are directly below us here, only much, much lower. Possibly in the levels beneath the ground—though I hope not. This is the part of the castle where prisoners are kept. I do know that much. The thing is, I don't know if any of the windows below me lead to empty rooms."

Wren took a part of the blanket in her teeth and jerked it twice.

"I see. You'd signal me. I hold the blanket and lower you slowly. You look, and if it's safe, then I hold still . . . yes. But how to send a message?"

Wren traced letters in the ash again: TALK ME. Her letters were huge and wavery and used up all the space.

Teressa frowned intently. Wren opened her mouth, a tiny whine escaping. Both Wren and Teressa sent hasty looks at the door, then Teressa swept the ashes smooth again with her fingers. "Can you try again?"

Wren lifted her paw and wrote DOG TALK.

"You're telling me something. I'm sorry to be slow, Wren. Talk, me, dog, t—oh. Could it be that one of *them*, your friends, that is, can understand you?"

Wren's head jerked up and down.

Teressa laughed softly. "Oh, do let us try. Anything, just to be trying. You will tell them that I am here and that I am so *sorry* about . . . what has happened, and then I will pull you back up. Then maybe you can spell out their message in the ash?"

Wren nodded again.

"Oh, you dear girl." Teressa hugged her tightly again. Then she drew back a little breathlessly. "Oh, I hope you won't mind, but *phew*. What have you been hiding in, stinkweed? Oh, what adventures you've had, and all on my account. I just wish—no, I will *not* think about that," she finished fiercely and turned to the blanket. "Gray. How I hated this ugly color, but now, what could be better? The wretched Lirwanis won't see you outside the window unless we make a noise and make them look up."

Teressa snatched up the heavy spoon from the tray and turned her attention to gouging a hole near one end of the blanket. "Luckily this thing is thin and badly woven. The Three Groves sewing mistress would have Andreus's weavers on bread and water for years for such shoddy work." Her voice wobbled. Then she hiccoughed and bent again to her task. With determined yanking she began tearing the blanket into three long strips, but slowly, so the sound would not carry beyond the room.

Next she knotted the strips securely together and fitted a

blanket-strip harness around Wren. Finally, she put the dirty tray down on the floor, balanced the table atop the bed, knelt on this at the high window, and lifted Wren up.

Cold air moved in through the window, and Wren tried not to shiver in fear. Teressa gave her one more hug, then set Wren on the narrow stone windowsill. The sides of the slit squeezed Wren's sides as Teressa helped her move out. At last all four of Wren's paws were dangling in the air, and Teressa wrapped the blanket-strip rope end around one of the table legs to help ease the weight.

Wren felt slightly sick as the blanket rope jerked downward, bumping her from time to time against the cold stone. She moved steadily lower . . . lower . . . past another window slit, where weak light leaked out. She glimpsed the inside of a tower room. Nobody was in view. Silently she moved past.

Lower . . . lower . . . It occurred to Wren then that if she chose an empty locked room, she'd never be able to get out. Ever. Fear dried her mouth, but Teressa, waiting for a signal, eased her lower still.

And then Wren heard a familiar voice.

"Let's talk about fun things," Tyron was saying desperately. "Good memories. How about the time we frosted those sniff-nosed heraldry prenties at the fair—"

Wren whined softly and jerked at her rope.

Inside the cell, Tyron broke off, then hissed: *"What was that?"*

Wren paid little attention. Her jerks had made the blanket rope bounce frighteningly. She began to rotate like a child's wind-up toy. There was a gasp from the near window, and a familiar hand reached out, grabbed at the blanket, and once more Wren was squeezed through a narrow stone window.

*"Wren,"* Connor said, and they all tumbled to the hard stone floor.

"Ooof." It was Tyron.

Apparently Connor had been standing up on Tyron's shoulders to reach the window. Except for a stub of a candle perched ridiculously on an iron torch holder attached to the wall, the boys' cell was completely bare. No table. No cot.

"Wren? Who is at the other end?"

*Tess,* Wren keened softly.

Connor grabbed Tyron's shoulder in a hard grip. "It's Teressa. She's at the other end of that blanket. An object-contact spell will work—*The Princess is now in our reach*."

"Hey! What's that noise in there," came a shout from without the door.

"But what about Idres—" Tyron gulped, looking at the door wildly.

"Leave me here, then, and get the Princess out."

*We'll come back for her*, Wren barked, as keys scraped in the door lock.

"Tyron, we *must* free the Princess while we have this one chance," Connor added.

"All right. Princess first—then we come back for Idres. Pact?"

Connor raised his hand in the honor sign, and Wren dipped her muzzle in her firmest nod.

Tyron squeezed his eyes closed and held out his hands before him. Tracing signs slowly with his fingers, he muttered softly. Connor stretched an arm toward the window, just grasping with two fingers the end of the blanket rope. With his other hand, he took hold of Tyron's shoulder.

"Grab his tunic," Connor said to Wren.

She closed her teeth on Tyron's hem and felt the swirl of transportation magic just as the door began to swing open.

# Chapter Twenty

*T*his time the magic vertigo lasted longer, culminating in that horrible worms-through-the-head sensation. Then Wren found herself standing in the familiar cottage belonging to those nice old people, Mistress Selshaf and Master Gastarth. She sat down. The vertigo dissipated rapidly, and Teressa dropped her end of the dirty blanket-rope, gave a cry, and swooped down on Wren, hugging her tightly and weeping soundlessly into her fur.

Wren let out a whiny yip, torn between joy at being free and frustration at being unable to talk to her friend.

"We *did* it, we did it," Tyron exclaimed.

Connor sat down abruptly next to the hearth. He seemed to be fighting the dizziness of the long transfer.

"Welcome back, young ones," said a sweet voice from the doorway to the kitchen.

Wren looked up as the brother and sister entered carrying trays of steaming food and drink. Tess's grip loosened slightly, and Wren saw a look of wonder on her friend's tearstained face.

"Who are you? And where are we? Wren—" Teressa turned back to her.

*We're safe,* Wren tried to bark.

Connor swiftly knelt on the floor next to Wren and Tess. "She says we're safe. I'm your Uncle Connor," he added with one of his funny smiles. "Though our birthdays are only two years apart."

"Come, eat." Mistress Selshaf gestured. "We have hot baths waiting."

"We are Selshaf and Gastarth," the old man said to Teressa. "Wren and Tyron visited us not long ago."

"Did you—who—" Teressa looked around in bewilderment.

"Tyron got us out." Connor indicated the magic prentice, who at that moment had his mouth stuffed with bread. "He's a student at the Magic School," he added.

Tyron scrambled up hastily and executed a creditable bow—if one discounted the bread still stuffed in his mouth. "Your Highness," he mumbled somewhat thickly.

Teressa laughed, her face flooding with delicate color.

Wren whimpered again, wishing she could talk, and Mistress Selshaf came over to her.

Crouching down, the old woman said kindly, "Wren?"

Wren looked up at those light blue, jewel-like eyes. For a moment a bright flash of something winked through Wren's mind—something strange, but not at all nasty. Then the Mistress's smile widened.

"You are a remarkable young person, Wren. You seem to have worn that shape very comfortably despite the long days and the danger. Shall we change you back now?"

Wren let out a loud bark that brought a laugh from her friends, then followed the Mistress into the little kitchen, where a big wooden tub of water stood. The Mistress's small hands were surprisingly strong as she lifted Wren and set her gently in the hot water. A few minutes of brisk scrubbing later, she brought Wren out and placed her on a stool. Murmuring words in a singsong voice, Mistress Selshaf touched a jewel around her neck with one hand and Wren's forehead with the other.

Wren fought a wave of severe dizziness; then a pang shot through her. Her perspective jerked upward, and colors glowed around her with sun-bright intensity.

"Here's a towel," the Mistress said. Her voice seemed to come through thick padding.

204

Wren shook her head, clutching at the towel. The Mistress helped to dry her, and Wren felt something slipped over her head. She could feel how clean it was, but oddly, it had very little smell.

She looked up again, and the Mistress pressed a hot, herbal-scented drink in her hands.

*Hands.*

"This will help the adjustment," Mistress Selshaf said.

Wren sipped and felt her two worlds melting together. Heaving a big sigh, she remembered everything that had happened—and leaped up on two legs to rejoin her friends.

For a moment she seemed too high, and staggered. Then she walked forward, fighting a brief urge to go down on her hands to speed herself along.

"Wren!" Teressa jumped up.

The boys greeted her, laughing.

Sitting down on the ground near the food, Wren caught herself just as she was about to push her face into a tempting bowl of soup. Catching up a spoon instead, she thought, *What a lot of bother we humans create for ourselves.* Then she realized Connor was talking, telling Teressa about their journey.

Teressa sat, her food forgotten, her eyes luminous.

". . . so then Idres pulled this long knife from her pack, and we fought against the baddies and lost. They brought us to the citadel. The rest is Wren's story," he finished, smiling.

Teressa turned that gaze to Wren. "Idres," she said. "I don't know who she is—but if she came to help and is still there, then we must go back and get her out."

Tyron choked, his brown eyes widening with alarm. "No. You—"

Teressa turned on him. "I can't *bear* the thought of someone having gone into danger for me and being stuck back there."

Connor said, "The three of us made a pact. We'll go back to find Idres as soon as we can."

"Then let me into it," Teressa said firmly.

"It's only fair—though what the King might say isn't tough to guess," Wren put in, glad to be talking again.

"Pact—" Tyron began, and then a shadow moved in the doorway.

Wren's head snapped around. Teressa gasped in surprise when they saw the tall, thin woman standing in front of Master Gastarth. Idres's face was pale as paper, and her dark eyes glittered with some deeply felt emotions.

"No need," Idres said in a low voice. Her eyes dropped as she came a little way in. When she looked up again, her voice was full of its old irony. "As you see, I managed to spring myself."

"What—how?" Tyron leaped up happily.

"When you left so abruptly, the castle was plunged into a chaos of searches, recriminations, and other pleasantries," Idres said, sitting down regally in a chair as if she were not as dirty as Tyron, Teressa, and Connor. "Andreus was furious. I expect things might not have been nearly so easy had not Verne and his allies chosen that exact moment to commence some sort of major magic attack on the border. Andreus went off to investigate. I tricked my door guard into opening the door and crashed a chair over his head . . . and eventually I slipped into Andreus's magic chamber and used his own sphere to dreamspell one of his minions into sending me here." She sat back in her chair, her tone careless but her posture tense and slightly wary, just as it had been during that long trek through Senna Lirwan.

Wren looked carefully at Idres. *Easy?* she thought, remembering those long stone corridors and the stamping Lirwani guards. *Maybe she's not telling us something.* Then, recalling the way Idres had suddenly produced a long knife from her pack just before they'd ambushed the Lirwani search party, and the cool, practiced way she'd used it, Wren shuddered. *Maybe it's just as well we don't hear the details.*

With conflicting emotions, Wren looked up at Idres's face again. Despite that detached manner, the woman was obviously very tired. *And she came straight here*, Wren thought. *To tell us she's free. She didn't have to do that.* Before she could further puzzle out Idres's uncharacteristic behavior, Idres spoke.

"You did well," she said, her dark eyes moving to each of the companions in turn. "And I thank you for wanting to return for me."

Tyron flushed bright red.

"Andreus will not be long in learning who you really are," Idres went on. "You are likely to see him again."

"Not soon I hope," Wren said stoutly. "Until I learn a few baddie-squelching tricks."

Everyone laughed at that, Teressa pausing to wipe her eyes again.

"Come, young ones, let us get you clean and ready for the interviews about to commence."

Tyron paused in the act of standing up. "Halfrid?"

Master Gastarth said, "I expect he will be along very shortly. Did you wish to be gone?"

Tyron shook his head firmly. "I thought about that a lot when I was stuck in the cell. But I'm not going to run off like some rabbit. If he wants to scuttle me, then he's going to hear some choice words first."

Mistress Selshaf nodded, her eyes glinting with hidden amusement. "All the more reason to be fresh in a new tunic, don't you think?"

"Yes, go," Wren spoke up. "I'll greet anyone who comes."

Idres rose from her chair. "I believe I will go home. If I may return tomorrow? I have some questions for you two."

"We will be here tomorrow," Master Gastarth said, bowing politely.

Idres half turned toward Tyron, seemed to hesitate on the verge of saying something, then walked noiselessly out into the night.

The boys followed Master Gastarth into one room, and Teressa went with the Mistress into the kitchen.

Wren sat, listening to the cheerful clatter of her friends'

voices and the musical ones of the old people, then sighed happily. *I have to admit, this is the best part of the adventure—having it come out all right and being warm and clean and full of good food.* She looked down at the plain gown of leaf green she'd been given; then she picked up a bowl of soup. She was halfway through it when there was a stir in the air, and a short, stout man with round red cheeks and a fringe of silver hair appeared. He wore a long white tunic with a purple sash.

Remembering Tyron's description of the magicians' formal clothes, Wren asked, "Are you Halfrid?"

The man gave her a beaming smile. "I am," he said. "And you are Wren? Are the Sendimerises and Ty—"

"Halfrid!" Tyron exclaimed from behind.

Taking no notice of Tyron, Wren marched up to the King's Magician and waved a finger under his nose. "It was ALL my fault," she said. "Tyron only went along with me because he thought he ought to, and anyway, *what* kind of a Magic School would scuttle a *wonderful* magician after just *one* mistake—"

"*WREN.*" Tyron's anguished yell was nearly drowned in Halfrid's surprised laughter. "Can't you let me take care of my own affairs?"

Wren turned on him. "No. You've been spending an awful long time in Connor's company, and you'll only muff it by hopping out with something noble. I thought it all out very carefully when I was running along those long Lirwani roads."

"Oh," Tyron said with heavy sarcasm. "And *you* trying to take all the blame *isn't* noble?"

"Not a bit," Wren replied smugly. "Since I'll be stuck back darning black orphan socks anyway, I thought I may as well do some good first. That's just being practical—"

A choking sound interrupted the argument, and both looked over to see Halfrid mopping his streaming eyes.

"Stop," he gasped, "before you two ridiculous urchins kill me." He paused as a fresh paroxysm shook him; then he sighed. "Tyron, you're not scuttled, and, Wren, you'll return to your sock-darning only if you wish to." He gave one last chuckle.

"Not likely—" Wren began.

"But you *said*—" Tyron burst out.

Halfrid turned to his heir first. "When did I *say* I would scuttle you?"

Tyron opened his mouth to reply, but for a time no sound came out. Finally he closed his lips and frowned; then he said abruptly, "Well, not in those exact words."

"I gave a command." Halfrid nodded. "What's the Third Natural Law?"

"No human being is perfect," Tyron muttered. "But what has that to do with—"

"And what is the sixth Crisis Rule?"

"That any command by a senior magician can be disregarded if one can show just cause—but wait," Tyron said. "I'm not a real magician yet, and I . . ."

His voice trailed off. Halfrid said gently, "There was yet one last test for you to pass, my heir, a test that could not be hinted at or it would be worthless."

"I don't understand."

Halfrid shook his head. "When I was a prentice about your age, Mistress Zhethrem, who was King's Magician then, gave me instructions that forced me to make a choice. I was gone three years on my particular quest, and I learned much during that time before I dared to return to face her down and defend what I thought was right. I put you into a similar situation with respect to Idres Rhiscarlan. You felt—like a good magician— that the Princess should be rescued without resorting to warfare. At the same time you strongly felt that Idres—as Andreus's former ally—should be consulted about the Princess's abduction. Your reasons were entirely practical. Just as strong, however unspoken, was your desire to see justice done in Idres's own situation. Because she had made it very clear she would not communicate with us, much less ally with us, I forbade any communications going to her.

"The night after the Princess disappeared we argued for a long time, did we not? You tried to persuade me to consult with

Idres on this one subject, and I held firm. And after a sleepless night you chose the course you felt was true, and left."

Wren nodded. "I think I understand. You could have stayed behind, figuring your position as his heir wasn't worth risking," she said to Tyron. "And after you and I first talked, and you knew I wasn't any magician, you *could* have left me behind. Or, after talking to Idres and getting a no answer, you *could* have gone back and turned me over to Mistress Leila."

"That part took me a bit by surprise," Halfrid conceded. "I confess I'd hoped to have Wren back within two days."

"You never really believed Idres would help us, sir?" Wren asked.

Tyron remained silent, head down and eyes intent on his tightly clasped hands.

"I thought she would refuse. But I did not think there would be any harm in Tyron's asking. I thought she'd send him off with some choice words to think over about getting involved. What I did *not* foresee was that you two would formulate the very same sort of plan that we in the Magic Council were discussing in secret. At the moment we were trying to determine who would be best suited to attempt to slip into Senna Lirwan on a rescue mission, you and Tyron departed on your own quest, sent on your way by outside powers greater than any of us here."

"Master Gastarth and Mistress Selshaf." Wren nodded sagely. "Idres said the same thing."

Halfrid glanced at the open door; four voices were still murmuring beyond. He said quietly to Tyron, "Master Gastarth and Mistress Selshaf—as they were better known many years ago—the Sendimeris twins."

Tyron's jaw dropped. Wren whistled, low and clear. "Even *I've* heard stories—"

She broke off when the others came through the door. Her eyes went first to Teressa, who was now wearing a gown of soft blue. Teressa smiled brightly and came straight to Wren as Halfrid bowed and greeted her.

Behind her, Connor walked more slowly. The old brother and sister followed him in, and the Mistress handed Tyron his bag of magic supplies.

"Good evening, Halfrid," Mistress Selshaf said.

"Good evening, Master, Mistress," Halfrid replied, bowing formally.

"How did the diversion go?" Master Gastarth asked, his eyes twinkling.

"On your signal, I initiated as splendid an array of illusionary mythical beasts, fire storms, and explosions as any found on a Cantimoor stage. I don't know yet why, but it worked. Andreus withdrew his entire force from the border, which made the war unnecessary—and gave us hope that the Princess Teressa might—even then—have freed herself. I brought the King and Duke Fortian back to Cantimoor, leaving the rest to return by conventional means under the command of the Princess of Eth-Lamrec. Then, despite everyone's questions and wild speculations, I came straight here. I wish to thank you on behalf of King and Council for your aid." Once again he bowed.

"Your thanks should properly go to these young people," the Mistress replied, smiling. "They contrived the Princess's rescue entirely on their own. We merely watched them when we could, and intercepted them when they tried to leave by magic. Getting across Andreus's border by magic is a tricky business. And now they are ready to return to Cantimoor. We know Princess Teressa's parents are eager to be reunited once again with their daughter."

Wren saw Tyron looking at the twins in bemusement and Halfrid raising his hands. She dashed forward, yelping, "Wait!"

All eyes turned to her.

Resolutely ignoring the tide of heat that flooded her cheeks, Wren said determinedly, "Even I know who the Sendimeris twins are, and one question I *always* wished that people in the stories had the sense to ask is this: why, if you're *that* wise and powerful and so on, did you leave us to grub across the mountains and get grabbed by those toad-walker Lirwanis? I mean, it was a good quest and one I was glad to make, but that's because I thought nobody else would do it. Why didn't you magic in and grab Tess yourself?"

Tyron covered his face with his hands, and Halfrid uttered another of his silent laughs, adding: "I must admit, those questions have been on my own mind. Not to mention the King's—as he's frequently told me."

Master Gastarth's eyes twinkled, and the Mistress gave a soft chuckle. "Because it was *your* quest, Wren," she said mildly. "We seldom interfere in such choices, for that is not our way, and you were very determined, were you not?" The Mistress turned her gaze to Halfrid. "We watched from a distance and aided the quest thrice. We watched for two reasons. The first because our time here is drawing to an end, and we hope to leave certain tasks in capable hands."

"By *capable hands*, you speak of these young people?" Halfrid asked quietly.

"We do," Master Gastarth rumbled. "Train them well."

"Second, we have watched young Andreus from afar. Our part of the tasks I mentioned will be to treat with the one who trained him. We have learned as much as we could about that unknown sorcerer by observing Andreus's actions and methods. But such actions as we take against that sorcerer, who has abused your countries and peoples so badly, is yet to come. And that is our own problem. However, your problems are, at least for now, solved."

Wren saw Halfrid's round face take on a sober expression. Beyond him, Connor's eyes were dark and intense. Wren felt Teressa's hand steal into hers and grip tightly.

"This house has served its purpose, and we will be gone from it soon. Farewell," the Mistress said in her singsong voice. She raised her hands, and magic washed gently over them all.

They appeared a moment later in the palace designation place, and a joyous pandemonium broke out. Teressa was borne away. Connor was immediately pulled in another direction. Halfrid transported Tyron and Wren to the school, where more crowds of shouting people waited, having been alerted by the King.


A week later Wren stood before a wall-sized mirror in a palace guest room, preening and posing. She heard a knock at her door. "Is that you, Tess?" Wren called happily.

She went back to admiring her new gown, a full-skirted dress, pale blue under and white velvet over. The overdress had tiny red berries and leaves embroidered along wide sleeves and hem. A glittering string of garnets had been braided into her hair, and around her waist she'd tied a wide scarlet silk sash with long dancing fringes.

"It is," Teressa said, coming in.

Wren sighed. "I *never* thought I'd ever have a real velvet dress." She turned and surveyed her friend. "Ooh—yours is even more wonderful."

Teressa looked tall and beautiful in white and gold and green, her hair threaded with a golden fillet. But she scarcely glanced at her own reflection. "Come, Wren. We haven't much time before we are summoned. Now that we're alone at last, what happened?"

"When? What?"

"With Halfrid." Teressa laughed. "They kept you at that school all week. Will you get to be a prentice there?"

Wren grinned. "Well, they kept me at the Magic School because Mistress Leila felt responsible for me, and she said your family would be too busy welcoming you back to have me underfoot."

Teressa wrinkled her nose. "I think she meant to protect you from the likes of my Uncle Fortian and my cousins. Mama would have let you come any time."

"You're probably right. And it's not as if I didn't have fun. The magic prenties are *all* interesting, or at least the ones I've met so far. Not a one like Zanna. And as for that Halfrid, every time he saw me for two days, he laughed and laughed. He's really a jolly sort. I'd thought he would be tall and grim, a little like that duke who took charge of Connor—"

"*That's* Uncle Fortian."

"—whew, what a pickleface. Anyway, Halfrid reminds me more of the pastry master in my old village in the mountains, who used to say he'd never be rich because he liked his own baking so much."

"Connor says you sat at the high table with the Masters that first night—" Teressa paused.

Unembarrassed, Wren smiled. "Right between Mistress Leila and Tyron. And *everyone's* eyes were on us, and I shoved my face into my plate. Some dog habits are hard to forget. Wow, did Tyron love that. Anyway, I did have my prentice interview, and Halfrid and the Masters asked me a lot of questions. Mostly about scrying, and signs, but also about reading, and history, and . . . oh, lots of things. Even why I wanted to pretend to be a pirate."

"And?" Tess prompted.

Wren grinned. "I do *not* have to go back to Three Groves. As of this morning, I am accepted as a magic prentice."

Teressa clapped her hands gently. "I'm so glad. Now we'll be able to visit one another often."

"So they're letting you stay?" Wren breathed with relief.

Teressa sank down on a chair, her face taking on the watchful expression that always accompanied discussion of Andreus. "They don't think he'll try abducting me again—just because he considers it clumsy to repeat a thing. Also, the magicians have some sort of new magic over the palace, strong enough to keep Andreus out for years, according to the Sendimeris twins. And if I leave Cantirmoor, it'll be in the company of a magician—at least until Andreus is finally defeated. So no more Three Groves. I'm home for good. And Mama says I may look at the records any time I like—"

She was interrupted by a knock on the door. A maid came in.

"Your guests, Princess Teressa," she said, and behind her entered Connor and Tyron.

The four friends looked at one another for a moment. Wren thought Tyron was almost unrecognizable in his clean white wool tunic, formal dress for the magic prentices, and his brown hose without holes in the knees, and shoes and sash. His hair had been trimmed and was neat and orderly. Next to him, Connor looked tall and princely in an embroidered blue tunic, new sword, dark hose, and shining new boots.

Both boys bowed to Teressa, Tyron awkwardly, until she came forward saying, "Please don't. Not when we're together. I expect I'll never get used to that, and I don't want it from friends."

"You summoned us?" Tyron asked.

Teressa flushed. "My father *summoned* us. I *asked* you to come—I know we won't be able to see one another alone for some time."

"May I first thank you both for not telling anyone my secret about talking to animals?" Connor said seriously.

"It's your secret to tell," Wren replied promptly. "Though I'd be proud if it were mine. And you both have to tell me some more about the Iyon Daiyin."

The maid appeared at the door. "Princess Teressa, the King has sent for you."

Teressa moved suddenly, giving each of them a quick, hard hug. "It's time for the ceremonies, and the banquet in your honor. That's my father's way of thanking you. And we'll all enjoy it. But for myself, I requested you to meet us here first so I could promise you that I will do anything for you, ever, my friends."

She turned and hurried from the room.

Wren and the boys followed more slowly. Another servant waited out in the hall to conduct them to the entrance to the throne room. Feeling constrained in the presence of this silent person, they did not talk during the long walk.

When they reached the golden doors with the stiffly standing guards at either side, and beyond them the glitter of gold and jewels and vaulted marble ceilings, Wren hung back a little.

"Hoo," she said uncertainly, staring down the long carpeted road to the other end of the room, where Teressa, now tall and proud, stood between her crowned parents. All along the sides of the room, velveted and bejeweled courtiers turned their eyes toward the door.

"Come, Wren," Connor murmured, smiling. "You'll do splendidly—"

Tyron added in a wicked whisper, "As long as you don't stick your face in the food."

Trying not to laugh, Wren huffed back, "Maybe I'm no longer a dog, but I can still bite!"

And smiling broadly, they walked in.